LAMBS: WORLD GONE DOWN

SURVIVORS: VOLUME 1

BENTON FORD

AMMFA PUBLISHING

For Wayno
A decent snack for any hungry T-Rex

SURVIVORS

VOLUME 1

It started as a normal day …

… but things quickly changed.

1

STALKER

He liked to think of himself as a fox stalking a lamb. A particularly tasty one, soft and young and unsuspecting, one he would slowly isolate from its flock until it was cornered, then he would slowly close in, and when the time came to strike, he would take his sweet, sweet, time….

He lowered the binoculars. Yes, he had seen her. For a brief moment, Juliet had come to the window, perhaps looking out at the empty driveway, wondering where her father had gone.

He won't be back. He's stuck at work, and you're alone. The way it should be. But don't worry, your Romeo is coming.

Lawrence licked his lips, thinking about how he'd soon be licking other things.

He was getting hard. He couldn't help it. Normally he'd have sorted himself with his hand, but today there was no need.

Juliet was waiting on her balcony for her lover to appear.

'I'm coming,' he whispered. 'I'm coming, very soon.'

He climbed down from the hedge, folded up the

stepladder and put it into the back of his van beside the trimmer. A little way back up the road he retrieved his council warning sign.

Maintenance in progress. Drive carefully.

He drove down the hill, past Juliet's house and onwards down the narrow country road until he came to a tiny side entrance so overgrown most people would drive past without knowing it was there.

He had planned everything carefully. There was a farm at the bottom of this lane, but it was no longer working, the land sold off to other farmers and the house converted into a secluded glass palace for some rich cocksucker from London who only visited for a couple of weeks a year. Lawrence had offered his gardening and maintenance services in the hope of being able to ditch his shitty council job, and now earned a decent bit on the side for keeping an eye on the place, doing general maintenance, and making sure no prospective thieves got their eyes on it.

He drove down the lane, parking his van out of sight around the back of the house. Then he climbed over a stile into the field that backed on to Juliet's father's place. The land conveniently bulged in the middle, meaning that by walking around the outside of the field, he could approach the house from the side without being seen. Once he had her, he could drag her quickly back across the field to the farmhouse and load her up into his van. The back of Juliet's house was visible only from the farmhouse, and Lawrence knew that was empty.

He'd have her gone and secreted away before anyone would ever know. And then … and then—

He still had his workman's overalls on, a utility belt around his waist. He had a piece of wire rope, a rag to gag her, and a knife to keep her quiet if necessary. Not that it would matter. The farmhouse was the only house nearby, and the valley would swallow up any screams.

Lawrence grinned. She was his. She was finally his.

The hedgerow was overgrown, the grass long. He could duck down and even if the back of his coat was seen, he might be mistaken for a badger, an escaped dog. Juliet wouldn't care. With Daddy out working late, she'd be watching television or doing her homework. Hell, there was a lot of shit going on up north which would keep the kids interested, even girls usually into Barbies and makeup and other bullshit. Lawrence had watched the news a fair bit himself, although most of it was the usual filtered speculation. He'd read some rumours on the Dark Web, but he went on there for other things, for the most part.

The house was ahead, above him, behind a low wire-framed fence but with the garage on this side, no windows. He had just reached the fence when a car rushed past on the main road, giving him a healthy reminder to keep his wits about him. It would only take one do-gooding idiot to spot him and everything would go to hell. He would never get another chance. A few more minutes and he'd be safe; she'd be his, and by dusk she'd be safely hidden away in his soundproofed shed.

He closed his eyes, dreaming about the soft feel of her skin, the gentle curves of her body. He'd get a day perhaps, at most, before the search put him in its radar. She had to be disposed of by then, no trace left behind, but a day was long enough. He'd have her, over and over—

Something shifted in the long grass nearby. Lawrence whipped around, but caught only a glimpse of something silvery as it dropped out of sight. The grass swished back and forth, indicating its position, and as he stared, a pointy serpentine tail flicked upwards, swished back and forth, then disappeared.

'What the actual fuck…?'

A sound like the tearing of flesh came out of the grass, followed like a growl. It could have been a dog with a rabbit, but there had been no sign of either, and that tail thing … for a moment Lawrence forgot everything he had been planning. He turned away, pushing carefully through the grass, trying not to disturb whatever it was until he'd had a good look. The tail-like thing whipped up again, so close he could have reached out and touched it. He paused a moment, then leaned forwards, peering over the top of the grass into the hollow made by whatever it was with its catch.

There was a dog, that was certain. Some kind of terrier, its throat ripped out, its stomach torn open, its guts spilling out onto the ground. He noticed the bloodied collar with its silver pendant, recognised the dog as Jimminy, who belonged to Mrs. Baxter, who lived on the corner of the estate. Poor bastard must have got out, and run into this … this … whatever the hell it was.

Its body was thin and lithe, like a fish. From overhead it was hard to see, it's skin a mottled dark green which blended into the grass of the field. Powerful back legs ended in hooked talons, which now held the dog's carcass down while smaller front legs ripped open the dog's chest and neck. A neck no thicker than Lawrence's wrist shifted back and forth, ending in a serpentine head covered in green scales. Its nostrils flared as though incensed by the fresh meat its needlelike teeth were tearing off the poor dog's bones.

'Mother of all that is holy—'

The creature paused. Its head flicked up, and in a moment it had lashed out, mouth snapping shut over Lawrence's forearm, teeth tearing through his coat and sweater to remove a chunk of flesh.

He stared as blood dripped on to the ground, then stumbled backwards, the pain still not quite registering over the shock, and the utter terror at what he had seen.

The creature's head appeared out of the grass, flicking back and forth. It caught sight of Lawrence and let out a low, threatening hiss, then took a couple of steps forwards. He backed away again, and found the fence surrounding Juliet's house at his back.

He thought of the shredded remains of a dog which he had patted affectionately a number of times. The creature was still watching him with its evil little eyes, head flicking back and forth as though assessing whether he posed a threat, whether it could take him down, too.

The opportunity to steal Juliet away and do delicious things to her had passed. He lifted a foot over the fence, though, stepping down onto the spongey, well-maintained lawn. He turned to climb over, the edge of the fence rubbing against his damaged arm, and the pain finally kicked in. He clamped his free hand over his mouth to stop himself crying out, tears welling in his eyes.

Hugging his bad arm against himself, blood soaking his clothes, he staggered across the garden to the back door.

'Juliet!' he cried. 'Juliet! Open up! Please!'

A light came on behind the frosted glass, and Lawrence felt all his last hope fading. This wasn't how it was supposed to go. She should be in the back of his van now, perhaps getting a little warm up for what was to come later.

The door cracked open, and a slender blonde girl wearing jeans and a blue Eden Project t-shirt peered out. Lawrence's heart lurched. She was an oil painting, even now, with worry etched across her face. Bright blue eyes, wide and innocent. Oh, the things he wanted those eyes to see—

'Uncle Lawrence? Oh my god, what happened? Are you all right?'

Lawrence stared at his eleven-year-old niece and felt the urge to cry. 'Juliet, you have to help me. There's something out in the field, something dangerous....'

2

BLACKOUT

'MRS. GREENFELL, your daughter's been late twice this week already, four times this month, and it's only the twelfth. You know two late marks count as an absence, don't you? Mrs. Greenfell?'

Kim clenched one fist beneath the table. The other hand held the strap of her bag so tight she could feel the frayed end stretching. Much more and it would break, then perhaps it would make a decent club to swing at Mr. Trower's head—

The wail of a distant siren distracted both. When Kim turned back from the window, she found Mr. Trower shuffling a pile of papers, their appointment apparently over. As she started to stand, he pulled open his top desk drawer and switched off an alarm flashing on the screen of a smartphone.

'I … I think—' Kim began, trying to keep her voice steady when her heart was thundering with an anger she was struggling to contain, '—I'll just let Emily chalk up a few absences if that's what she needs, if that's what it takes to keep her on track. She's not had a good run of it since her dad walked out—'

Mr. Trower tilted his head and gave Kim a sour look, as though to say, *whose fault is that?* 'There are currently seventy-six pupils at Bloomfield being raised by a single parent. Most are coping fine. It might help if your daughter made more effort to fit in, and they say that conformity starts at home—'

The siren had come closer and was now loud enough to make it hard to hear his words. On the corner of his desk lay a newspaper with a blurry picture on the front of some kind of prehistoric animal. NATIONAL HEALTH AGENCY NOW BELIEVES VIRUS ORIGINATED WITH SAURODS, the headline read.

'Well, if we're done here?' Kim said, suddenly feeling an urge to cry. It was easier than picking a fight, which would get her in the school's bad books, along with her daughter.

Mr. Trower flapped a dismissive hand at her as though she were no more important than a speck of dust, and Kim, chastened, headed for the door. She had one hand on the handle, when Mr. Trower cleared his throat.

'Mrs. Greenfell?'

'What?'

She turned. Trower was holding his phone in his hand, his face grave as he stared at the display. 'Go straight home,' he said.

Kim gave a solemn nod, then headed out. Her fingers, still shaking, slipped on the door handle, and it took two tries to close it. *God, I need a fucking drink.* Emily, the only person sitting on the line of plastic chairs in the corridor outside, looked up from a science textbook that barely hid a fashion magazine lying beneath.

'All right, Mum?'

'Let's just get going.'

Kim walked quickly past, and heard Emily fall into step behind her. Her daughter caught up with her as she reached a set of double doors leading outside.

'Mum, what did old Trowel say?'

Kim pushed through the doors, then stopped and waited for Emily. As Emily stepped outside, Kim jabbed a finger into her daughter's chest.

'Show some fucking respect for once,' she said. 'If you could damn well grow up, I wouldn't have to come down here. Can't you try a little harder? Just smile once in a while, and do what they want without making a goddamn song and dance about it. I can't deal with this, Em.'

Emily, head lowered, peered up through jet black dyed hair gelled against the side of her face. 'By cope you mean drink yourselves to sleep, then bang some pill to keep you awake until lunchtime, when you—'

Kim lifted a hand, but before she could lean into the slap, her anger left her in a sudden rush, a soul departing its body. She sagged sideways, and might have fallen if Emily hadn't grabbed her, pulling her into a hug.

'I'm sorry, Mum.'

'Em, please.'

'All right, I'll try. I'll carry some boxes for old Trowel or mark out the lines for sports day or whatever.'

Kim could barely bring herself to speak, she held her daughter close, remembering a time which didn't feel all that long ago now, when she'd only needed one arm to hold her daughter, and her husband, Emily's father, had still been around.

'By the way, Mum, you can't say fuck in front of me. That means I can say it.'

Kim laughed through tears. 'You say it more than me

already. Come on, let's ditch this place. We'll get pizza on the way home, or whatever trash food you like.'

'There's that new burger place in Kidbrooke. It's not far out of the way.'

'Sure.'

Emily pushed her mother away then gave a playful grin. 'I have enough zits already. Might as well fill out the gaps that are left.'

'You don't have many.'

Emily lifted an eyebrow. 'That's because I cover them with concealer. And you never notice, because you're always—' She turned away. 'It doesn't matter.'

'Come on,' Kim said. 'Let's just go.'

The car always made her focus. She gripped the wheel hard enough to leave her knuckles white and steered out of the school car park into traffic. It was busier than usual this evening, perhaps due to the sirens she had heard earlier. But then, this was London, and it was rush hour. And despite what was happening in the north, that was there, and this was here. They had just come to a standstill when a military helicopter flew low overhead, angling away towards North London.

'Woah, you see that?' Emily cried. 'Nearly took the roof off the car.'

'Yeah, I saw it.'

'You reckon it's gone to shoot a few more of those things? Those—'

Kim thumped the steering wheel. 'Maybe,' she said, a little louder than was necessary. 'I don't know, do I?'

'Dad would.'

'Don't start this again.'

'Mum, I'm just saying, perhaps you should give him another chance—'

'Your father and I are over.'

Emily looked away, out of the side window. Kim squeezed her eyes shut for a moment then looked over at her daughter. Every harsh word … it burned.

'Em, I'm sorry.'

A half shrug, but Emily didn't look back. 'You know, this kid from class, Barry Davis, he said his dad took him up there last weekend, trying to get a look.'

'Up where?'

'Up to Manchester. To the edge of the zone.'

'I'm sure he was lying—'

'He said they were shooting people who tried to leave. Said he saw someone take a bullet. The front of their head just exploded—'

'Emily!'

Emily looked up, eyes wide. Chestnut brown, like her father's. Like her hair, before she dyed it. She was so beautiful, was Emily, as beautiful as her father had been handsome, before he wrecked himself.

'Em—'

'Please stop saying sorry. I know your generation is in denial, pretending there's nothing going on. Blackout zones "for our own good". It's all government horseshit. You should see some of the SnipVids that are coming out of Manchester.'

Another helicopter buzzed overhead, this one so low its skids were barely above the line of cars as it angled downwards ahead of them, and then suddenly it was dipping sharply sideways into a residential area, momentarily disappearing from view before a deafening explosion sounded, the shockwave rocking the car. Kim was too stunned even to move as a plume of black smoke rose from behind a line of houses, and fragments of debris rained down on the windscreen of the car.

'Mum, that's not good.' Emily had tears in her eyes.

'Let's forget the burgers and just get home, shall we? That helicopter … it just crashed.'

'It just crashed.' Kim felt like a soundbite, but her tongue was dry, her senses feeling like someone was holding her underwater. 'It just … crashed.'

'Mum, please, I'm scared.'

They weren't alone. Other cars were attempting to turn around, away from the crash site. A few cars ahead, doors opened and a handful of people got out. Some ran towards the crash, others away, while the rest stood uncertainly, hands running through their hair, unsure what to do.

'Mum! I want to go!'

Emily was right. Whatever had caused the crash, it was nothing to do with them, and there was nothing they could do to help. As the traffic across the street lurched forwards, Kim slammed the car into gear and turned into a gap.

It was a significant detour, but it was worth it. Sirens were everywhere, police and fire engines roaring past them far faster than was safe on the narrow, crowded commuter road. Kim took what shortcuts she knew, turning up narrow residential streets to avoid potentially busy intersections, even cutting down a one-way street to avoid a notoriously busy roundabout. As she pulled into traffic just short of Thames Tunnel Three, she began to think they might make it home at a reasonable time tonight. Too bad if they couldn't get the dinner Emily wanted. There was some leftover spaghetti, some sausages in the fridge—

A shadow passed above them, something silent Kim didn't get a good look at. She craned her neck to see, but Emily was reaching across her, trying to grab the wheel.

'Mum, look out!'

The car in front had braked sharply. Emily pushed Kim aside as she jerked the wheel to the right, the car's wing missing the back of the nearest car by a hair's breadth. Kim let out a gasp, but before she could take the wheel back, the headlights of an oncoming car flashed out of the darkness. Brakes squealed, horns blared. Kim squeezed her eyes shut and waited for the impact.

'Did you see it, Mum? Did you see it? They shot it down. They shot it out of the sky.'

Kim opened her eyes. The oncoming car had missed them, and they were somehow still moving, descending into the tunnel in a line of slow-moving traffic. She glanced in the wing mirror, saw the tunnel entrance receding behind her. Her fingers shook on the wheel and she gripped it tighter, wishing, oh wishing, she had something to drink. The line of cars had slowed to a crawl, horns blaring up ahead.

'Mum? Did you see it? It was one of those flying—'

A muffled explosion cut off Emily's words. Kim glanced in the wing mirror again, in time to see the tunnel entrance folding downwards like a closing mouth. In an instant, the block of grey sky over east London was gone.

3

HOUSE

IN THE POTTING SHED, the bell was ringing. Alfred Lammonby set down the hoe with the broken handle he had been patiently repairing for the last hour, and pressed the intercom button beside the door.

'Yes?'

A hiss of static. Then: 'Alf? It's June. The Master wants a word. Can you come up?'

Alfred closed his eyes for a moment. Another of the Master's "words". Perfect. All Alfred needed to break his concentration, reward himself with a long trudge up to the house, attend a pointless meeting, and then another long trudge all the way back down again.

'I'll be there in five minutes,' he said, but as soon as June hung up, he swore like an old sailor and knocked a cup of nails across the floor.

Then minutes later, he staggered through the back door into the staff utility quarters, pulled off his wellington boots and set them down on the mat behind the door. Wincing, he rubbed at his bad knee. At seventy-three he should be long retired, sitting with his feet up, perhaps doing a little fishing. Lord Evans had promised Alfred a plot of land all for himself, a reduction in his duties to a few ceremonial activities, and a comfortable retirement package as a thank you for fifty years of dutiful service.

And then Lord Evans had died, leaving his son, Richard, to take over the estate, and he had reneged on everything.

The spiteful little bastard.

Richard was sitting at the table in the drawing room, still wearing his outdoor boots, one raised over the other, dropping mud onto the carpet. He had some trampy thing with him, all blond hair and flesh showing where it shouldn't be, feet up on one of the sofas along the wall as though she owned the place.

'Sir? You requested to see me?' Alfred lowered his head a little into a respectful bow.

'You took your time. When I call, I expect promptness. This isn't a fucking holiday camp.'

'Yes, sir.'

'You won't have seen the news. There's been some kind of outbreak just north of Birmingham. Typical with our fucking government, but a media blackout has been put in place so it's hard to know exactly what's going on. However, in case it's military, I want you to prepare the bunker at the end of the grounds with enough provisions for a couple of months. I know my father kept an inventory just in case, paranoid that he was about a nuclear war. Whatever he had on it, double it. I'm not taking any chances.'

'Yes, sir.'

Richard stood up. He was a wiry little man who stood a full head shorter than Alfred's six-three. Lord Evans had been short too, but he had possessed a dignity and a grace of which Richard had inherited none. Richard's eyes were dark, pitiless seeds, his mouth a sour, twisted grey line. Alfred had never liked him even as a child, but it had been June who had spent most of her time with him. She had never liked the boy either, Alfred knew, but unlike Alfred, she had been forced to hide her dislike, smothering him with motherly attention that his own mother had, due to her aristocratic duties, been unable to give.

'You've served my family a long time, haven't you, Lammonby?'

'Yes, sir.'

'Can't he say anything else?' the tart on the sofa said suddenly, leaning backwards on the chair, exposing a white triangle of cleavage. 'Yes, sir, no, sir, three bags full, sir?'

Alfred chose to say nothing.

'My father considered you a confidante, and a friend?'

'Yes, sir.'

Richard leaned close. Alfred smelled whisky. Richard's breath tickled his ear.

'Don't fuck this up,' he whispered. 'This could be it, Lammonby. The great disaster my father foretold. I'm counting on you. You won't let me down, will you?'

'No.'

'Good. Now get on with it. I want the bunker prepared by the end of tomorrow.'

~

'At least let Lilian and I help you,' June said, as Alfred reached for another box of canned goods, wincing as his back screamed at him. Nine loads so far, and he was feeling every step. He had tripped on a root last time, almost dropping the box. He had a dozen more to do, and that was just to stock the larder. Sooner or later he would stumble again, but an order was an order.

'No,' Alfred said, shaking his head. 'You have your duties. I can't burden you. This is my task.'

'He's gone too far this time. I mean, he won't even let you use the truck.'

'The master said that if something bad is going down, we need to save petrol. He gave me the trolley.'

'But the wheel has a puncture. You know what he's doing, Alfred. Don't pretend that you don't.'

'I have my duties.'

June grabbed his arm as he tried to pull away, and as he looked back into her defiant face, he wondered if his love for her had ever burned so bright. She was every day of seventy now, but to Alfred she looked as lovely as she had on their wedding day, forty-seven years ago.

'You know what that little so-and-so is doing. He's trying to—'

'I know exactly what he's doing,' Alfred hissed. 'But I'd rather he broke me than you or Lilian. He thinks he can run me into the ground, but I'm made of sterner stuff than that.'

Shaking her head, June sighed. 'You were,' she said.

~

Had it been a summer house perhaps, or a potting shed, or anything other than what it was, the bunker could have been pleasant, idyllic even, set in a grassy, shady grove of mature trees at the far end of the house gardens. All that was visible above ground was a dome of concrete with a heavy steel door set into one side which opened inwards to reveal a steep set of concrete stairs leading down into darkness. Down the stairs was a short, low corridor, designed to keep potential assailants in single file, which led to another door, thicker than the one above and designed to be blast proof. To the best of his knowledge, Lord Evans had never done a practical test on the door's impregnability, but it hurt like anything to haul open each time, and was almost as difficult to close.

Inside the door, which could be bolted from the inside, was a small lobby room designed as a decoy. There was everything one might expect of a bunker here, a small kitchen, a shower unit and toilet with a plumbing system that exited near a pond two hundred metres away in a lower section of the gardens. There was a fold-down bed, and a desk. The walls were concrete, but the floor lined with tiles.

Through a hatch in the kitchen floor, however, was what appeared to be a small underfloor larder. This however, slid on rails to the side, revealing a second hatch, and beneath this a ladder.

Alfred hated this section. Not only because it was hell on his shoulders and back to climb down, carrying a few cans at a time, but because he was now nearly ten metres under the ground and hated every second of it. Even when he reached the bottom and opened a door onto a spacious living section with a second, larger set of everything above and with beds for up to five people, he hated what it represented. The walls had been painted, but they were still concrete, and an air filter in the ceiling was the only thing between them and suffocation. It looked good on the surface, but on the literal underneath it was a place for desperate measures, somewhere to hole up while the world went to hell.

Alfred remembered when Lord Evans had ordered it built, nearly thirty years ago, when Richard had been just a child. For nearly six months construction crews had worked solely at night, excavating the land and laying down the bunker, equipping it with everything Lord Evans had considered necessary at the time. For decades, Alfred had been required to give it a once monthly clean, dusting everything down, making sure the filters worked, the toilets flushed, and the taps ran clear. After the lord's death, Richard had ordered all activities to cease, so now, after five years of inattention, the bunker was stuffy and dirty, the air filters coated in dust.

Climbing down, Alfred placed the cans he had brought on a shelf and inspected the bunker's components.

Nothing seemed amiss. It was a little grimy, but the filters appeared to be working. The water from the taps ran clear, and the lights all switched on. The electricity system was connected to the house, which now ran on more recently installed solar panels. There were plenty of spare bulbs, and the fridge, which he would soon start to fill, was cool.

As a man of duty, the events in the outside world were none of his concern, but he had to admit, that the master's sudden request had left him a little spooked. In one corner of the bunker was a television—a modern replacement of the old box that had stood here until a year prior to Lord Evans's death—and Alfred found himself reaching for the remote in a bracket on the wall. He needed to check that it worked, after all.

The first couple of channels he flicked over were the usual filler—varieties, game shows, reality this and that—which June enjoyed on an evening off. Alfred was a man of books, and classics at that; little written in the last fifty years held much interest for him, not when there were so many of his own contemporaries he was yet to read.

The next channel was a news loop. A middle-aged reporter wearing a construction site hard hat stood in front of a building on flames in the background, although it looked slightly off kilter, as though it were a superimposition.

'The government is advising everyone north of Birmingham to stay at home,' the reporter said. 'We will bring you updates when we have them of the nature of the outbreak. At the moment, very little is known. It is thought that the attack is of a biological nature….'

Alfred changed the channel. A couple more of fluff, shopping, commercials. Then another news station, a local one.

'We are evacuating,' a young female reporter said into the camera. 'It's possible that soon we will be forced to go off the air, but stay tuned to our social channels for text updates.'

A sudden explosion came from somewhere in the background, and for a moment everything shuddered. Alfred expected the station to go off the air, but the woman's face reappeared, leaning close to the camera. 'We're hearing there might be a breach,' she hissed. 'We're unsure what kind. I advise you to take shelter, and to stay at home until you hear further instructions. Stay safe—'

The connection broke. Alfred sighed. He flicked past a couple more shopping channels and a black and white film, then switched the television off.

At least he knew it worked.

He replaced the remote in the bracket and headed for the ladder. It would soon be dark, and he had several more loads to do.

Whatever was going on, he felt that following the second reporter's advice would be for the best. They were safe here on the grounds of the house, and it wouldn't do to panic.

Richard had taken away June's television a month ago,

claiming that it was a distraction from her work. Since then she had spent most of her free time listening to old records on a record player in their quarters.

He didn't really know what he could tell her, not yet.

It was best to carry on as normal, for now.

4

HILLTOP

ONE MINUTE the class were enjoying a picnic beside the stone circle at the top of the Clent Hills, and the next, the *pat-pat-pat* of multiple explosions came popping out of Birmingham city centre as though someone had dropped a giant firecracker. Columns of smoke rose from a dozen burning high-rises as more explosions sounded. The ground shook beneath their feet.

Claire Hopgood, form teacher for Lower Sixth Class 2, had spent much of her adult life watching horror stories on the news, and sometimes, over a glass or two of wine, had absently wondered how she might react if such a disaster ever befell her: would she run screaming for cover, or stoically and heroically start marshalling and barking orders?

They did fire drills at school, of course. And when the prearranged time for the alarm to sound had come, Claire had carried out her duties like the rest, summoning the lacklustre enthusiasm to blow the whistle at the right time, to order her class out into the corridor, to lead them gamefully to pseudo-safety.

On the day when the world truly went to hell, though, at first she could do nothing. She stared dumbly at the distant puffs of smoke, felt the bangs—so, so much louder than they ever sounded on the television—ripple through her, and she stayed silent, even as the black dots of helicopters flew over the city, the staccato rhythms and the flashes of gunfire seemingly everywhere. Even as some of her pupils began to scream or duck down behind the standing stones, she simply stood still, useless and immobile, as the city in which she had grown up began to disintegrate.

It was actually Pauly, the driver from Don Jones Coaches who reacted first. Claire felt a tug on her sleeve, and when she could bring herself to turn, she found Pauly standing there, his face ashen, breathing hard from having hurried up the hill from the car park.

'I heard those explosions,' he puffed. 'Do you think we should head back to the bus?'

Claire could only nod. Then, as though broken out of a trance, a rush of adrenaline flooded through her and she found herself galvanised into action.

'Get back to the bus!' she shouted. 'Quickly! Duck your heads!'

It sounded stupid with the explosions still so far away, fifteen miles as the crow flew, but what if it was just the precursor to worse? It was forty minutes by coach, but a helicopter could cover the distance in a fraction of that. Worse of all, though, was that Claire had no idea who was on who's side, who or what the explosions were aimed at, and who the helicopters were here to either massacre or save.

But there was safety with cover, and cover meant the electric bus in which they had come on today's history school trip.

Panic did crazy things to people, however, Claire was quickly finding out. Some kids had run for the trees, others still cowered behind the stones, while more—a stupidly high number, she thought—had actually walked in the direction of the explosions, craning their necks to see more.

'Miss, can you see those dots?' Danny Rainer said, pulling a phone out of his bag, pressing it to his lips and issuing a command for the camera function. A phone that was banned on school trips, not that it probably mattered now, Claire thought.

'Danny, I trust you. Go and bring Daisy, Ishy and Mick back here. We need to get back to the bus.'

Get back to the bus. It was a mantra to hold on to, one that gave her a modicum of comfort when she sensed she would soon have none. She thought of her house on Siding Street in Birmingham's south, her terrier Reggie who would be panicking by now, probably peeing on the carpet in the hall. How close was Siding Street to the explosions? She thought they were too far north, but more were coming now, spread out, pops and bangs and more columns of smoke.

And then something let out a sound that Claire knew in that moment that she would remember for however long she lived. Something preternatural, something both haunting and awe-inspiring at the same time: the shriek of some kind of bird, an animal with lungs more powerful than any known. Something that couldn't, shouldn't exist.

She had heard the rumours, of course. Everyone had. But she had no more believed it than she did any other hairbrained conspiracy theory. And even if scientists were making crazy shit in labs, it wouldn't get far if it ever got out. The kind of things she was reading about weren't invisible little things like viruses, they were big, monstrous things that ripped and tore, and this world no longer belonged to them. They wouldn't last five minutes among humanity.

And yet the dots that Danny Rainer was pointing at, soaring high above Birmingham city centre, fitted what descriptions she had heard. And they were, to her horror, coming closer.

'Miss, Miss, are they birds? What kind are they?'

'Danny, I told you, go and get Daisy and the others. They've gone too far down that slope. It's dangerous—'

Someone began to scream. Claire spun around, almost tripping over a protruding root, sticking out a hand to touch one of the standing stones to give herself balance.

It felt so ancient, so powerful, so secure. She wished she could hold on to it forever, let its solidity comfort her, but two girls were standing up on a bench, one with a pair of binoculars held to her eyes, the other screaming at her, trying to snatch the binoculars away even while being fended off.

'Lisa! Connie! Get down!' Claire shouted, but her authority meant nothing now the world was collapsing in on itself. She might as well no longer exist.

Lisa Margate, the girl with the binoculars, pulled them away from her eyes and got down from the bench. Her face was ashen, her mouth agape. She dropped the binoculars with a hard thump which sent the other girl, Connie Hart, into a frenzy, scrabbling in the dirt to retrieve the binoculars. As she held them up, Connie cried, 'You've broken one of the lenses, you stupid fucking bitch!'

'Connie!' Claire shouted, increasingly aware of her ineffectiveness. Lisa had fallen to her knees, her skirt tearing on a corner of the bench. She lifted her hands as though she meant to cover her eyes, then just flapped them in the air around her face while shaking her head slowly back and forth.

Eighteen kids. Eighteen sets of parents she would have to answer to if she didn't get them back on the bus. Most of them were harmless, but Connie Hart's dad was a rich, arrogant wanker. Getting on his wrong side was *not-a-good-thing*.

It was the focus Claire needed to galvanise herself. Ignoring the dots on the horizon that moved like birds and were slowly approaching, she began to run back and forth across the hill's crest, waving kids back towards the car park, summoning reserves of authoritative anger she hadn't thought she possessed until now.

And they started to listen. Most, at any rate.

Danny had managed to get Ishy and Daisy back to the bus. Connie was still berating Lisa, pushing her in the chest and making her cry, but both were backing up towards Pauly, who was standing at the top of the path back down. Jenny Coates and Tim Parkson, the alpha couple everyone knew were sleeping together, had reemerged from an overgrown area a little way down the slope. Tim fixed his belt as he ran, Jenny pulling at his arm.

Where was Mick Williams? The idiot kid who had scrapped into the Sixth Form with two Ds and a sob story at the interview with the headmaster had been with Daisy and Ishy but had disappeared. Claire thumped the side of her thigh. She would leave him behind if she had her choice. Since getting into the Sixth Form by the skin of his dirty teeth, he'd done nothing other than be a total pain in the arse. He'd survived two behaviour warnings and if he didn't get back to the bus in five fucking seconds he'd get another—

'Miss? Miss?'

Danny Rainer stood behind her. Claire shook her head. 'What?'

'Those aren't birds, Miss.'

Claire had the children to consider. Bombs, helicopters, those things scared her, but she could make sense of them. Flying things that were not birds, she couldn't.

'Danny, please get on the bus.'

'Miss, look. Please, Miss. Like, I know what they are. I saw something on Flip-Chat—'

I can't look, Claire wanted to say. *If I look I'll lose my mind, and I just found it. I can't look.*

'Miss, we have to go.'

Danny reached for her arm then pulled back as though breaking some unspoken code. He shook his head, then backed up, turned, and ran.

Claire turned, cupping her hands over her mouth to holler for Mick, but no sound would come. Something massive swooped out of the sky, dropping into the bushes just beyond the crest of the hill. Claire knew what it looked like, what it could be, but couldn't process its existence in this world. This was her world, damn it. This creature's world was gone, in the past, and yet here it was, dark, forest green, covered in the tufty beginnings of feathers over scaly skin, the size of a glider, the backdraft from its wings so powerful Claire staggered back, finding one of the standing stones behind her, cold against her back. Her hands shook so badly she could barely control them, and her heart felt set to explode out of her throat. She stared at the bushes as a muted scream reached her, and she didn't think that Mick, wherever he had gone, was coming back.

'The bus,' she gasped, as the bushes shook. 'Get to the bus….'

If any other members of her class were still outside, then they would have to fend for themselves. As a dark shadow momentarily passed over her, and then the sky above filled with something massive and dark that she dared not look up at, she understood that the world had flipped on its head. The role of teacher as it had once been was now obsolete, and if she were lucky enough to see the dawn of another day, nothing would be as it had been yesterday, and wouldn't ever be again.

5

CHANGES

THE SIRENS WOKE Alan Graf from an uneasy slumber. He had fallen asleep in the chair by the window again. Light peeked around the drawn curtains, and for a moment he felt disorientated, unsure of both the time, and the day itself.

The clock read just after seven. Alan pushed himself up, feeling an unfamiliar muscle ache in his shoulders. That was it—a patient had come in late last night, a big guy, stumbling about, complaining about dizziness. He'd fallen, and it had taken three of them to get him up off the floor. The doctor had diagnosed complications related to severe diabetes, but after helping get the man into a ward, Alan's role had ended. He remembered getting home two hours later than his shift should have ended, checking on Dad, then slumping into the easy chair with a cup of tea to take a moment to relax for a few minutes before bed.

He had knocked the tea off the table at some point in the night, and a grey-brown stain had soaked deep into the carpet. Alan just stared at it, too tired to rouse himself to fetch a sponge and some cleaning liquid. He would get to it when he could.

Like a lot of things.

Another siren howled in the distance. He recognised this was an ambulance; the one that had woken him was fire. He hoped that whoever was misfortunate enough to be expecting them wasn't hurt too bad, and wondered if he would encounter some result of it later, on his evening shift.

For now, Dad was the priority. Moving stiffly, Alan went to the hall and cracked Dad's door. The air filter purred, the heart rate monitor beeped, the non-invasive ventilation machine hummed. Dad, pale and thin, his face little more than a stubbly, creased mask over bones, sat propped up in bed, his eyes closed, the ventilator mask over his mouth and nose. As he did every day, Alan watched for Dad's breathing, ignoring the gentle background noise of the machines until he saw for himself that the old man still lived.

Only then did he enter the room.

'How are we feeling today?' he said in a low voice, adopting his best ward manner for Dad, aware that the slightest surprise could be the end of him. 'A little better?'

It was unlikely, but Alan had seen miracles on the wards that he hoped one might one day follow him home. While he knew in his heart he was only providing palliative care, nevertheless he still dreamed of Dad one day being strong enough to get out of bed, to walk alongside Alan down to the river where they had spent so many good days, perhaps throw a line out over the water like old times.

'That's good,' Alan said, covering his mouth, aware the tears were coming. He mentally went through the list of morning jobs—change Dad's incontinence slip, feed him breakfast, turn him, give him a bed bath, then switch on the radio or the TV to provide a little entertainment, check the machines, administer his medicine—while backing out of the room and gently closing the door.

By the time he was in the kitchen making coffee while heating up the baby food that Dad now lived on, his eyes were so watery he could barely see. He drank one coffee quickly, then refilled his cup while chewing down a piece of toast—nothing tasted good anymore—then returned to Dad's room to start his duties.

When he was finished, leaving Dad comfortable and clean, a radio drama playing gently in the corner, he went back to the living room and checked his work schedule. He needed to get Dad's ventilation machine serviced soon, which the government wouldn't pay for. Was there some way he could squeeze in another shift? The money would help.

He was about to make another coffee when an almighty explosion came from somewhere nearby. Alan staggered, reaching out for the back of a chair to steady himself as books slid from shelves and a framed photograph fell off a sideboard and struck the edge of the old fireplace lintel, the glass shattering. As other rumbles sounded, each a little farther away, Alan roused himself and hurried through to Dad's room.

Dad's eyes were open, moving gummily around the room. Alan knelt beside him, a hand on Dad's arm, and whispered comforting words until Dad's eyes closed again, and the heart rate monitor attached to his finger began to slow.

Alan let out a taut breath. A close call. But what had made that noise? It sounded as though a gas storage facility had exploded, but there were none anywhere near their part of town. The only other thing he could think of was perhaps the sewage pipes, but would an underground explosion have made that kind of commotion?

After convincing himself that Dad was all right, he went to the front door and peered out through the spy hole. The street was busier than usual, a couple of dozen people hurrying past, all heading south. No cars though, but when he opened the door and looked up the street, he saw one had overturned near the north junction with Leicester Road, blocking access.

Something about the scene outside made him uneasy. Dad was his priority, and he wanted no part of anyone else's problems, but as he started to close the door a young boy he recognised who lived nearby came running across the street, waving a hand at him to wait.

'Mr. Graf! Mr. Graf! You're a doctor, aren't you? There's a man hurt up there.'

A nurse, but he guessed the boy's father might have hammed him up a little. He paused, wanting to refuse, but the boy's face was desperate. Alan wondered if he had some personal connection with whomever was hurt.

'All right,' he said. 'I'm coming.'

The boy had already run back across the street, perhaps trusting in Alan's status as a medical professional. It was worthy, he supposed, and his conscience couldn't refuse. He slipped on a pair of shoes and grabbed a jacket—not for him, but for a possible patient—and hurried down the steps to the street.

Something felt different about the world this morning to the world he had put to bed last night. An unfamiliarity, an uneasiness. Alan tried to identify one thing that would label how he felt, and it seemed to be the lack of traffic noise. Sure, there were sirens still wailing in the distance, and the roar of fires perhaps started by the explosions, but of regular traffic, usually a constant background hum, there was nothing. He looked south down Porter Road to the junction with Abbot Street, and let out a gasp.

Four cars had been involved in a pileup. One completely blocked Porter Road, while another had somehow lifted off the ground and now sat stacked on top of a parked car nearby. He started to head that way, wondering if he could help, then remembered the boy and turned back. The boy was standing by the overturned car at Porter Road's north end, beckoning to him.

Ellis, that was his name, Alan remembered now as he hurried up the street, not quite walking, not quite running, but somewhere in between, a reluctant man trying to look the opposite. Ellis Webster, so close to the name of the boy who had given rise to the sport of rugby—allegedly, at least—so many years ago. Alan's thoughts were briefly interrupted by memories of school games, in particular of the try he had scored playing prop against Darwent Secondary that had lifted his school to an unprecedented semi-final in the Midlands Under-15s. He would never forget looking to see Dad, fists clenched, standing by the touchline, screaming with joy.

(That's my lad! That's my lad!)

For a moment he was derailed, stopped in the middle of the road, overcome by the grief he knew was coming.

'Mr. Graf! Hurry! I think his leg's trapped!'

The boy's voice galvanised him back into action. He reached the overturned car and squatted down beside a flopped, bloody body, half in and out of the car, lying in a circle of shattered glass and splattered blood.

'Can you help him, Mr. Graf?' the boy was saying over and over, so much so that Alan wanted to snap at him to shut his mouth to let him think. It took him a moment to recognise the way the body had twisted, and understand that for this man there was no hope.

'Should I call an ambulance, Mr. Graf?'

No ambulance could come quick enough. The man was breathing, blood bubbling up out of his nose, but wouldn't for much longer. Alan shook his head.

'It's too late.'

'That's Mr. Fredricks, my dad's boss,' Ellis said. 'He gave Dad a raise last year. Dad was well pleased—'

Alan filtered the boy out. His eyes glazed over as he stared at the mangled body, the breathing slowing until finally, with one last cough, Mr. Fredricks gave out. Alan pushed himself stiffly to his feet and looked around.

'What happened here?'

Ellis, staring at the body, ignored him.

'What happened—'

A shriek that Alan could only describe as inhuman echoed up the street. He heard the distinct sound of large, flapping feet, like a giant running duck. He turned to look up past the line of parked cars along the side of Leicester Road and saw something that left him speechless. For a moment, as he watched the running creature, his mind wouldn't compute what he was seeing. The thing was nine or ten feet tall, running with its head lowered, a thick, meaty tail swinging back and forth. It ran on two powerful legs, two shorter arms dangling at its sides. Its head was the size of a dustbin. It had big, stupid eyes, and a pouting mouth. Two nostrils that could easily have accommodated a man's arm flared as it exhaled, and when it opened its mouth Alan saw teeth built for grinding grass, like a horse's. The whole creature was a kind of light orange, patchy scales covered with tufts of fur, not unlike the skin of a pig.

He was still staring at it when a deafening, *rat-tat-tat* came from up the street. Red spots appeared across the creature's body, and it briefly became a moving art project before the heavy machinegun fire began to break it apart. Alan could only stare as it twisted under the barrage, its skin popping and greenish red blood spraying out, before falling sideways, landing on its back in the middle of the street. For a few seconds the gunfire continued, until the creature was a bloodied, unrecogniseable mess. Then an uneasy calm fell over the street. The stench of copper hung heavily in the air, smoke appearing like a funeral veil to cover over humanity's sins.

'Did you see that?' Ellis said from nowhere, making Alan jump. 'That was a hadrosaur, wasn't it? A real one. Not like a model. That was a *real* one.'

Alan said nothing. His acute awareness of danger meant he was more concerned about where the gunfire had come from than a creature that no longer posed any threat.

A hiss of static filled the air. Ellis let out a cry of alarm and Alan clamped hands over his ears.

'This is a public service announcement,' came a mechanised voice through a loudspeaker. 'A citywide curfew is now in place. You are required to return to your homes.'

From somewhere far in the distance came the sound of more gunfire, then a louder explosion. A series of sirens rose up as though in opposition.

The world had changed. Alan turned and started walking back to his house, aware that Dad might have heard the gunfire and become alarmed. The room was soundproofed as best as Alan could, but not well enough.

He was nearly there when he realised Ellis was trailing along behind him.

'It wasn't what I thought it would look like, Mr. Graf,' he said. 'I didn't think it would have fur, did you? And it looked like it couldn't walk too well, like one leg was bigger than the other. And you know what was strangest? The way it didn't seem to show any fear, as though it wasn't evolved enough to know to be afraid.'

Alan stopped. Halfway across the street, he turned back, about to tell Ellis to go home, when the façade of a three-storey terrace on Leicester Road, just up from the junction, suddenly exploded outwards, showering the street and the line of parked cars with glass and chunks of masonry.

Alan could only stare. The world had most certainly changed. Without a word he turned and hurried for his front door, the patter of Ellis's feet on the ground behind him as the boy, lost and without comfort cried, 'Mr. Graf! Mr. Graf! That was my house. That was *my* house!'

6

ESCAPE

AT FIRST, everything was pitch black. For a while, a long, low grumbling continued, distant and muffled like a stomach growl concealed beneath a thick coat, joined at times by the slow crunch and tortured creak of metal. Petrol fumes filled Kim's senses, and beneath her hands she felt the sharp gritty sensation of recently pulverised rock mixed with shattered glass.

Too stunned even to speak, for a few seconds nothing seemed to happen, then the lights began to click on, smart phones, internal car lights, even a flickering torch, and the first early screams of panic rang out from nearby.

'Jeff's not breathing!'

'Help me! My leg's trapped!'

'I can't move!'

'Help!'

'Mum?'

Kim tried to twist in her seat but a white hot lance of pain raced up her side. She reached up a hand inch by slow inch, until her fingers touched the plastic casing of the inside car light. It was too low, the roof buckled, but when she clicked it, the inside of the car filled with a dim but welcome light.

'Emily? Are you all right?'

Instead of her daughter, it was the groan of the compressed car roof that answered. Kim pressed a hand against it as though that would help, and tried to twist around again. The pain was still there, but a little less than before.

'Mum? Mum, I'm here. What happened?'

The answer was obvious, but Kim knew her daughter. It wasn't about the tunnel collapsing; that was clear. There was more, so much more.

'I don't know, but we have to try to get out of here. I don't know how much has come down, but if the rock shifts….'

She couldn't say it. She reached up and angled the mirror to see Emily's face. A streak of blood ran down from a cut beside her daughter's eye.

'You're hurt!'

'It's okay. It's just a scratch.'

'Can you move?'

'Can you?'

Kim remembered something her father had always said when she was child on the frequent occasions when she would get frustrated trying to figure something out, trying to do something before she was ready. *How do you climb a ladder, Kimberly? One step at a time. Deal with the first rung, then deal with the second.*

She began to shift herself about, one body part at a time, looking for pain, looking for compression. Her left thigh ached, but she could still move her toes all right, so hopefully it was just a bruise. A rock had come through the side window and cut her arm, but it wasn't deep, and on the plus side, the door had popped open.

People were already moving past, trying to find a way out. Distant sirens blared, and blind flashlights flickered across a mess of damaged cars. From the look of things, they had got lucky. Most of the rockfall had been on the northbound lane. Their car had taken direct hit from a lump of fallen masonry, but on the northbound, there was nothing but a slope of broken rock where cars should have been.

'Emily, are you trapped? We have to get out of here.'

'I think I'm all right. The roof … Mum, what's happening?'

'I don't know. Come on.'

She rolled sideways out of the open door. She hit the ground hard, cried out, then pushed herself back up. Her left thigh was agony, making it hard to straighten her knee or put weight on that foot, but she had broken her leg during a hockey tournament aged fourteen, and it didn't feel like that. Just bad bruising, maybe.

She hoped.

The back door opened easily and Emily climbed out. Other people came running past as they struggled away from the car, one man asking if they were okay before hurrying on without waiting for the answer. The air was a haze of smoke and dust, flickering lights strobing through it. Everything smelled of concrete and petrol, and the gentle yet menacing patter of falling stones reminded Kim that the tunnel might not be done collapsing.

'Come on.'

'Wait, my phone.'

'Emily, leave it.'

'It has a light. We might need it.'

Feeling a flood of pride at her daughter's common sense, Kim waited while Emily grabbed her phone off the back seat. Holding on to her daughter, she tried to limp forwards, but made it only a couple of steps before losing her footing again.

'Come on, Mum!' Emily said. 'It's not much farther.'

An ominous rumbling began to grow behind them. Sheer desperation made Kim ignore the agony in her left thigh as she struggled forwards, Emily half supporting, half dragging her. The muscles in her left leg were unresponsive, meaning she had to swing her foot forward from the hip, each step sending bolts of pain up her leg. But with each movement forwards, the light at the end of the tunnel drew closer. People were still pushing past them, drunkenly running into partially buried cars, tripping and falling over each other. With a sudden deafening tear, part of the roof to their left broke free, crashing down on the trapped cars and the people still struggling to free themselves.

'Mum, don't look, please.'

Kim had tears in her eyes. 'It should be me … saying that to you.'

'Don't look, Mum.'

Emily was crying, Kim too now. They struggled past the body of a man who had been crushed, his chest cavity opened out into bloody butterfly wings. His eyes were stretched wide, his grimace almost a smile, rapturous.

The road began to slant uphill, towards the tunnel exit. Kim slipped, and she looked down to see water running past her feet. At least she thought it was water, until she caught the smell.

'Faster, Mum!'

Emily was trying to run, Kim lolling forwards, her bad leg like a concertina beneath her. She wished she could just cut it off and be done with it, but she sensed she would need it if she wanted to survive what was going on. *Run, Kim, run.*

A sound like someone flapping a massive blanket came from behind them, just as they reached the overturned tanker. The heat at their backs was breathtaking, and then Emily, brave, brave Emily, was pushing Kim sideways, past the buckled door of a service tunnel entrance and into a narrow stairwell as the world plumed orange.

'Cover your mouth!' Emily shouted, pushing Kim ahead of her, into the stairwell. Emergency lights flickered. The air stank of oil, and Emily was pushing her from behind, trying to will her up the stairs.

And from somewhere, Kim found a last desperate measure of strength. She took Emily's hand and pulled her daughter up with her, and together they struggled up the stairs as below them the sounds of fire raged. The heat and smoke followed them, but another light came from above, natural light, what was left of the evening.

The service doors already stood open, swung back to reveal a fenced in maintenance access road set back from the top of the tunnel exit. To their left, the top of the tunnel had caved in. Below, smoke plumed from the rubble. People still came running out, some blazing torches, their clothes and hair set alight.

Together, they struggled back along the fence to where the maintenance road angled down to a closed gate. They slumped down with their backs against the cold metal, watching the sky fill with smoke, still hearing the screams and explosions coming from the entrance into hell from which they had narrowly escaped. From somewhere across London came the *rat-a-tat* of automatic gunfire, the *dut-dut-dut* of helicopter blades, and then the piercing wail of some kind of animal.

Emily was fussing with Kim's leg, trying to remove her shoe, but now that they were out, the pain had gone, replaced by a terrible, mortal fear, one that they had experienced more than just some horrific disaster, but a turning point in the way things were and had always been.

'Mum, what happened in there?' Emily said. 'What just happened?'

Kim closed her eyes. 'The world went down,' she said.

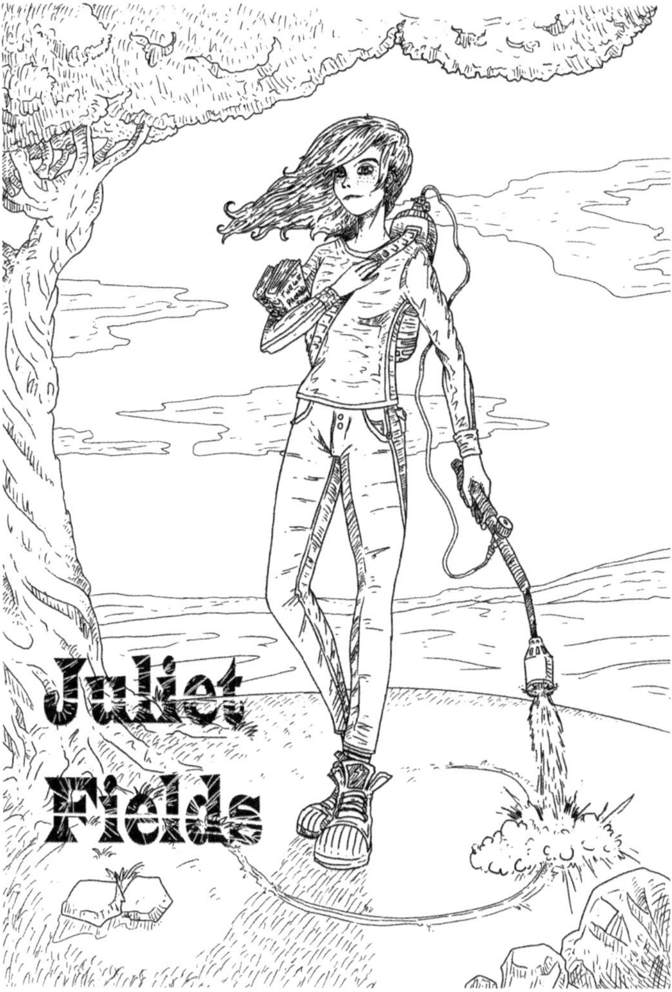
Juliet
Fields

7

VISITOR

Juliet had been going to first aid practice at the village hall for the last three years but no amount of practicing on dummies could have prepared her for the real thing.

The front of Uncle Lawrence's sweater—*what was he doing here, anyway?*—was soaked with blood, and it had taken Juliet a minute to realise where he was actually hurt. The blood was coming from his forearm, from a deep, jagged gash that pooled and dripped the dark stuff all over the ground. Just the sight of his bloodied clothes made her queasy, but Dad had told her so many times how a patient needed a doctor to be calm. And if she ever hoped to follow in his footsteps and become a doctor, she should start practicing now.

Calm, calm, calm.

It was far easier in theory than in practice.

Uncle Lawrence was cowering in the porch, injured arm held against his chest. She backed away, waving him after her, trying to get him to the kitchen before he dropped too much blood on the carpet.

Would it wash out? Could she get it out before Dad came home?

At least the kitchen had tile floors, which would be easier to clean, and their medical box was there, under the sink. She had last seen it back in April when she'd been stung by a bee in the garden and Dad had smeared her arm with Anthisan.

Uncle Lawrence, who'd been here more times that she could remember, drinking beer in the kitchen with Dad, was different this time, and it wasn't just the injury. He looked nervous, like a wild dog, caught inside and cornered. She had to pull out a chair for him—one he'd sat in hundreds of times—and push down on his shoulders to make him sit.

Her fingers were a trembly mess. She couldn't even grip the cupboard handle cleanly so ended up gripping the bottom edge of the cupboard and pulling it open there.

The medical kit was where it always was, nestled in among the pipes under the sink. With Dad being a doctor, it was far bigger and had more stuff in it even than the one Mrs. Wilberg brought to first aid practice.

She pulled it out, ripped off the lid, and then spilled half its contents on the floor.

'Pills,' Uncle Lawrence gasped, practically hyperventilating. 'Get me some pills.'

He must mean painkillers. Juliet tried to clear her mind, tried to concentrate. Uncle Lawrence was pale, his face drenched with sweat.

'I can call Dad,' she said, alarmed at the tremble in her voice. 'He will … he will know what to do.'

'No. No, no.' Uncle Lawrence shook his head. 'You. You have to do it.'

Juliet shook her head, but she was starting to remember now what she had been taught. Clean the wound. Stop the bleeding. Compression. Words and phrases she had heard over and over buzzed around her head like annoying flies.

She pulled a cloth out from under the sink and soaked it under the cold tap. Or should it be the warm? She couldn't remember, if she had ever known. It would have to do.

'Clean the blood,' she said, handing it to Uncle Lawrence.

'I can't,' he gasped, a weird, desperate inflection in his voice. 'You do it.'

She didn't want to get blood on her clothes, but the floor in the back hall was spotted and the tiles had smeared patches. She reached out for his arm, pulling it away from his stomach. The bloody gash had stuck to his sweater, and he cried out as it ripped free. Juliet held his hand with her left and wiped at his forearm with her right.

A section of skin perhaps three inches long had been ripped up and now flapped uselessly. Blood had pooled beneath and darker spots indicated puncture wounds. He howled like a dying man as she first wiped around it, trying to identify the extent of the injury, then flapped the piece of skin back down, like a lid she hoped would close the door on the bleeding. As blood spread out around it, she knew that only one thing could be done.

'Sutures,' she said.

'What?'

'It's what Dad says. It needs to be stitched. I'll have to call the hospital.'

'No, wait!'

Cleaning the wound was one thing, but there was no way Juliet could sew up Uncle Lawrence's arm. As he continued to protest, she went to the phone in the hall and lifted the receiver out of the cradle. The clock display on the phone's smart screen said just after five. Dad wouldn't be home until at least seven, and he hated her calling him at work. Instead, she searched through the phone book until she found a number for the local hospital reception. When she pressed dial, however, a message appeared on the screen:

NO SIGNAL.

She checked the settings, but the local reception was giving her no bars, and the Wi-Fi refused to connect. She switched the phone off and on again, but the same thing happened.

'Juliet?'

'There's something wrong.'

'What?'

'I can't get a signal.'

She had her own phone, one set up just for calls, blocking the internet Dad said was poison for kids. She retrieved it from the living room, but the same. No signal.

'Something weird is going on,' she said, coming back into the kitchen. There's no signal. Perhaps there's a signal mast down or something. If you can wait, I can ride my bike into the village—'

'No!'

Uncle Lawrence put up a hand so quickly that his wound started to bleed more profusely than before.

'You can't go out there,' he said. 'What if that thing … what if it's still there?'

'I can ride pretty fast—'

'No!' Uncle Lawrence shook his head. 'You didn't see that thing move. What if it … what if it—'

'We can wait for Dad to get back—'

'No!' Uncle Lawrence shouted again. 'You … Juliet … you have to do it.'

She stared at him, sweat streaming down his face, his

clothes covered in blood. She didn't think she'd ever been more scared.

'Please, Juliet.'

Dad wouldn't hesitate, and he'd be ashamed that she had. She nodded. 'I'll try.'

'You'll need thread.'

There was none in the box, but they had a sewing kit in a drawer in the living room. She ran to get it, pausing by the door where she thought to take off her socks to avoid getting blood on the carpet, then figuring she'd rather get blood on her socks and the carpet than on her bare feet. This was her uncle's blood, and Dad always said Uncle Lawrence was … dirty.

She got the sewing box and came back.

'Hold a needle over the gas hob,' Uncle Lawrence said. 'Sterilise it.'

She did as he said, then then threaded a piece of white cotton through the eye, feeling this crazy euphoria at the thought that she should have asked him his preference of colour.

'Just do it,' he said.

Her hands were slick with his blood, and she wanted to wash them but had no choice. Trying to hold his arm steady, she lined up the needle, trying to imagine that this was nothing more than an item of clothing, two pieces of leather, perhaps, not a bloodied flap of skin she had to reattach to the flesh of his arm.

'One, two, three,' she whispered, then plunged the needle in.

Uncle Lawrence howled, pulling backwards, ripping the needle free. He gasped and spat, nearly falling off the chair.

'A rag,' he whimpered. 'I need a rag. To bite down on.'

She fetched him a new dishcloth out of a packet, rolled

it up and put it into his mouth, cringing at the way his tongue briefly brushed against her fingers.

'Okay,' he mumbled. 'I'm ready.'

He sounded anything but, and Juliet only wanted it to be over. This time, when she pierced the skin, Uncle Lawrence just let out a muffled scream, but held his arm in place. She glanced at his face, saw his eyes rolling, barely holding on to consciousness.

Get it done.

She began to pierce and pull like she was sewing the hem of a dress. The flap of skin was crescent shaped, and she worked her way around the semi-circle until the wound was covered over. Along the line of the stitches, blood pooled and dripped, but it was starting to crust over. The skin already looked like it was dying out around the line of the tear, but it was better than nothing.

By the time she was done, Uncle Lawrence had slumped in the chair, his eye closed, his breathing hoarse. Blood was still oozing out in places, so Juliet cleaned around the wound as best she could, then took a bottle of Dettol out of the cupboard and wiped along the tear, each dab of disinfectant bringing a weak twitch from her uncle.

She understood the basics of medical practices from Dad, who talked about nothing else, and knew that the biggest danger now was infection. She went through the kitchen drawers until she found a box of tablets that Dad had collected over the years. Most were over-the-counter goods like allergy tablets, headache pills, laxatives, even sleeping pills, but near the bottom she found a packet of prescription meds Dad had got for an ingrowing toenail a couple of months ago but not needed after the infection cleared up on its own. She popped two pills out of the packaging and pushed them through Uncle Lawrence's lips, pouring a little water after to make him swallow.

Then, she set about dressing his wound with a bandage from the medical box.

By the time she was done, he was snoring loudly as he lay slumped in the chair. There was no way she could move him to a bedroom, but afraid he would slip and hit his head, she lowered him to the kitchen floor. She turned him sideways to make sure his airway stayed clear as she had been taught, then rolled up an old towel and propped it under his head.

Then she set about cleaning the blood off the floor and her hands.

By the time she was done, with everything except Uncle Lawrence cleaned up as best she could, and having showered and changed into clean clothes, it was nearly half past eight.

She was starving, and Dad still wasn't back yet. The network was still down, meaning not only that she couldn't call, but that he couldn't call her either. Perhaps something had gone on at the hospital, a big accident or something. She tried the TV, wondering if there was something more dramatic happening, but their TV ran on the same signal as the phone and was also blank.

She was really starving. There wasn't much in the cupboards except some dried spaghetti, but Uncle Lawrence wasn't likely to move very far and the shop up in the village shut at nine. She just had time if she pushed it. They didn't sell much more than packets of pasta and tins of beans, but she had a craving for outside company, to be around someone other than Uncle Lawrence. And if there was something going on, she could find out more.

She got her coat and pulled on her shoes, but as she reached the front door, she stopped. Something was scratching at the wood outside, loud enough to make the door shake. They had no cat or dog, and it wasn't like a wild animal to do something like that.

As the door shook again, she took a step back.

Whatever it was that was out there, it really wanted to get inside.

8

REQUEST

'I'll tell him you're sick. He can't keep pushing you like this, Alfred. It's too much.'

Alfred lifted a hand to protest, but the little bit of something June had sprinkled into his tea was starting to have its effect. June watched him as his eyes closed, his shoulders dropped, and he slumped back onto the pillows.

She made him comfortable, then went back downstairs, briefly listening at the door to the drawing room, where Master Evans was entertaining Melinda, his current girlfriend. She had considered sprinkling a little something into their drinks too, but the Master was as sly as a fox and would know something was up. Everything he did was carefully measured, organised, carried out to precision. He knew exactly how much he was drinking, what effect it ought to have, how far he needed to go before he could have his way with his girlfriend. Just as he knew how hard he was pushing Alfred, how little Lilian enjoyed his advances, and how frustrated June felt at his constant complaints.

Sometimes she felt like they were nothing more than a

line of long-suffering stepping stones upon which he was gleefully jumping. Sooner or later, however, one would come loose and sink, and he wouldn't like it if he was standing upon it at the time.

At least that was how she liked to think.

What was more likely was that he would drive them all into the ground and then replace them. They were only the house staff, after all.

But things were afoot beyond the expansive grounds of Carlton Manor. This morning Benjamin Adams, their regular grocer, had arrived with the warning that future deliveries might become difficult. Something was happening in the north, he said. Something that the media was hiding, but a night-time curfew—unprecedented since the last world war, had been put in place in all major cities, and people reported receiving draft call ups, even as lines of troops were seen moving through the cities after dark. It seemed remarkable in such an age that no one could know what was going on, but all it had taken to regress the world fifty years was to bring down the phone networks. There were intermittent reports of rogue networks popping up, but the wider internet and all major service providers had been off the air for the past week.

June, who had never been one for internets or phones or anything of that ilk, hadn't been so much bothered. The news had affected Lilian the most, who feared it would be more difficult to keep tabs on Harry's whereabouts without her discreet access to his social networks. The fear that he would find her was still there, despite June's assurances that the security at Carlton Manor would keep her safe.

Dave, the groundskeeper, however, had called June just this afternoon to tell her his salary had not been paid. She had so far kept the news from Lilian. She didn't need the stress, particularly with Melinda due to go back to the city tomorrow. June could only hope that Master Evans would be too busy with aristocratic matters to bother her granddaughter any more.

She had just returned to the kitchen when the bell tinkled, signaling that the Master needed attention. June frowned. He had taken a bottle of whisky to the drawing room with him, and she had hoped that would be enough for the evening. Once, her duties had officially finished at eight p.m. five days a week, six on Saturdays, and Sunday had been a day off. Now, she was on call whenever Lord Richard wanted her, whether she liked it or not. As he had told her the one time she had tried to complain, there weren't many manor houses about which would hire a seventy-year-old housekeeper.

She hurried to the drawing room before the bell could ring again, gave a polite knock, and then cracked open the door.

Melinda was draped across one of Lord Evans's finest armchairs like an ugly throw rug, her top undone. Richard was sitting on the edge of the hundred-year-old billiards table, smoking a cigar.

June let her face show no emotion. She took a breath and stepped into the room, hands folded across her waist, head bowed.

'Yes, sir? How may I help?'

'Melinda dropped something behind the bureau,' the Master said. 'That one by the wall. Go and fetch your idiot husband then pull it out and find it.'

'Sir, Mr. Lammonby has retired for the evening. He has a migraine—'

'I don't care if he's got fucking rabies. Get his wrinkled old arse down here to help you pull out that bureau.'

Melinda sniggered from the armchair, one heel tapping

against the seat cushion. The bottle of whisky lay nearby, empty.

So, this was how it was going to be.

'Sir, I don't believe it is that heavy. If I remove the drawers, I can manage it myself.'

Richard hopped down from the billiard table and sauntered over, swaying, the glowing head of the cigar drifting back and forth like a faltering ship heading for shore. June waited, too afraid to move. So far, Richard's cruelty had been played out like the opening moves of a cagey chess match. He had feinted and pressed, but had yet to make a full bloodied attack. He had spat more spite in a single day than June had heard in a lifetime of servitude under his father, and his demands had become increasingly erratic and overbearing. Endless unnecessary tasks in unrealistic timeframes, and vicious putdowns when said tasks were completed late.

Now, though, he looked different. No more the petulant child who had thrown more tantrums growing up during his summers home from boarding school than was natural of even the most spoiled of children, he had true harm in his eyes. And June dared not look away.

He stopped less than an arm's length in front of her, surrounded by a cloud of cigar smoke, a wet stain on his shirt front stinking of whisky. June's own father had drunk himself to death and she despised the smell, but could do nothing other than hold the gaze of the man she had first held as a newborn. His gaze had been strong even then, and though she had done her best through the years to soften it, sometimes there was nothing that could be done.

Richard took the cigar from his mouth and moved it forwards through the air until it was so close to June's cheek that she could feel its heat. She tried not to tremble as its smoke got into her eyes, forcing tears he didn't deserve to see.

'When I was growing up,' he said quietly, 'I knew you weren't my real mother. I saw her, I watched her, with him, and I wondered why she never came to me, why she treated me like I didn't exist.'

'That's not true—'

'Oh, but it is. I might have been a legacy to her, an achievement, maybe, but I was never a son. You cared for me, and you looked after me, but why you, and never she? And then I realised. Duty. You did what you were ordered. You did what my wonderful father paid you to do.'

'I loved you—'

'Loved. You might have once, when I was young, pretty. But like a dying flower, whatever dutiful love you had slowly faded as I grew older, and you knew, and I knew, that I was not your son, and that we were bound together only by duty. You never fought for me to stay when they sent me away, because in your way, you were happy. It meant your duty was done.'

'Richard, no—'

His hand came up quickly, slapping her across the cheek. Not overly hard, but enough to smart. Behind him, Melinda was a shadow as she got up and sauntered away into an adjacent room.

'If your lazy husband won't come down, call the girl.'

'Lilian? She's preparing for breakfast.'

'I don't care. Call her now.'

'But—'

'Now.'

June nodded. She had no choice. She went to the door and pulled a cord that fed into the wall, hoping the medicine she had given Alfred was strong enough to keep him asleep.

Richard had wandered over to the billiards table and was idly knocking the balls back and forth with his hand. June waited, wishing Alfred was beside her, if not to help then to offer his support. She felt like a caged animal, looking out through the bars, unable to do anything as a fire rose up to consume her.

A light tap came on the door, and it opened to reveal Lilian, her eyes wide, inquisitive. She had a graceful, natural beauty in the same way that her dear mother—June's daughter—had possessed. Lamblike in so many ways, but June didn't dare to think what those eyes had seen behind closed doors, before she had found the strength to run away from Harry.

'We need to move the bureau,' June said.

'Yes, Mrs. Lammonby,' Lilian said, maintaining her formalities in Richard's presence.

June led Lilian over to the offending item of furniture. She waved Lilian to take the far end, and was about to order her to lift when Richard called out, 'Wait!'

He stubbed out the cigar on the edge of the billiards table, then wandered menacingly over. June could barely contain her beating heart as he walked to Lilian's end and stood behind her.

'I need to make sure you do it right,' he said, a smug smile on his face. Lilian, leaning over, her hands gripped on the bureau's edge, met June's eyes. All June could do was give a slight shake of the head. Whatever was coming would be unbearable, but to show any kind of dissent could make it much, much worse.

'On three,' June said, voice trembling. 'One, two, three.'

They lifted, shifting the bureau forward a few inches. Richard, instead of looking behind it as one might, pressed in close behind Lilian, his eyes over her shoulder not leaving June's, a thin, defiant smile on his face. Lilian, frozen in place, was also staring at June as Richard's hands rested on her hips, then slowly rose up over her body until they were cupping her breasts through her clothes. A single tear ran down Lilian's cheek, but she didn't move, even as Richard's fingers squeezed.

'It makes me happy to know I inherited such fine staff from my father,' Richard said, his grin widening. 'Such fine staff indeed.' Then, as though tired of the wicked spell he had cast over them, he let go of Lilian, leaned over and said, 'Ah, there it is.' He reached down, picking something off the floor that neither of them could see, then turned and walked towards the doorway Melinda had gone through. Lifting a hand without looking back, he called, 'Put it back, won't you? Make sure it's not out of place.' Then he was gone, a door slamming behind him.

June and Lilian replaced the bureau in its original position. And then they headed back downstairs to the servants' quarters, June supporting a weeping Lilian, wishing there was something she could do, but knowing in her heart that there was not.

9

BOMBS

Get to the bus.

It was a mantra for school children that transcended time and space, a universal, indisputable rule. And now, as Claire screamed it at the last fleeing teenagers with all her remaining breath, she wondered whether there was any point.

The bus was no protection against that thing, that scaly, flying thing. She couldn't even bring herself to say what it looked like, because it could not, should not exist, not here, not now, not in this time and place. Its wingspan was as wide as the bus was long, if not more, and that pointed, compass-like head with its rows of teeth would have no trouble punching through glass, the resistance little stronger than that of the ribcage of the boy it had torn to pieces in front of her eyes as she howled her ragged, failing mantra at the kids still running, because there was nothing else she could do.

Simon Reynolds. Not a good kid, not a bad kid, just an average kid, one of those ones she rarely spoke to outside of formalities because there was no need. He did his work, handed it in, got middling but good enough grades. He liked playing darts and going fishing and wanted to go to York University. His best friend was Pete Smith from the Fifth Year because they lived next door to each other. His mother worked in Lloyds TSB and his father was an administrator at Virgin Trains, and now she would have to tell them—if she survived this herself, of course—that their son had been ripped to pieces and eaten by something out of a Hollywood film, and no, there wasn't anything left for them to bury or cremate because it hadn't been quite appropriate—for obvious reasons of rather self-serving personal safety—to interrupt the creature while it was feeding.

Her legs gave way beneath her and she crashed to the ground, quickly recovering and pushing herself back up, staggering onwards in a kind of drunken zigzag, her legs like boneless tubes of meat.

Get to the bus, she tried to scream again, but her voice was gone now, and she was reduced to a gesturing shadow, flapping her arms aimlessly like the half cut remains of a flower blowing in the wind.

Some of the kids, perhaps trained by an online home education in the fantastical, were actually doing as she wanted, running, heads low, towards the bus. Others had lost their minds. She saw a couple cowered by the standing stones, as though a lump of ancient rock was any protection at all, while one clown stood out in the open, a smartphone raised towards the sky, seemingly videoing the creature as it rose up into the air, wheeled in a tight semi-circle and then dive-bombed into a stand of trees where three other kids were attempting to hide in the thin brush. As the creature landed among them, one managed to get away, but the other two disappeared into a flurry of claws and a ripping, tearing beak.

Claire, barely able to breathe let alone speak, backed up, staggering down the grassy slope as she watched the creature methodically dismantling the bloodied remains of two of her kids. Then, as though aware it was being watched, it lifted its elongated diamond of a head, twisting sideways, and one palm-sized eye seemed to focus on her.

The air cooled, the wind falling still. Claire existed inside a helium balloon, the only sound a gentle background hum. She stared at her death, grimly aware there was not a single thing she could do or say to avoid it. Someone was pulling at her shoulder, but it didn't matter, there wasn't time. Less than fifty yards separated her from the creature; it could cover the space with one flap of its gigantic wings.

And then it did, its wings billowing out, not the taut sheets they always appeared in pictures, but flexible like tarpaulin, giving it an explosive lift, and in a moment the creature was airborne, shooting straight upwards almost too fast for Claire's eyes to follow. She let out a sobbing gasp as Pauly leaned close.

'We've got to get to the bus!'

It was the mantra that sprung her back into action, aware now that the creature had not come for her but was headed skyward to attack a similar creature coming in low over the Clent Hills, perhaps to ward it off the fresh food supply. Claire retched into the ground then let Pauly pull her backwards, one of his hands closing over one of hers to place it over the cold metal of the door handle.

'Quickly, Ms. Hopgood. Before it comes back.'

'How … how many?'

He paused a moment, and she realised he was counting. 'Seven,' he said, his voice a mixture of despair and hope, grateful for those who had made it but heartbroken for those who had not. Eleven kids. Eleven of the pupils in her charge, still out there.

'I have to check.'

Pauly's hand closed over hers. 'No. We'll drive up the path a ways, see if we can see any others, but we can't get out of this bus. You saw it, didn't you?'

Claire nodded.

'Is it real? I mean, it can't be, can it? Perhaps it's some sort of machine.'

The thought hadn't crossed her mind, but as she remembered the way the creature had torn her kids apart, she shook her head. There was no way something like that was manmade. Even if they could … and she didn't doubt they were close … no one could surely be so cruel.

'Ms. Hopgood, we have to close the door.'

Pauly's voice was just the safe side of panicked, somehow holding it together. Claire nodded. She stepped backwards, onto the bus, letting Pauly's hand guide her. She forced herself to look away from the hill into the bus, and at first her breath caught in her throat as she saw no one, before realising they were all crouched in the aisle, holding each other down.

The door slid shut, making her jump. She leaned back against the folded emergency seat in the stairwell as Pauly started the engine and turned the bus onto the tarmacked lower section of the path that led up to the top of the hill.

Almost immediately one of the kids started screaming. Jenny Coates, always so cool and suave as she sauntered through the school corridors like she owned the place, was now reduced to a jibbering wreck, wailing at the top of her voice that they were going the wrong way, that they had to go back. Claire was spent, so left it to Tim Parkson to try to calm her, pulling her back down, physically putting a hand over her mouth, snapping into her ear that she had to shut up or more people might die.

As the bus bumped up the track, two figures appeared at the top of the hill, standing among the stones.

'Mick and Andy!' Danny Rainer shouted. 'That's Mick and Andy!'

The two boys came running between the stones, heading for the path down. The bus came to a stop at the top of the tarmacked section, blocked by a hedgerow, the path leading through a stile and then becoming gravel. Claire forced herself to stand, pressing the door control.

'Miss, don't!'

I can't leave them, she thought she said, but may have not. She took a step out of the bus and lifted a hand to wave, feeling like she was stepping over a threshold between heaven and hell, the world that was warm suddenly turning dark.

A shadow fell over the two boys, and then a great green blur dropped out of the sky. Mick Williams flung himself forward, but Andy Dunworth, overweight, lazy, always sitting out of games with some vague ailment, was too slow. Massive claws closed over his back, pulling him up into the air. The creature shifted, off balance, and from a height of fifty feet Andy fell. His flailing body hit one of the stones with a thud that made Claire shiver, and as he landed, inert, on the ground nearby, she dearly hoped he was unconscious or even dead, as the creature dropped to reclaim its prize, only this time to begin dismemberment on the ground.

Mick was halfway to the bus. A second creature swooped low, but aborted its dive after a warning screech from the bloody beak of the first. Mick, looking over his shoulder, tripped.

Something in Claire's circuitry ignited. Without

thought, she pushed away from the bus, climbed over the stile and raced up the path. She felt like she was floating, treading water in a bubble. She reached Mick, pulling him up to his feet. The class idiot, the one that teachers had to berate for sleeping, the dumbass who hung onto his Sixth Form place by the skin of his teeth, stared at her, tears in his eyes.

I will not die for you.

The thought was like a thunderbolt. She grabbed Mick by the arm, fingers squeezing far harder than ordinarily would have been acceptable, but the old world order had been swept up and thrown in the air by one swoop of the ripping, tearing monster's wings.

'Get the fuck up, Mick.'

He did. His eyes met Claire's only briefly. 'I don't want to die, Miss. Me and Andy, we were in there, mucking about. That thing, it got Roger and Kai. It … it fucking … it fucking ripped them up.'

Claire closed her eyes. Roger Stevens and Kai Park. She might shed a tear for them later, if she had a chance. If she was still alive to do it.

'Move. The bus. Get to the fucking bus, Mick.'

He ran. Claire took one look back up the slope at the thing that was eating one of her kids, picking out his entrails, twisting them around and snapping them up like human spaghetti. Claire retched again, eyes filled with tears, stomach with revulsion, and mind shrouded by a veil of madness, then turned and ran.

Mick had made it to the bus. Claire stumbled inside, then looked up at Pauly. 'Go,' she whispered.

He nodded. There was nothing else that needed to be said. Ten kids that were dead or missing, but she had a duty to the eight on the bus. The rumble of the engine was masked by sobbing from the aisle. Tim was shouting at

Mick, calling him a faggot, telling him Andy was dead because they couldn't help playing with their dicks. Danny was telling Tim to shut up, and Tim was telling Danny he'd knock his teeth out. Connie, bizarrely, was berating Lisa for dropping her binoculars.

Pauly turned the bus around, backing into a large signboard, knocking it over, perhaps an indication that he wasn't quite all together either. The bus bumped over something, a marker rock or bollard perhaps, then started downhill.

'Tim, leave him!' Daisy shouted, and Claire looked up from the stairwell just in time to see Tim Parkson swing a fist into Mick's face. Mick grunted, sitting down hard on a nearby seat, blood dripping from his nose. Danny was pushing Tim back. Daisy was crying. Connie was crying, Ishy was screaming. Everyone was breaking.

'Shut up!' Claire screamed, voice cracking. 'Just shut up and sit down!'

Pauly looked up at her, eyes offering sympathy, holding onto his own sanity simply by doing the one thing he knew best, steering the bus out of the car park and down the access road, maintaining a preternatural sense of calm, as though nothing at all was wrong, that the world wasn't about to turn dark and dangerous in a way no one could have imagined.

They bumped over a cattle grid out onto the main road. Driving through a pretty village, it felt like everything was hunky dory, that they hadn't just left ten kids to die at the claws of a pair of prehistoric flying creatures. The signs that something was wrong were starting to appear, though. People stood in their front gardens, or out on the road, and as the bus rumbled up to a junction Claire saw an overturned car, its front bashed in. Someone lay on the ground nearby, bleeding, untended.

Pauly saw it too, but Claire shook her head. 'Keep moving,' she said.

They rounded a corner, the road angling uphill as it came around the side of the Clent Hills. Birmingham appeared again in the distance, and Claire's breath caught in her throat. Explosions popped across the city, puffs of smoke billowing up into the air, the bangs of delayed explosions making the bus's windows shake. Claire stared, tears in her eyes as a high-rise in the city centre tilted and collapsed, sending up a plume of dust.

'Where are we going?' Pauly asked, voice trembling. 'Ms. Hopgood, where are we going?'

Claire shook her head. 'I don't know,' she said. 'But we're not going home.'

10

LOCKS

Mark Caine woke to the unfamiliar sound of silence and knew something was wrong. There should have been the bleep of machines, the footsteps on the hard tiles of the corridor outside the room, the cursing of overworked prison doctors. Instead, as he lay still and listened, all he heard was the distant creak of a swinging door, perhaps triggered by the wind through a window left open.

He leaned over and pressed an emergency alarm button on the side of his bedframe. That would bring them running. He could claim a violent headache after the hammer blow perhaps, or an unnatural ache in his stomach where the warders' boots had left their hard plastic signature.

Neither did the button light up as it should, nor did it even have that give it should have had when it was functional. There was just the immobile hardness of dead plastic.

The power was out. Mark pushed himself up. There was a headache, a spinning of his vision, a sudden dizziness and an urge to vomit he couldn't ignore as he leaned over the side of his bed and let last night's spoon-fed meal come out onto the floor.

Neither Arthur Sawyer's homemade mallet nor the boots or batons of the warders trying to stop Mark from ripping off Sawyer's head in response had caused as much damage as he had milked them for, however. The mallet had given him concussion but not fractured his skull, while the beating ached but was mostly cosmetic. He had fancied a few days in the infirmary, just to get out of the cage for a while, assess his options. Sawyer's attempt on his life couldn't go unanswered; however, his sentence only had two more years to run. He had overheard the warders talking about an extra five years being added as a result of the altercation; he needed to keep his head down.

Something, however, wasn't right. He got up from bed, stretching out his stiff legs, rubbing his side where the warders' boots had bruised his ribs. The doors all had electronic locks, but as he nudged it with his foot, it swung open.

The corridor was empty. Perhaps there had been a staff strike? Yet there seemed to be no one in any of the other rooms. He walked down the hall, looking for someone, anyone, who might know something. Doors hung open, trolleys of medical supplies had been knocked over. A computer monitor had fallen off a desk and been damaged, its back casing popped off, broken into two parts.

Mark rubbed his eyes, trying to shake off the feeling that he had forgotten something. The grogginess he felt was a clue, when he hadn't felt too bad before, even when they brought him in.

That was it. They had put him under last night in order to perform a routine brain scan. Whatever had gone down must have happened while he was sleeping it off. His room was pretty isolated at the end of a corridor, and if the power was out there would have been no alarms.

As he reached the end of the corridor and started down a set of stairs beside the now-defunct lift, his thoughts turned towards escape. If the power was down, if the locks were no longer operational, and there were no more guards, perhaps he could walk out the front gate.

Just two years left to run. But what if … what if the dust up with Arthur Sawyer ended up costing another few years of his life? He was thirty-eight, nine years into an eleven stretch. Getting out one day had kept him going all this time. Getting home, getting back to Amanda, to Hannah and Evan, already fifteen and thirteen. He'd missed most of their lives already; he couldn't miss any more. He might as well be dead.

He went downstairs, along corridors and through doors that had once needed multiple pass codes or keys to open them, out of the infirmary and into the prison's front courtyard where the warders and the guests parked. He'd only been here a handful of times, on strictly supervised work duties. Now, he stood among a scattering of cars still left, wondering where the people were. The main gates, just a couple of hundred yards distant, stood open.

Where were the people?

There were cars here, so there had to be people. Mark paused, letting his senses adjust to the sudden overload of sensation. It had been years since he had stood alone, surrounded by nothing but the whisper of a gentle breeze, the cawing of a distant bird. A moment to let his guard down, to allow himself to think unencumbered by the always present thoughts of self-preservation. Violence in the prison was rare, but it only took a moment. Look away at the wrong second and it could be you with a knife fashioned out of cloth and broken glass slashing across your neck.

He let his guard down. He let himself see the world for what it was.

And he saw.

One car had rolled, its windscreen smashed. A black smear in the middle of the courtyard could be blood. And out beyond the gates, in the mists that never seemed to relent over this section of Dartmoor, dark lumps lay scattered across the tarmac, lumps that could have been bodies. A piece of metal pipe lay nearby, rusty, jagged at one end, the points of metal bloody, clumped with something. He walked over, stood above it, looking down.

Something or someone had died at the end of that pipe, or at least been badly maimed. It looked like a solid weapon in the absence of any other, so Mark reached down, picked it up, hefted it in his hands. Its hollowness gave it lightness, its length gave it power. And the jagged end made it deadly.

A car nearby had its door ajar. Mark leaned inside, but there were no keys. The lower dashboard had already been removed, the wires hanging loose, as though someone had attempted to hotwire it already and failed. He opened the glove box and found a rag with dirt patches he guessed had been used for wiping down the footwells. He ripped it into two strips, and tied one piece around the end of the pipe to give him grip, the other around his head, covering the sticky plaster over the shaved patch of hair where Arthur Sawyer's mallet had landed. As he climbed back out, he caught a look at himself in the wing mirror. He looked like a mechanic gone mad.

A rustle of movement came from behind him. Instinctively he dropped to his knees behind the car, peering through the window glass as a door opened in the building on the other side.

Out stumbled a prison guard, a baton in one hand, the other held against his stomach as though he had suffered some injury. He pushed the door shut, then leaned back against it, gritting his teeth. With one hand he fumbled in his pocket, looking for something.

He had just withdrawn a key when the door at his back reverberated. The guard let out a cry of fear that cooled Mark's blood, straining his feet against the concrete path, a look of horror on his face as whatever was behind the door slammed against it again. The door shook. The guard let go of his baton, trying to hold the door shut while getting the key into the lock.

As the door burst open, Mark ducked out of sight. A wail of pure terror filled the empty square, followed by the shriek of something inhuman. When Mark dared to look up again, he caught a momentary glimpse of an outstretched hand, fingers clawing at the concrete, as what was left of the guard was pulled into the darkness of the corridor.

Mark's heart pounded. He wasn't about to wait around for whatever was in there to come out. He gripped his pipe club with one hand, pushed off the side of the car with the other, and ran as hard as he could for the open gates to the prison. The mist, always so imposing, for once felt like an old friend, waiting to hide him from whatever horrors he was leaving behind.

Only as he reached the first of the shapes lying on the road that led away through Princetown towards the bleak hills of Dartmoor, did he realise that some kind of battle had ensued, and that he might be in as much danger outside the prison as he had been inside.

The people lying around him had been horribly

mutilated, clothing shredded, bodies ripped open. Whatever had dragged the guard back into the prison, there had to be more of them or similar out here.

Determined that he wouldn't become another trough for some unseen creature to feed, Mark gripped his weapon across his chest and ran, away from the prison, away from the bodies, looking for somewhere, anywhere, he could be safe.

11

MONSTERS

'Is there not somewhere you can stay? An aunt or uncle? Someone I can call?'

Ellis shook his head. 'Please, Mr. Graf. I don't know. Please, help me find Mum and Dad.'

'I can't. I don't … have time.'

Dad would need turning soon, his instruments checked. Alan stared at the collapsed building in dismay, eyes glazing over. A fire raged among the ruins, and chunks of masonry continued to fall from the surrounding structure. If Ellis's parents had been inside … there was nothing he could do.

Ellis was starting to cry. 'Mr. Graf, I'm scared.'

Alan didn't want to admit to the boy that he too was scared, more scared than he could ever remember being in his life. So scared that if he stopped too long to think about things, his head would take a leaf out of Ellis's parents' house's book and collapse in on itself.

'We have to stay calm,' he told the boy. 'If we panic, we increase our risk of harm, of worse injury.'

He sounded like he was reading out of a textbook, and

that in part was what it was, a paraphrasing of an emergency room procedures manual he had long ago had to learn. Years in and around emergency rooms would help, but this was something else.

'It was a hadrosaur, wasn't it?' Ellis said. 'That thing? It was a … hadrosaur.'

The boy began to cry. Trying to focus on something other than his destroyed home, Alan knew the boy might go into a form of shock.

'You'd better come in,' he said. 'Just for a moment. Just until we find someone we can call.'

He led the boy into the house, then opened the door to the small living room at the front and waved Ellis inside. The boy looked around, uncertain, but Alan pointed at a bookcase by the far wall.

'Find something in there. I have some, uh, classics you might like. Sit down. I'll bring you … a drink. Coffee? I mean, juice? Or I have milk.'

Around the wards, directing ill, injured and grieving children was second nature. Here, in his own home, where no one ever set foot except occasionally a specialist to check up on Dad, it felt awkward, stilted. As Ellis stared at him, he found he had nothing to say.

'Juice, please, Mr. Graf.'

The world was getting shot up outside yet Alan felt like he was running a bed and breakfast. He nodded, stepped back, closed the door.

In the kitchen he found a half-finished carton of orange juice. It was a day or two outside its best before but it would be all right for now.

He was halfway through pouring a glass when a loud bang from outside made the house shudder. A glass he had taken out of the cupboard to fill with water for himself slipped from the worktop and shattered on the tiles. He gave a frustrated grunt, pulled open a cupboard and retrieved a dustpan. He was halfway through sweeping up the mess when a door banged in the hall.

Leaving the dustpan on the floor, he went to check. The living room door was open. Alan leaned inside, but the room was empty.

'Uh … Ellis? Where are you?'

Another door creaked. Dad. Alan ran past the stairs to the door to Dad's room. Ellis stood beside Dad's bed. He lifted a hand towards Dad's arm.

'What are you doing in here?'

Ellis dropped his hand and spun around. 'I—I—didn't mean anything. I got scared.'

'Get out!'

Ellis backed up, deeper into the room. Alan backed away, realising he had left the boy nowhere to go.

'Get out of here!'

Ellis dodged past Alan, head lowered. 'I'm sorry!'

Alan went to the front door and pulled it wide, planning to order the boy outside. He was met by a scene out of an apocalyptic film. A house across the street was a raging inferno. On the corner, another building had collapsed. A scattering of people ran about like ants, lost, nowhere to go.

Ellis was standing by the living room door, one hand over his mouth. He looked about to cry. As Alan came forward, the boy shook his head.

'I'm sorry, Mr. Graf—'

'Just stay in there. Don't move.'

Alan went to check on Dad, but there was no change in his condition. His eyes remained slits, barely awake. Ellis, to his credit, hadn't touched anything.

He went back into the kitchen, finished tidying up the broken glass, then remembered the drink he had offered

Ellis. He scooped it up, marching through to the living room.

The room was empty.

'Ellis? Where are you?'

There was too much anger in his voice aimed at a boy whose family might be crushed beneath a fallen building, but Alan couldn't help it. He hadn't asked for this. Dad was his priority, the only thing that mattered.

A small head poked out from behind the arm rest of the sofa facing the window. Ellis shuffled out from between the sofa and the bookcase and stood up with his head bowed like a kid caught shoplifting.

'I'm sorry, Mr. Graf. I was scared.'

Alan sighed. 'It's okay. Here. Drink this.'

Ellis didn't move. How old was he? Nine? Ten?

'I'm not going to hurt you.'

Ellis shuffled forward. Alan had no time for games. He put the drink down on a side table at the end of the sofa and went back out, closing the door.

One way to deal with the boy would be to get hold of his parents. Alan worked shifts, and had been doing nights the last couple of weeks. They would surely be at work.

He found his phone on the table beside the door and pulled up the map application to search for their address, but his phone had no signal. Frustrated, he opened his settings, but there was nothing. No Wi-Fi, no roaming mobile, nothing.

He had a landline, but the phonebooks he remembered Dad using as doorstops when he was a kid had gone digital years ago. He looked up, into the mirror hanging inside the front door for him to check his appearance before he left for work. Forty-eight, prematurely lined, tufts of grey hair around his ears, bags beneath his brown eyes, unshaven. He looked like shit.

And he had the feeling things were going to get worse.

He went to the door, first peering through the spyhole, then opening it a crack. The fire still raged across the street, unchecked, the flames now licking at the adjacent roofs. Ellis's parents' building was little more than a heap of rubble, as though a giant had punched down out of the sky.

Sirens blared in the distance, but they sounded miles off. Alan opened the door a little wider, looking up and down the street. His instinct was to stay inside, out of sight. He could see what was left of the dinosaur lying in the road up by the junction. A stray dog had appeared and was tugging at a piece of loose flesh.

There was a sudden blur of movement as something rushed past Alan, down the steps and out onto the street. Alan turned, startled at the sight of Ellis racing up the pavement. Oblivious to any danger, Ellis sprinted across the south junction, coming to a stop outside the ruins of his house.

'Come back!' Alan shouted. 'Boy … come back!'

Wasn't this what he wanted, though, to be rid of responsibility for the child? For a fleeting moment Alan considered stepping back inside, closing the door, and forgetting ever encountering the boy.

Ellis began clambering up over the pile of rubbish, pulling away rocks and broken boards, screaming his parents' names.

What would Dad have done? The inert, failing body held only the ruins of a man now, but once Dad had been brave and strong. *Sometimes you've got to man up,* came Dad's voice in Alan's head. *Sure, he's bigger than you, but that means you've got to hit him twice as hard as he hits you.*

Alan looked around for something that might make a useful weapon, but the best he could come up with was an umbrella with a metal handle. He felt ridiculous as he stumbled down the steps beneath a blue, cloudless sky, the umbrella held in his hands like a club.

Ellis was still climbing over the rubble on the other side of Abbot Street, opposite the junction. Alan looked up and down the street as he crossed, afraid of what he would see, but instead of Armed Forces vehicles and prehistoric creatures there were just haphazard lines of abandoned cars, and the remains of a couple of other destroyed buildings that had slid forwards into the street.

'Get down from there!' Alan shouted. 'You'll hurt yourself!'

Ellis paid him no attention. Alan picked his way through the rubble, looking for a way up. He felt something soft underfoot and looked down, terrified of what he might see, but it was only the cushion of a half-buried sofa, its red plumage flecked with grey concrete dust.

Ahead of him on the rubble heap, Ellis dropped down out of sight. Alan shouted after the boy, but his voice was drowned out by the whirring of a helicopter's blades as it flew low overhead. Alan ducked, covering his ears, until it passed beyond the roofs of the houses opposite.

'Ellis?'

The rubble was shifting dangerously, unstable. Alan clambered over a shattered window and saw Ellis squatting in a hollow, pulling at something buried under a lump of masonry.

'Come out of there,' Alan said. 'It's dangerous.'

Ellis pulled backwards and Alan gasped at what came free in the boy's hands. A human arm, severed at the shoulder, the ball of the humerus poking out, the shredded remains of a red, knitted sweater surrounding it like the petals of a nightmarish flower.

The boy screamed and dropped the arm, then tripped backwards, falling into a bowl of rubble beneath a large piece of leaning wall that hadn't broken up. Ellis scrambled away from the arm, pushing against the section of wall as it creaked and groaned.

'Ellis, give me your hand—'

The wall was about to fall. Ellis was catatonic, eyes on the severed arm. Alan pushed himself into the hollow, grabbed Ellis by the collar, and pulled him backwards as the section of wall tumbled down, filling the hollow and burying the severed arm with broken masonry.

Ellis was shivering, gone into shock. Alan slapped his face, wanting a reaction, and got one, the boy turning to stare wide-eyed into his own.

'Stay with me, Ellis,' Alan said. 'We have to get down from here.'

'Mr. Graf … Mr. Graf … that was my—'

Whatever he meant to say, a thunderous roar from up the street obscured all other noise. Alan looked up as something monstrous advanced between the abandoned cars. His hands shook, his stomach churned, and he pulled Ellis against him, as much to comfort himself as to protect the boy.

Alan didn't care much for dinosaurs. He knew the familiar names—triceratops, stegosaurus and the like—but anything beyond a selection of plastic models you might find in a cereal packet he was lost.

The thing wasn't a T-Rex because it had bigger arms, but otherwise it might well have been. As tall as a two-storey building, it had back feet the size of motorcycles and a head the size and shape of a small car. A massive tail swung back and forth as it advanced, knocking abandoned cars out of the road. Its head hung low, massive nostrils flaring. Alan couldn't see its eyes beneath overhanging windshield-like flaps.

As a very young boy, Mum had always warned him about plants in the woods near their home. 'Red means danger,' she told him. 'It's nature's way of telling us not what to eat.'

By the time he was old enough to point out such anomalies as strawberries and tomatoes, Mum had drunk herself to death, leaving Dad to bring him up. Nature's way always seemed about right, though, and Mum's words came back to him now as she watched the stalking monster, which wasn't just red but a dark, crimson red, like a spot about ready to burst, a warning button on nature's own landscape. *Death comes this way, and there's no way to escape.*

Ellis was whimpering. Alan clamped a hand over the boy's mouth, careful to keep his nose clear, but tight enough to make the boy struggle. Aware it was their only chance, that there would be no running from this thing, he held Ellis close and gently shrank back behind the torn and shredded remains of a protruding mattress.

The creature came level with them, the crunch of its feet over debris fallen in the road making Alan feel sick. His stomach wanted to expel its contents, but he held them down, holding on to Ellis at the same time, hooking his legs around the boy's to keep him still.

The creature grunted, pushing at a pile of rubble nearby, making the mattress shift. The shredded tangle of cloth and springs slipped forward, and for a moment Alan was staring right into the creature's left eye as it followed the mattress's fall. Then its head dipped, there was a tearing sound, and it lifted again with a flopping body held in its teeth. As the creature turned, its tail knocked against the rubble pile, dislodging much of the debris. Alan, still holding on to Ellis, slid down towards the road amidst a cascade of crumbling masonry. The creature's tail swung again, barely passing over the top of their heads, then it padded off up the street.

For a long time, Alan couldn't move. Even after the creature turned out of sight, he held on to Ellis, slowly relaxing his hand over the boy's mouth until he heard Ellis whimpering in fear. He looked down to see tears in the boy's eyes, but held his tongue where words of comfort wanted to be. There was nothing he could say. Things weren't going to be all right. They were very, very wrong, and they were going to stay that way. That way, or worse.

He started to get up. He had barely lifted his head above the nearest chunks of rubble when the sound of scampering feet came from the way the dinosaur had come. Others were coming, smaller ones, a dozen or more, barely bigger than dogs. In fact, were they not hairless and narrower across the back, they could have been dogs. They had snouts with flaring nostrils, overlarge eyes and pointed ears.

They hurried in the larger carnivore's wake, quarrelling over some morsel fallen from its mouth. Another pulled something out of the rubble and began to chew on it: part of a human torso.

Scavengers, Alan realised, but at the size of Alsatian dogs, they might be brave enough to attack a human, especially in a pack. He clamped his hand back over Ellis's mouth again, holding them both still. The creatures argued over the meal, snapping and snarling, until one got hold of it and made a dash up the street. A couple of others followed, while the rest spread out, peering under parked cars, nosing into toppled rubbish bins, looking for other things to eat.

Then, as one ran up the stairs to Alan's front door, he

realised his error. In his haste to catch up with Ellis, he had left the door ajar. As he watched, frozen in terror, one of the doglike things nosed through the front door and disappeared inside.

In a moment Alan was on his feet. He pushed Ellis away, the boy forgotten. As another creature followed the first into Alan's house, a single guttural word fought its way from his throat.

'Dad!'

12

FIENDS

No one seemed to know what was going on. Abandoning their cars, people fled on foot, leaving roads blocked for those still trying to find a way through the traffic. It was impossible to be heard over the blaring of car horns and broken alarms, the screaming of people, the background thud and boom of bombs falling, exploding.

It made sense to keep off the main streets, but they were hopelessly lost among suburbs made unfamiliar by the maelstrom of panicking citizens. Even where they found no one, there were overturned cars, heaps of luggage piled outside front doors before being abandoned, cats and dogs wandering the streets, searching forlornly for their vanished owners.

As they limped around a corner and found themselves in a cul-de-sac where two cars had collided in the middle of the street and another had driven through a fence and been abandoned among muddy tyre marks on an otherwise pristine front lawn, Emily wondered if it made sense to find somewhere abandoned and hole themselves up. Kim was limping badly, putting on a brave face for her daughter, but Emily was wiser than her mother ever gave her credit for. She had grown up behind a mask of petulance and rebellion that her mother had been unable to see behind, but she had grown up nonetheless, and was capable of looking after herself. Kim was wittering into her ear, but she had no more survival instincts than Emily had herself, and Emily's instinct was telling her they had no chance of making it home, and it was better to find cover.

'It can't be far,' Kim said, gritting her teeth with each step. 'We'll recognise something soon.'

'Mum, we're lost. You know it, and I know it. We have to get off the street.'

'We can't just break into someone's house.'

'These people have gone. They must have known something us poor types didn't.'

'It's not right!'

A pair of men came running out of an open front door up ahead, black bags slung over their shoulders. One of them clocked Emily and Kim, then bolted, following his companion into an alley that led between houses. Looters. At the first sign of trouble, what hid under the surface had risen up to add to the chaos. Emily shook her head. People were fuckwits.

We deserve everything we get.

A fighter jet rushed overhead, fast and low, the roar of its engines pushing them to their knees. Emily threw a middle finger at its departing back, but it was already a distant dot, and a moment later it was out of sight.

'Fuckers,' she hissed. 'You probably started all this.'

'Emily, language!'

'Yeah, Mum, that's going to help us, isn't it?'

'We're not animals.'

'Not yet.'

They headed down the alley that the looters had taken.

Emily peered over a wooden backyard fence at a sheepdog running in mad circles, howling with each turn.

They know better than we do, she thought. *Animals aren't stupid like us.*

The ground rocked with a nearby explosion, knocking them sideways against the fence. Emily held on to Kim as she cried out, clutching at her leg.

'You have to rest,' she said. 'You'll make it worse.'

'I'm fine.'

'Mum, if your leg goes, I can't carry you. We need to rest, at least have a look at it.'

'It's not safe.'

'And you think our house will be? It might not even be there anymore.'

Whether it was or wasn't was irrelevant, Emily thought. Her mother was clinging to the hope that whatever was going down was a moment, and would pass, but Mum was old, she had her head in the sand, just like the teachers at school. They denied everything, all the blackout zones, the rumours, the grainy videos from people sneaking into government compounds at night. No, there were no giant beasts. It was all a lie made up by kids with their heads in devices.

Well, fuck you, world. Look what you were hiding.

They emerged from the alley onto another quiet cul-de-sac that backed onto it. Here, a family was busy loading suitcases into the open boot of their car, the father dragging one with a broken wheel across the front lawn while the mother shouted at two young girls to hurry up.

'We have to leave him, Julie. Sorry.'

'Who'll feed him, Mum?'

The mother turned and flapped a hand at the nearest bush, then howled in frustration. 'Just let him out, give him a chance.'

There it was, the same feeling that Emily felt, that she felt like she had always felt, even before shit went crazy. Like she was trying to push a rock uphill, while everything was conspiring to push it back down. That frustration that made her want to lash out, hit stuff, to swear at her teachers, to abuse her own mother.

This is the world you built. And we're the ones who've got to clean up your shit.

'What the hell are you looking at?' the mother shouted, and Emily realised the woman was talking to her.

'Don't talk to my daughter like that,' Kim shouted back, fingers clenching Emily's shoulder tight, trying to summon some conviction into her voice.

'Go fuck yourselves,' the woman shouted. 'Julie, Amy … *get in the car!*'

'Sandra—'

'Shut up! Just *shut up!*'

'Mum, come on,' Emily said, pulling Kim away as the woman began berating her husband, hands gripping her hair as she kicked out at carefully manicured shrubs that had likely been her pride a month, a week, maybe even a day ago.

They stumbled out to the main road. A line of abandoned cars blocked the traffic in both directions. Some doors had been left open, belongings scattered about.

'Should we tell them there's no way through?' Mum said.

'They'll figure it out soon enough. It's not our problem—'

Mum stumbled, falling to her knees, letting out a cry of pain.

'Are you all right?'

'I'm … I'm fine.'

'You're *not!*'

'I am!'

'Mum, please.'

Emily began to wrestle with her, pushing her on to her back. Mum eventually relented, letting Emily undo her jeans and slide them down.

'Oh, Mum.'

A vicious purple-black welt covered most of her lower thigh, the skin mottled and misshapen.

'It's just a bruise.'

'That's more than just a bruise, Mum.'

'I'll live.'

Emily couldn't bring herself to speak. She stood up and looked around, searching for somewhere safe they could hole up. Not far up the street was a curry restaurant, its doors open, a closed sign hanging in the window.

'Mum, let me help you up.'

Kim howled as Emily lifted dragged her up. Supporting her mother, together they limped along the street. They had barely got inside the restaurant when Kim's strength gave out. Emily strained under her weight, lowering her into a booth seat behind the door.

'Just stay there a minute,' Emily said, pulling the door shut. 'I'll go and see if there's some ice or something.'

'I'm—'

'No, you're not!'

The restaurant had half a dozen tables, and a counter bar at the back. Looters and vandals had already been here: half the bottles were missing, many of the others smashed. The ground was a nightmare of broken glass on wet, slippery tiles. Emily, shaking her head at how quickly people turned into scumbags at the first opportunity, stepped around the mess as best she could and headed into the kitchen.

A swinging door gave her access, lodged open by a fallen fire extinguisher. She stepped inside, immediately pausing at a scrabbling sound from around the corner to the right. Food debris was scattered across the floor. Nearby was a large walk-in fridge-freezer. She stepped over a pile of smashed vegetables and reached for the handle.

Movement made her pause. She glanced to her right, freezing at the sight of the thing in front of her.

It was little bigger than a chicken, but lean and wiry, a long, whip of a tail snaking out behind as its serpentine head dipped and rose over whatever was its meal, just out of sight beneath a wheeled trolley. As it shifted, front claws ripping at flesh, Emily covered her mouth to suppress a gasp.

A human shoe, knocked loose, lay among scraps of some kind of pinkish meat.

Skin.

Barely able to bring herself to move, Emily glanced around for a weapon.

On a worktop nearby was a block of heavy-duty meat cleavers. Keeping one eye on the animal's back, she leaned sideways, reaching out until her fingers closed over the nearest hilt. Then, slowly drawing it free, she turned around.

The serpentine creature was engrossed in eating what was left of the man lying half out of sight behind the trolley. The walk-in fridge-freezer door was just inches in front of Emily. She reached out, pulling it open.

The creature continued its feast, undisturbed.

Emily slipped inside, pulling the door half closed. An ice-machine stood just inside the door, its power still turned on. Emily pulled a clear plastic bag off a roll, then slid open a glass lid to reveal a container of ice-cubes. She scooped some up into the bag, then twisted the bag's top closed to keep the ice together. Then, leaning against the door, she slowly pushed it open—

With a snarling hiss, the creature leapt at her, a blur of motion. Emily had no chance to even see it clearly, but she reacted on instinct, leaning back as it passed in front of her chest, then swinging back out of the walk-in fridge-freezer and slamming the door shut before the creature could gather itself for another attack. She leaned back against the door, hearing a faint scrabbling from inside. If it really was what it looked like, they were cold-blooded, weren't they? Wouldn't it die?

The walk-in fridge-freezer had a lock handle. Emily twisted it, the sounds of the creature inside growing fainter.

She didn't dare to look at the corpse slumped in the corner. Wiping sweat off her face, she went to find her mother. As she emerged from the kitchens, however, the sound of raised voices came from the restaurant floor.

'Just give us what you've got. We won't hurt you. Now, bitch.'

Emily froze. The two looters they had seen coming out of the house earlier stood over Kim. One with his hood down was a fair-haired older white guy, mean and gnarled, tattoos up the side of his neck, a scar by his eye. The younger one was a black guy, a hood still covering most of his face, but he looked more scared than dangerous.

'Fucking show us what you have,' the older guy said to Kim, kicking out at her leg, making her scream. 'A woman like you, she don't go nowhere without her purse.'

Emily looked down. In one hand she still held the knife, but in that moment she froze, her fingers opening. The knife fell, striking a metal cupboard handle on the way down, causing a ring which made the two men turn.

'Hey!'

'Emily!'

The older guy didn't hesitate. He darted for Emily, shoving tables out of his way as he came rushing forwards. Emily jerked, striking the cupboards behind her, knocking a line of ornamental elephant models to the floor. She scrambled for one, wanting anything as a weapon, but the nearest fell through her hands.

The man reached the counter quicker than she might have imagined. His hands reached for her, one finger hooking over the cuff of her sweater. She ripped it free, then ironically the man slipped on the fallen knife, losing his footing. He crashed sideways into the counter as Emily backed away towards the kitchen.

'Leave her alone!' Mum cried.

'Watch that bitch,' the older man shouted over his shoulder, pushing himself back upright. 'You got any money, girl? Or anything else?'

'Fuck off,' Emily said, reaching behind her for another knife as she backed into the kitchen. Her hand closed over nothing. Her panic rose. Where were the knives?

She didn't dare turn around. The man was in the doorway. His face a mass of stubble, scars, and tattoos, the kind of guy who had gone to places someone like Emily might consider romantic, storybook. He was a fighter, a criminal, maybe a dealer, an enforcer, perhaps even a killer. And he had her trapped.

'Life sucks right now, doesn't?' he said, leering at her. 'I'll tell you what—'

Emily shifted sideways, feeling the handle of the walk-in refrigerator under her fingers. She twisted, leaning away as the door swung open.

'Ah, fuck—'

The creature leapt out, landing on the man's chest. He grabbed its neck with one hand, trying to pull it away, but a three-toed claw slashed one side of his face, the flesh soughing off, his left eye gone in a smear of blood. Howling, he fell back against the wall, the creature getting hold of him now with its teeth, ripping and tearing. Whatever words he might have tried to scream were lost as it ripped out his tongue, leaving only a dull, chilling bellow. Emily, backing away, found one of the other knives and gripped it tight. With a shriek, she pulled it free from the block and swung it hard at the creature's back.

It connected with the middle of the creature's backbone, sinking deep, severing its spine. The creature let out one solitary wail then fell away from the man, landing on its back as the man crashed down on top of it. Emily stared at the two twitching bodies, their blood spurting in a mixture of crimson and green. She dropped the second knife and wrapped her hands around herself in a bid to control the shaking.

'Graham?' came a voice from behind her, jarring her back into the moment. She turned to see the younger black guy walking towards her, a ceramic vase held upside down like a makeshift club, his eyes filled with horror. 'Graham? Are you all right?'

Emily looked from him to where Mum lay back in the booth seat, her eyes closed, and a terrible rage rose inside her.

'You fucking bastard!' she screamed, reaching for the closest weapon, which happened to be a wooden chair upturned on a nearby table. 'Get the fuck away from my mum!'

Emily flung herself forwards. The man turned and bolted, but the restaurant door had closed and he slammed against it, fumbling vainly for the door handle. Emily swung the chair hard, crashing it against his shoulders and back. Unlike her movie-led perception of such things, it didn't break like she might have expected, but landed with a sickening thud. The man cried out, slumping to his knees. Emily swung the chair again, this time connecting with his face. He slumped sideways, landing on the restaurant carpet, arms flopping uselessly, tongue lolling. Emily, breathing hard, clothing flecked with the blood of both man and beast, lifted the stool to deliver a finishing blow.

'Stop! Emily, please! That's enough!'

She lowered the stool. Mum was staring at her, eyes wide, mouth open.

'Emily, you'll kill him.'

'I want to kill him. He hurt you.'

'He didn't hurt me. Please, Emily. We're not monsters. Not yet.'

Emily let go of the stool. It bounced off a nearby table and came to rest on the floor, not far from where the young man lay, groaning. Emily stared at him, at a bloody welt around the side of one eye, at the flecks of blood which had stained the beige carpet. She thought about the anonymous man lying in the kitchen, Graham's face ripping apart, and the creature she had killed.

'Mum,' she whispered, and began to cry.

13

BAIT

I CAN'T LET it in. Whatever it is, I can't let it in.

The repeating thought was a like a bell in Juliet's mind as she went through into the living room, climbed up on the wide sill and peered out of the protruding bay window at the front door to the left. Out of sight behind the big, ornamental postbox Dad had bought himself as a Christmas present last year, she only caught glimpses of whatever was scrabbling at the door. She hoped it was a dog, perhaps a wild one from one of the local farms, because she had heard they sometimes had puppies grow up in the surrounding woods that ate out of the pig troughs. She wasn't scared of dogs because she could outrun one on her bike. Uncle Lawrence seemed to think it was something else, though, but maybe he was mistaken. Dad said he smoked this stuff called "wacky baccy" which made him paranoid. Dad said never to believe anything Uncle Lawrence said unless you saw it with your own eyes, but Juliet had always enjoyed his stories. They were funny, and he was harmless enough, even if he was a bit weird.

She decided to take a chance, see if she could get a

look at whatever was outside. She went back into the kitchen and looked in the fridge. There was half a joint of ham left from yesterday's dinner, and she agonised over taking it. Dad would be mad, but these were special circumstances, kind of like when an ambulance needed to drive down the wrong side of the road. Dad was a doctor, he would understand.

Uncle Lawrence was where she had left him. His eyes were closed and he looked asleep, even if he was groaning and muttering as though having a bad dream. Juliet checked his bandage to make sure it hadn't come loose or that any blood was seeping through, then hurried back to the living room.

She climbed up onto the windowsill and opened one of the small windows along the top, the ones Dad said it was okay to leave open during the day because they were too high up, and too small for a burglar to climb through. On tiptoe she could only just reach, pushing her hand with the ham outside and tossing it to the ground by the front door.

Almost immediately something darted away from the doorway, so fast Juliet's eyes couldn't focus on it clearly until it paused to take the meat in its jaws. She blinked, shrinking back from the window, and might have fallen had one hand not still had hold of the open upper window frame. The creature, disturbed by the noise, looked up, hissed at something unseen, then took the lump of ham in its jaws and ran off. It crossed the driveway and dove into the long grass verge in front of the hedgerow, disappearing from sight.

Juliet's heart pounded. She stood still, staring at the grass verge for a couple of minutes before she could bring herself to move. Then, very slowly, she closed the window and locked it, then climbed down from the windowsill.

A dinosaur. It had been a little dinosaur. She could

dress it up however she wanted, that it was a kind of crocodile thing, or a lizard walking on two legs with an extra-long tail, but she would be kidding herself. It had been a little dinosaur, one of those ones that you saw on TV shows that were never the main focus, but always buzzing around in the background, kind of like birds over a lion enclosure at a zoo. Filler dinosaurs, perhaps, would be how Dad would call it. Extras in a bigger film.

Yet it had ripped open Uncle Lawrence's arm and had tried to get into the house.

For a few moments, Juliet just dawdled, unsure what she should do. Dad would be home soon—*wouldn't he?*—but if there were strange creatures running about, what if he had to work late? If there was one, there might be more.

Finally summoning the will to move, she went into the kitchen to check on Uncle Lawrence. To her dismay, he had rolled onto his back, his eyes half open. He groaned, his forehead soaked in sweat. Juliet reached down to touch his skin, and pulled her hand away with a gasp. He was burning up.

'Water,' he croaked.

She took a glass from the drying tray by the sink and turned on the cold tap. Nothing came out. Juliet, frowning, turned the hot tap, but it too was dead. Shaking her head, she went into the bathroom where she had taken a shower just twenty minutes before. Both the bath and the sink taps were dry. Desperate, she took a cloth from a cupboard under the sink and wiped it around the bath, collecting as many drips as she could and squeezing it into the glass, but it was barely a centimetre's worth of liquid, not enough.

She spun around, trying to think. There was water in the toilet, but that was dirty, wasn't it? And their cistern was up in the loft. The hatch was locked with a key, and she had no idea where Dad kept it, but would that water even be drinkable? Uncle Lawrence was hurt. She doubted it would help.

Back in the kitchen, she found a six pack of Coca Cola in one of the cupboards, and a couple of bottles of red wine. Were either suitable for a sick man? Again, she shook her head. She didn't want to make him worse.

She glanced at the clock. Ten to nine. She just had time to make it to the shop if she really hurried. Her bike was in the garage, accessed through a door from the house, and Dad always kept the garage door shut. If she got ready and opened it really quickly, she could get out to the road before the dinosaur spotted her. It had been fast, but her bike was faster.

Decided, she went into the kitchen and looked in the top cupboard over the fridge for Dad's spare change pot. An old tea caddy with an elephant design, he usually kept enough in it for bread, milk, whatever they might have run out of and needed to go up to the shop for. When she opened it, however, there were only a couple of coppers at the bottom, nowhere near enough to buy bottled water.

Perhaps if she promised to pay Mrs. Clark in the shop back tomorrow? Juliet shook her head. Mrs. Clark was an old battle-axe, never particularly friendly at the best of times, and tight as a duck's butt, watertight. Juliet remember going up there for two-penny sweets when she was little with her friends, and having Mrs. Clark make them count out every bag, even Annie Solton, whose parents were poor and had only ever given her enough for ten sweets. No, Mrs. Clark would tell her to get lost.

She noticed the bulge in Uncle Lawrence's jeans pocket. It had to be his wallet. Juliet grimaced. It was technically stealing, but he wouldn't mind, would he? She was going to buy the water for him, after all.

'Uncle Lawrence, sorry about this,' she muttered, squatting down, and slipping a hand into his pocket. 'I'm just borrowing it, okay? I'll get Dad to pay you back.'

Uncle Lawrence didn't appear to understand. He continued to groan, his head lolling. Juliet pulled the wallet free and turned him onto his side again, pushing the towel back under his head.

Standing up, she opened his wallet. There were a few notes inside along with some cards. As she pulled some notes free, however, something else fell out with them and fluttered to the floor. She picked it up and turned it over, frowning.

It was a picture of her, taken when she was much younger, perhaps seven. A summer's day, when Dad had got the paddling pool out in the back garden. Juliet, in her new mermaid designed one-piece swimsuit, stood straight, her hand lifted to her forehead in a salute as she beamed at the camera. Her body glistened with water from the pool.

She frowned. She knew this photo. It was in one of Dad's albums. Why would Uncle Lawrence have it? Then, rubbing the paper with her fingers, she realised. This wasn't a photograph, but a picture someone had taken of the photograph, and then printed out. The image was slightly grainier than the original, the colours slightly faded.

But why would Uncle Lawrence have it? She knew he was fond of her. He had given her fifty pounds in a card for her last birthday, and Dad had been almost angry, telling him to take it back. Uncle Lawrence didn't have any children, Dad had explained later. He liked to spoil Juliet because he didn't have a daughter of his own, but it wasn't right to spoil someone else's daughter, even if she was your niece. In the end, Dad had let Uncle Lawrence give her the money, but had taken all but five pounds away to put into her savings account.

That had to be it. Uncle Lawrence clearly liked her even more than Dad had realised. Perhaps he thought of her as his own daughter.

She put the picture back into his wallet, but left his wallet on the table.

If he thought so much of her, she owed it to him to try, to make sure she got to the shop on time.

Stuffing the money into her pocket, she leaned down, wiping Uncle Lawrence's brow with a tea towel.

'Don't worry,' she whispered into his ear. 'I'll be back soon. I'm going to look after you, Uncle Lawrence. I'm going to make sure you're all right.'

14

WARNING

LILIAN LAY ON THE BED, trying to force herself to get up. The sun shone gloriously, mockingly, almost, through the open drapes of her attic bedroom window, but the promise of another fine summer's day wasn't enough.

Melinda, the dirty skank Richard like to call his girlfriend, but whom Lilian had discovered was on the payroll like the rest of them, was getting a car back to Exeter this morning. Much as Lilian disliked the rude, coarse woman, she didn't want her to leave. She would gladly put up with Melinda's exaggerated wails of pleasure at all hours of the night, her sharp, barbed comments over breakfast, and the way she created extra work for them all by leaving things lying around, neglecting to flush the toilet, to make her bed, because the woman's presence kept Richard occupied.

Once Melinda was gone, he would turn his eyes back towards the door of Lilian's little attic room, and his sinister knock would come at night.

It was Harry all over again. Harry, whom Lilian had come here to escape from, seeking sanctuary after years of horrific abuse it had taken all her strength to leave behind. Her grandparents had promised Lord Evans was a kind and warmhearted man, and he had been. He had accepted her without any questions asked, bringing her into his employment. Treating her fair, she had worked hard for him, and slowly had begun to find her footing in the world.

And then Lord Evans had died, and Richard, his son, had inherited the property.

There was only so long she could brush off his advances, ignore the gentle knocking on her door, the slurred purr of his voice compelling her to let him in. Sooner or later, she would have no choice but do as he asked. She had seen the way his frustration at her passive rejection was growing, the greater harshness with which he treated her grandparents as a result. In the end, she would have no choice. She would do what was necessary to keep them safe.

Until last night, however, when his hands had got the better of him, he had never let on to her grandparents that he had dark designs on his mind.

Now, Grandma June was livid, banging around the kitchen like an untethered bull. Lilian had talked it down as a once off, as a result of too much to drink, but what if June told Grandfather Alfred? He was old, his strength fading, and Richard treated him badly enough already. If he found out, what if he said something to Richard? Lilian wouldn't be able to live with herself if Richard punished her grandfather in some way.

She forced herself out of bed, dressed, and headed downstairs. She had prepared the breakfast things last night, and June had served this morning. From the sound of the raised voices in the dining room, Richard had a nasty hangover. Melinda was berating June for overcooking something, but Lilian couldn't bring herself to get involved. Instead, she went looking for Grandfather.

She found him in the pantry, loading bags of flour and rice into a wheelbarrow. Clearly struggling under the weight, she silently began to help, assisting him to lift the bags out of a storage locker and set them down.

'Thank you, dear,' Alfred said.

'Where are you taking them?'

'The bunker.'

'I'll do it.'

'No. Lord Richard tasked me.'

'I don't care. It's too heavy for you.'

'He won't like it.'

'He's busy with breakfast and Melinda. We can go together.'

She didn't wait for him to protest, taking up the wheelbarrow, pushing it out through the open side door and down a paved path into the gardens. The bunker was at the very end of the gardens, so Lilian set the barrow down while she assessed the easiest route. The central area of the gardens was a vast lawn, but the grass needed cutting and it had rained yesterday, making it spongy. Lord Richard would be angry too if the wheelbarrow left depressions in the grass.

Around the house and the garden's northern end was a maze of flowerbeds, patios, and fountains. Some areas had steps, others were paved slopes. Lilian planned her route, aiming for the trees along the northern hedgerow where it was shady, and the ground was rockier.

Hard work at the house had given her arms strength, so she gritted her teeth, lifted the wheelbarrow and set out, aiming to do the rest of the journey in one go. Alfred had appeared out of the pantry and was following her, but Lilian was converting her anger into effort as she marched down the path between the flowerbeds, making him struggle to catch up.

She couldn't help but notice the weeds among the flowers as she went. The hedgerows needed cutting back, and patches of dandelions were starting to mottle the lawns. She had only served under Lord Evans for a few weeks before his untimely death, but he would never have allowed it. Richard was like a slowly spreading cancer, corrupting and souring everything around him.

Head down, lost in her thoughts, she didn't notice the man climbing through the hedgerow until he jumped down in front of her.

'Oh!'

The man's fall had spent him sprawling, but now he climbed up, brushing himself down. He was dirty, clothing ripped and torn. Behind several days of stubble he looked to be about thirty. His sky-blue eyes might have been attractive in better circumstances, but his face was pockmarked with sores. His hands, fingernails caked with dirt, were bruised and scratched, as though he had fought for his life and then escaped through a bramble patch. As he stared at her, mouth working silently, Lilian dropped the wheelbarrow with a heavy thump and stepped back.

'Help me, please.'

'Who are you? What do you want?'

The man didn't appear to understand. He looked at her, then looked around, eyes taking in the house and grounds.

'What is this? Some theme park?'

'Hey you, you're trespassing!' Grandfather Alfred came up behind her. He had found a cane from somewhere and was waving at it about like a weapon. 'You're not allowed in here.'

'They're coming,' he said, looking from side to side as

though whomever was coming might appear at any moment. 'You can't stay here. They'll see you.'

'Who?'

'They came into Marshdown last night. I don't know who they were, but they shot the place up, burned it.'

'What are you talking about?' Alfred said. 'What a load of rubbish. If anything had happened in Marshdown, we'd have heard about it.'

Marshdown was the nearest town, nine miles to the east. A bus stopped a hundred yards from the entrance to the grounds.

The man looked at the wheelbarrow. 'You have food. Do you have water? May I have some, please?'

Lilian was about to offer to run back to the house, when her grandfather said, 'What does this look like? This is private property. Get out of here. We have a groundskeeper, you know. He has legal permission to shoot intruders on sight.'

Lilian wasn't sure that Dave Brussells, the groundskeeper in question, would agree, but her grandfather had a natural authority to his voice that clearly convinced the man. He looked over his shoulder, turned back to Lilian and Alfred, and gave a little shake of his head.

'Go fuck yourselves,' he said. 'You'll get what's coming to you in time. We all will.'

He turned and sprinted off down the slope from the hedge, across the wide, flat lawn, and into the woodland area to the south. A few hundred yards through the trees and he would come out on a small forest road, Lilian knew.

'Grandfather,' she said. 'We should have helped him.'

'We can't help everyone,' Alfred said. 'We're not running a charity.'

'But what if what he said was true?'

'I'll have a word with Benjamin when he comes with the morning delivery,' Alfred said. 'I'm sure he'll put our minds at rest. Certainly that man was some kind of escapee, perhaps from a hospital. We had a lucky escape. I apologise if he offended you with his ghastly manners and unpleasant language, my dear.'

Grandfather Alfred was so achingly sheltered that it brought tears to Lilian's eyes. She turned away so he wouldn't see her, trying to erase the memory of Harry's swinging fists, Richard's pressing hands, the black, soulless eyes on both.

'It's okay,' she said. 'Thank you for your concern. Now that he's gone, though, we should hurry up with these bags to the bunker.'

'Yes,' Alfred said. 'You're quite right. I'll ask Mr. Brussells to make a sweep of the grounds later, to make sure he's gone.'

'Thank you,' she said.

Grandfather Alfred leaned on his cane. He frowned, giving a little shake of his head. 'I'm sure it's nothing to worry about, my dear. Nothing to worry about at all.'

15

ROADBLOCK

THE DISTANT THUNDER of bombs falling on Birmingham were like muffled firecrackers. Pop-pop-pop-pop-bang-bang-bang. At first they had headed north, but as they left Clent Hills behind and approached Hagley, they had been able to see it, and the columns of smoke rising over their city had been too much for many of the kids. Claire, desperate just to find some way to reset, had instructed Pauly to turn the bus west.

Now, with Birmingham behind them, she was trying to establish a level of temporary calm. The problem was, everyone had experienced enough trauma in a few short minutes to last a lifetime. While some pupils were curled up in their seats, sobbing into their hands, others were talking too fast, talking over each other, speaking without listening, trying to reason out what they had seen, to make sense of it all.

A fight broke out between two, Tim Parkson piling into Danny Rainer's seat, swinging a haymaker as he shouted something too rapid-fire for Claire to understand. In normal circumstances she would have had to rush to the back of the bus and break it up, but she had no energy left. She hoped a couple of the girls would stop Danny getting too bad a beating, but as Tim's head popped up above the seats, his nose bloodied, Claire tutted in surprise. In what would normally have been a no-contest, trauma had given Danny strength, sapping it from Tim. Danny, snarling, caught Tim with another punch flush in the eye, and Tim backed off, howling some vague threat in an attempt to save face, letting Jenny Coates pull him back into his seat.

'There's some kind of road block,' Pauly said.

Claire leaned forwards. Red traffic cones made a line across the road. As the bus approached, two men climbed out of a car and walked to the centre line. They wore military fatigues, but something about them wasn't right. They were too ... *small.* The only time she had ever seen soldiers in real life they had been bulkier, laden down with gear. Both men wore helmets, and one carried a rifle across his chest, but otherwise they could have just stepped out of a surplus store.

One waved his hands for the bus to slow down. Pauly started to apply the brake, but Claire put a hand on his shoulder.

'No. This isn't right. I don't think they're soldiers.'

'What do you want me to do?'

Claire took a deep breath. 'Go straight through.'

'Are you serious?'

'Yes.'

'But what if they don't move?'

Claire gulped. 'They'll move. They'll have to.'

'I can't!'

'Pauly, those aren't soldiers. I have a bad feeling. We can't stop. We just can't.'

'All right.'

Claire felt almost dizzy, and knew she was running on

pure adrenaline. Whatever the men wanted, it wasn't good. They had guns, there were girls on the bus … it wasn't good.

Pauly started to slow, and for a moment Claire thought he was going to back out. The roadblock closed to a hundred, eighty, fifty, thirty yards—

'Hang on!'

Pauly slammed his foot down. Rather than roar into acceleration, the bus groaned as it gradually began to increase its speed. They were going no more than thirty, thirty-five, but the bus was big, and the men were small.

The man with his arms out backed off when he realized they didn't mean to stop. He grabbed the other man's shoulder, but the gun came up, pointing towards the bus, and let off a muffled *pop-pop-pop*. Three thumbnail sized holes appeared in the bus windscreen. Claire dropped down into the stairwell, cowering behind the dashboard. A second later the bus bumped as the right tyre rode up over something and cones scattered out of its way.

From the rear, kids were screaming. Claire looked out of the side window to see what had happened, but only caught sight of one man lying by the roadside, speaking into a walkie-talkie. She looked up at Pauly, wondering if he knew what had happened, and let out a desperate gasp.

Pauly was slumped in the driver's chair, head lolling to the left. A growing patch of red on the front of his white shirt showed where the bullet had struck.

Claire jumped up as the bus lurched sideways. She grabbed the wheel as Pauly's hand fell away and he slumped against the side window. Yanking the wheel back straight, Claire found herself sitting half on and half off of Pauly's body as she steered the bus back into the centre of the road.

'Miss, is he dead? Is he *dead*?' someone shouted, but

Claire could barely hear over the screams of the others and the ringing in her ears. Her cheeks and throat felt filled with blood, her face flushed with heat. Her heart was hammering faster than she thought it was possible. Squeezed beside her, in death Pauly's bowels had opened, letting out a rancid stench.

A car, abandoned, had been turned sideways across the road. Struggling with the awkwardness of the bus's wheel, they were on it before Claire could even find the brake pedal. Kids screamed as they slammed into it, the bus jerking forward. Claire struck her head on the wheel, sat upright, feeling dazed, her vision a blur. Something sticky ran down the side of her face. Her fingers came away wet with blood, feeling upwards to a gash on her forehead.

'Sit down!' she shouted, aware from the rearview mirror that a couple of kids had made their way farther up the aisle, but more because she needed the harshness of the sound to shock herself into clarity. It worked; her vision cleared, and she steered the bus back into their lane, settled her foot on the accelerator, and gradually increased their speed.

She didn't know the area, had no idea where they were going. It made sense to keep away from the city if it was being bombed, and if there were people who might or might not be soldiers setting up roadblocks, even smaller urban areas could be dangerous. All she knew was that she had to keep her surviving pupils safe.

They came to a junction where a sign indicated the Shropshire Hills Area of Outstanding Natural Beauty. It was a moorland area she had gone with her father as a child, but it had been twenty years since she had been anywhere near. Twenty-five miles.

The tank was nearly full. Pauly had been well prepared.

A sudden lump rose in Claire's throat. She blamed herself for the deaths of her pupils, but deep down she knew it had been beyond her control. Pauly, though was dead because of her decision. If she'd told him to stop, he might be alive.

Or they might all be dead, or those men might be raping the girls right now.

Or—or—*or*—

Claire gripped the wheel with both hands, ignoring the blood dribbling down her face. Something told her she'd be making more difficult decisions before long. People's lives would depend on whether she got them right.

She followed the signs for the Shropshire Hills, accelerating hard through the few villages they passed. In some places nothing looked amiss: two old women were talking outside a village store, and a man was changing a car tyre in the driveway of a pretty cottage. She wanted to stop, to ask for help, but whatever tidal wave of apocalypse that had overwhelmed them at the Clent Hills would soon reach them here.

Other things she saw convinced her she was right. A man carrying a suitcase out to a car. A small village school closing early, the teachers ushering little children out of the gates. An older woman pointing in the direction of Birmingham as she spoke to a bearded man, tears in her eyes, a hand rubbing her forehead.

They passed through the last village and came to open moorland. Pretty, conical hills stood in front of them. Claire accelerated uphill, the bus bumping too quickly over the uneven road. They were approaching a building set in its own grounds, overlooking the landscape, a car park to the side. A pub. Goddamn, she needed a drink, even if there were few things less appropriate right now. Where there were no safe places to stop, it was as good as any, and would at least have food and drink. She pulled the bus into an empty car park and killed the engine.

From behind her came the weak sobbing of a couple of the kids, but otherwise there was silence. Most of them had to be screamed out by now. Even though she had spent the last hour pressed against the slowly cooling body of their dead driver, Claire didn't think she could scream any more. Maybe later, if she tried to sleep, when the nightmares came.

Claire was the first to step down from the bus, out into a chilly, overcast afternoon. She made it only a few steps across the car park before her strength gave way and she slumped to her knees, grazing the palms of her hands on the tarmac. Slowly, the pupils came after her one by one, each moving tentatively like astronauts stepping out on to the surface of an explored planet for the first time. She looked up, watching them as they slowly came closer, the heartbreakingly few survivors.

Danny Rainer, his face flecked with blood, had one arm around Daisy Cale, who was sobbing into a handkerchief, eyes bloodshot. Ishy Gupta stood beside her, Ishy with her tan skin and chocolate brown hair, perfect features and catalogue-model-bound stature, now reduced to a hunched, bedraggled wreck. Seeing such deconstruction in a girl whose confidence had been almost insulting, Claire was actually glad to see the defiance in Mick Williams's face as he stood beside a stunned, wide-eyed Lisa Margate, his fists clenched as though ready to punch out the next impossible monster which appeared to prey on his classmates. Beside them, Connie Hart's eyes blazed with anger, while completing the circle, Jenny Coates and Tim Parkson, holding hands, had lost the aura of elitism that surrounded them in the school corridors. Tim's left eye had swollen shut, his cheek had a vicious graze, and Jenny's intricately woven plaits, the envy of many younger pupils, had come unfastened and hung half unwound, matted with leaves, soil, and blood.

'Miss, are you all right?' Danny, assuming the role of spokesman, asked.

Claire looked up at him. She wanted to berate him: what a stupid question. *I'll never be all right again*, she thought, but the earnest look in his eyes defied her.

She nodded. 'I think so,' she said.

'What do we do now?' Mick asked. 'I wanna go home.'

'We can't go home.'

'Miss—'

Claire put up a hand, and whatever shred of authority she still retained made the protester—Ishy, maybe, but Claire was still too dazed to focus on anything—fall silent.

'We can't go home, not yet. It's not safe. I think you … I think you saw that.'

It felt insulting to patronise them with the brutal deaths of their friends, but if they were going to survive, they had to get smart, and real fucking fast or they would all be dead. She had seen enough already to know that what had come on over the last couple of hours wasn't about to blow over. It could get a lot worse before it got better.

If it ever does, a horrid, mocking voice whispered. *This is humanity done. Get used to it, and start saying goodbye to everything you've ever held dear.*

'Miss, if we can't go home, what are we going to do?' Jenny Coates said. 'Those bird things—'

Jenny nodded at the pub. 'We'll see if there's someone in there who can help us. We have to be patient, keep our heads down.'

She was well aware of the irony of preaching cover when they were standing in the middle of an open car park, but at least here they could see anything coming.

There was no cover, no trees, nothing to hide any of those things. Up here, their biggest threat was other people.

It felt like lifting the sky just to get back to her feet.

From far in the distance came the muffled *crack-crack-crack* of a series of explosions.

'Miss, I'm scared,' Connie said.

Claire nodded. 'Me too. Come on, we have to get to cover.'

16

SLAUGHTER

The fog had closed in, turning Princetown into the set of a horror movie even before Mark came to the first bodies lying in the road. They were unrecognisable; mutilated, half eaten. Mark, even with his stomach empty, found himself retching up bile as he encountered them, flies crawling over the older corpses, maggots churning in grey masses inside ripped open body cavities.

Whatever had come through here had been swift and decisive, leaving nothing alive. Indiscriminate, the corpses of men, women, and children lay all around, splayed out on the ground, slaughtered.

At first Mark was hesitant to get too close, but his own survival instincts were kicking in, and in order to live he needed to know what was making all these people die.

Something had happened to make these people panic and come out on the street. He came across cars with their doors still open, cases piled inside, their unlucky owners lying dead nearby, torn apart.

No single animal could have done this. And if there

had been a large number, there would be evidence of them somewhere.

He found what he guessed was the faeces of one of the animals responsible in a heap on a street corner. The stinking black mess was the size of a small dog. Even flies seemed reluctant to touch it, as though it were something alien, poisonous. He gave it a wide berth, continuing up the street.

Up ahead, a car had overturned, its boot popped open, its contents spewed across the road. A middle-aged couple had tried to climb out. The man had made it to the street but lay face down, his feet in the air against the underside of the car. The woman was in the process of climbing out, like a submarine sailor emerging above water. Her head lolled, blood splashed across her face.

Mark stopped.

Four bullet holes had fractured the windscreen, two each. Mark looked closer at the bodies. The woman had been struck in the chest, the man in the stomach and thigh. Both had bled out while trying to escape.

Mark dropped down behind the car, blood thumping in his ears. Not killed by some unseen animal. Shot.

He knew little about guns, but more than most. Keeping still, his eye scanned the ground until he saw it, a little metal object lying on the road.

A spent bullet casing.

His knowledge of guns wasn't good enough to identify the weapon from its bullet, but he knew what it wasn't: a shotgun cartridge. That meant it was at the very least gang-owned, maybe military.

He carried on up the street. Finding more bodies, he inspected them one by one, and even though these had been partially eaten, he found an exit wound in one unfortunate man's back, meaning the same thing.

An execution.

The danger of the streets rose another level. Mark kept down, checking his options, the club held ready.

Footsteps from farther up the street drew his attention. He crept to the edge of the overturned car and peered around the front bumper.

The front door of one of the terraced houses opened and a family came bustling out, making for a car that sat at the kerb nearby. A man, woman, two kids around ten or twelve years old. The boy was whimpering, the woman hassling him to be quiet as they piled suitcases into the back of the car.

They were almost done, climbing in, when something came racing out of an alleyway opposite. Mark braced himself, not wanting to watch them die, but it was only a dog, some mongrel breed, shaggy and unkempt. A pet, forgotten, perhaps—

The woman screamed. The dog had a hold of the boy's ankle and was dragging him backwards, away from the car as he tried to hold on. The man came running around and tried to hit the dog with a smaller suitcase, but the dog just darted sideways and the man struck the road instead, the case popping open. The dog snarled at him as he tried first to gather up the clothes that had spewed out, then to strike at the dog with the half-closed suitcase. The dog snapped at him, then went for the boy again. From the car, the girl was now screaming, the woman crying.

Mark stood up before his little internal warning voice could talk him out of it. He shouldered the club and ran towards the group. At the sight of him, the man gasped and backed away, falling back over himself. He was portly, overweight, flabby chin hidden by a wisp of beard. Some clipboard type, a coordinator or inspector. Someone who'd never so much as lifted a spoon in anger at anyone more threatening than his wife.

With a powerful swing of his shoulders, Mark smashed the dog's ribcage. Even as the concrete shards on the pipe end ripped the flesh from its stomach, it turned and came at him, eyes wide, rabid. He stepped back, wrong-footing it, and this time got it on the side of the face. Its jaw hanging off, it still wouldn't die. Mark swung again, and this time it did, collapsing in a bloodied heap at his feet.

'Are you all right? What happened here?'

The girl was helping the boy into the car. He had a vicious gash on his ankle, and Mark felt a momentary sense of regret that he hadn't moved sooner. He had done what he could, though, and they were no longer his problem. If they wanted to survive, they had to get resourceful, and fast.

'Thank you,' the man said, his eyes darting across Mark's face, filled with distrust.

'What happened here?'

'A herd of—' the girl began, but the man slammed the back door shut, cutting off her words.

'We were told to leave,' he said. 'But we waited. Other people were out in the street, packing their cars. And then we heard shooting. Are you from in there?'

Mark didn't need to know where "in there" meant. There was only one place.

'I didn't cause this,' he said.

'Someone did.'

The woman leaned out of the car. 'Jerry, hurry up!'

'I'm sorry,' the man said. 'We've got to go. Before … before—'

Mark lifted a hand as the man backed away towards the car.

'Who was shooting?' he asked.

Jerry shrugged. 'I didn't see them. But there were a lot. A lot of guns. It sounded like the army.'

'I didn't see any dead soldiers.'

'Jerry, come on!'

Jerry looked around. His eyes held Mark's.

'It's not the guns you have to worry about,' he said. He reached the car and pulled open the front door. Then, as though remembering manners no longer needed, he said, 'Thank you. Good luck.'

Jerry slammed the front door. The engine started up, and the car made its way up the street, winding between bodies and other debris.

An ordered evacuation gone bad. Maybe. Mark shouldered his club and headed on up the street.

He found more bodies, more signs of abandonment, but the only living people he saw were distant, fleeing before he could reach them. Night came on. Initially reluctant to enter a stranger's house, no matter how abandoned it appeared, in the end he had no choice. He chose a small house at the end of a terrace, with windows facing three directions. The front door was locked, but a back door in a small, neat garden that encircled the house's three sides was open.

Mark went inside, did a quick sweep of the house, then went through each room, checking carefully to make sure no one was holed up. There was no cellar, but there was hatch leading into a cramped loft, and he checked in there too, making sure the place was clear. Only then did he lock and barricade the back door, and only then did he allow himself to relax a little.

The power was off, but the water was still running.

Mark cleaned himself up, then ate what he found in the fridge—a bowl of cold baked beans covered in clingfilm, and a plastic tub of unfinished spaghetti Bolognese. As he sat at a narrow kitchen table to eat, he stared at photographs stuck to the fridge of a family of three on a fishing trip, a young girl in a ballet costume, a woman holding a new baby, a terrier dog lying on grass with a dirty orange ball in its mouth.

He wanted to sleep, but he didn't dare, so he pulled a chair close to the window in a cramped upstairs bedroom, put a pillow under his head and leaned against the wall, planning to keep watch. A couple of street lights blinked on, but most stayed dark. He saw two cars pass at half hour intervals, one speeding, bumping over a dark shape lying in the street, the other moving slowly, it's exhaust scraping along the tarmac.

~

He hadn't planned to sleep but he had, and was woken by a woman screaming. He sat up, nearly fell off the chair, and caught hold of the windowsill to steady himself.

A figure was staggering up the street, stumbling from side to side, wailing at the top of her voice.

A small alarm clock with a cartoon design and battery-illuminated hands told him it was just after midnight.

The woman—he couldn't tell her age, only that she was an adult—came on up the street, until she was almost level with Mark's window. One reason he had chosen this place was because it was on the edge of the village, with views back up the street and out on to the moor. The woman staggered past, still screaming. It sounded like someone's name, but Mark couldn't tell, and he wasn't about to open the window to find out. He watched her, morbidly fascinated, as she came to a junction where the road led out across the moor.

And then the impenetrable black that was the moor began to move. Mark shrank back, breathless, too afraid to move as the creatures swarmed out of the darkness, running on two legs, narrow heads low to the ground, long tails high in the air, smaller front arms hooked forward, claws just above the ground. They were waist high to the woman as they passed, dozens of them, spreading out through the streets, some stopping to pick at the bodies fallen outside, others running on, looking for other meals.

Somewhere, a dog howled, the sound wild with horror. The woman, however, had stopped screaming.

She lay in the road, outside, what was left of her. A dozen or more of the creatures had taken it upon themselves to dismantle her, flesh, bones, organs, even clothes. They engulfed her, and when they moved on, there was nothing left but a dark patch in the road, and a few dismembered pieces. Her head, severed at the neck, lay like a forgotten football, and although her eyes were invisible in the gloom, Mark felt sure they were watching him, condemning him, damning him.

He shivered. In minutes the creatures began to return, racing past his window, back out onto the moor, disappearing into the darkness. He clung to the window frame, too afraid to move, watching them until they had all gone, a couple of stragglers, one moving with a limp, the last of them.

The street was still once more. The dog howled again, but the woman, what was left of her, remained silent.

17

INTRUDERS

In his desperation to get back to his house, Alan stumbled and fell twice, the first over a jumble of masonry, and the second over frustrating nothing, his legs and his nerves conspiring against him as he tried to get back before the creatures got to Dad. Hands bleeding, hip aching from a bad landing, he rushed up his steps and through the front door, hollering Dad's name.

The sound of falling tins came from the kitchen, at once a horror and a relief. Alan ran to the doorway, saw the creature in there, a blur of serpentine, nosing through the cupboard under the sink, half an unfinished tin of curry sauce spread across the floor. With no idea what else to do, Alan pulled the door shut, trapping the creature inside, then turned for Dad's room.

The bleeping of Dad's heart monitor was a momentary relief, but where was the other creature? Alan peered into Dad's room, saw nothing, Dad still lying inert on the bed, eyes half closed, but alive. Gloriously alive. Alan closed the door, heading for the stairs.

The thing in the kitchen, all scales and bony limbs,

couldn't weigh more than a stone or two. Alan, though, his impressions of such things warped by too many CGI disaster movies, had no idea how strong it might be. Would it attack him or flee? If the other was upstairs, he needed a weapon.

He pulled open a cleaning cupboard at the bottom of the stairs and pulled out a broom, then tossed it aside. Too light, too weak. A plastic handled mob. Same. A dustpan he threw aside with a scream of frustration.

'Mr. Graf?'

He pushed the door shut and turned. Ellis stood by the front door. He held up a small fire extinguisher, the size of a two-litre flask. Hard, heavy, metal.

Alan felt a knot in his stomach. He had ignored the boy, left him behind. Now he wanted to hug him.

'Thank you,' he said.

He told Ellis to stay at the bottom of the stairs, then he took the fire extinguisher and went up, one finger on the trigger like a gun, the other on the base in case he needed to use it like a club.

His bedroom: clear. Dad's old room, before Alan had moved him downstairs, also clear. Alan swallowed down a sob as he looked at the lines of Dad's old books, dozens of the thrillers and spy novels that Dad had loved, some he had even read to Alan at bedtime after Mum had gone out drinking with her friends. Too grown up, so that Alan had barely understood, from Dad's tone alone he had grasped the excitement of each story.

'Mr. Graf!'

Ellis's voice was filled with desperation. Alan spun, almost skidding down the stairs. Ellis pointed at Dad's closed door.

'I heard something move. I think it's in there!'

Alan's heart lurched. He had checked, but there were a

dozen places it could have squeezed itself into behind Dad's machines and monitors.

He kicked the door open, lifting the fire extinguisher.

The thing was on Dad's bed, standing on Dad's legs. Its maw was bloodied, and as the door swung open, its head dropped, teeth closing over Dad's shin.

'No!'

Alan pulled the trigger. Foam engulfed the creature, which gave a birdlike screech, twisted and fell from the bed, landing on its back on the floor, quickly scrabbling back to its feet. Alan howled in rage and threw himself forward, slamming the butt of the fire extinguisher against the creature's head. The first blow left it stunned, the second knocked it down, and two more left it blooded and dead.

'Dad … oh, Dad….'

Alan clambered over the dead creature to check on Dad. Dad's eyes were closed, his head shaking from side to side. Dad's face was covered with a fine orange powder from the fire extinguisher, and Alan brushed it away, aware it could cause suffocation. Dad seemed to be breathing okay, but his heart rate was rapidly increasing. Alan turned to the wound, recoiling in horror at the vicious gash on Dad's leg.

That Dad had been lying flat on his back and wearing pajamas had saved him from a bite wound far worse. The cloth and Dad's shin bone had saved much of his flesh, but the skin had been scraped away from an area nearly two inches across, the bone exposed.

With Dad's life in danger, Alan's emergency room experience took over. He raced to a cupboard, pulling out what he needed to sedate Dad and lower his heart rate, then set about attending and dressing the wound. At some point as he worked, Ellis came and pulled the creature's body away, then began to clean up the floor around Alan's feet. For his part, Alan ignored him, his focus only on Dad, aware that a moment's hesitation could be fatal.

Even under sedation, Dad twitched and groaned as Alan worked, as though in the grip of some horrible nightmare. Alan, tears in his eyes, bandaged the wound then set up an antibiotic drip. As always when he tended to Dad, he tried not to let the memories swamp him. Dad, a grin on his face, waiting at the end of the street as Alan took his first bicycle ride without his stabilisers, Dad picking him up from school with a smile, asking him how tests had gone, Dad telling him Mum would be fine and then closing the bathroom door so Alan wouldn't have to watch her being sick. Dad sitting beside him on the bed at night while the sound of breaking plates and furniture came from the other room, the bed pushed in front of the door, a book held close, Dad's voice in his ear as he read so he couldn't hear over Mum raging. Dad telling him not to worry, that Mum was with the angels now, that none of it had been her fault, that she had always loved him, even if she'd never found time to say.

'Live, Dad, live,' Alan implored the old man, leaning close to his ear, briefly hugging him tight, too tight, feeling the warmth in the failing body, holding on to a fading, fading hope that everything might still be all right, even when the blood on his clothes and the thing he had killed convinced him it wouldn't be that ever again. The good days, such as they had been, were done.

Finally, satisfied he had done everything he could, he pulled up a chair and sat down next to Dad's bed, feeling exhausted. He reached out for Dad's hand, his heart momentarily breaking at the frailty in Dad's fingers, the papery feel of the skin. The man who had lifted him into the air and spun him around, laughing while Alan squealed with delight, reduced to this, a hollow, cardboard cutout of a man.

But he was alive. He was still alive.

Movement in the doorway made Alan look up. Ellis stood there, watching him.

'Mr. Graf? I'm sorry to bother you, Mr. Graf. The other one is still in the kitchen.'

Alan closed his eyes briefly, then stood up. The fire extinguisher was still by the door, where he had left it, but most of the spray was exhausted.

'Mr. Graf? What should we do?'

There was a back door, but the only way to access it was to walk to the end of the street, go through the locked gate into the rear alley, and walk back along the terrace to his house. There was too much danger outside, and he didn't want to leave Dad a second time.

'We need to get it outside.'

'Can we kill it?'

Alan looked at the fire extinguisher. He could still use it as a club, but the spray had given him an advantage. If he missed, and the creature bit him, he might not be able to care for Dad.

'We need to lure it out,' he said.

'We could put some food on the front step,' Ellis said, eyes brightening. 'Then we could shut the door on it.'

It was a simple, childlike idea, but it might just work. Everything he had to lure it with was in the kitchen, however.

'It's a meat eater,' Alan said. 'We need some meat.' He shook his head, trying to think clearly, but his mind was fogged. 'Maybe next door?'

'There's the other one,' Ellis said.

Again, the simplicity. Alan looked up. 'Where did you put it?'

'It's in the living room,' Ellis said, then quickly added, 'but I didn't get any blood on the carpet. I found some bags in the cupboard in the hall.'

'Let me see.'

Ellis had somehow squeezed the thing into a black refuse sack. Alan baulked at the sight of it, its head bashed in. Already it stank, a mixture of blood and something else, an alien kind of warmth. Alan had seen a lot of dead bodies, but this was somehow far worse than someone dying on the operating table. This was something that shouldn't be, that shouldn't exist.

He dragged the bag out into the hallway. It was heavier than it looked, perhaps three stone.

'Do you want me to open the door?' Ellis asked.

Alan almost said yes, then he looked at the boy, saw something in his face. A desperation. A need to be useful, to justify himself.

'How old are you, boy?'

'Ten, sir. I'll be eleven in January.'

So young. Too young to be involved in something like this.

'Go into the living room,' Alan said. 'Close the door, and keep it closed.'

'I can help—'

'You might get hurt. Please.'

Ellis looked at him for a moment, then nodded. 'I can help you clean up,' he said, and Alan could have laughed if the situation wasn't so grave. There was a … there was a dinosaur in his kitchen, another dead one in a bag at his feet, and the boy sounded like this was nothing more than the aftermath of a big party.

Alan nodded. 'Sure,' he said.

Ellis looked at him a moment longer, then went into the living room and closed the door. Alan took a deep breath, then opened the front door and peered out into the street. It was clear now, both of people and prehistoric animals. The door opened inwards, so Alan pulled away his jackets from a hook behind the door, then kicked away some unopened circulars to give the door the widest possible opening range. Then he dragged the bag out on to the step and dumped the contents onto the ground.

The creature was a mess. Alan could only stare for a few moments, unable to fully comprehend what he was seeing. The thing was reptilian, yet among the scales there were tufts of downy feathers. And despite its legs being no thicker than his wrists, it had three huge, hooked talon-like claws the size of his middle finger.

He put the fire extinguisher down in the hall, near the bottom of the stairs. Then he took a broom handle from the cupboard. Heart thundering, he went to the kitchen door, depressed the handle until the mechanism clicked, then retreated down the hall, climbing a few steps up the stairs.

'Hey!' he called. 'Come on!'

At first he thought it might have got back out on its own, but after a moment he heard the rattle of fallen tins, and then a serpentine face poked out, beady marble eyes looking around. Alan shivered; it was all he could do not to run up the stairs and lock himself in the bedroom.

'Hey,' he said again, voice lacking conviction. 'Hey … get out of there.'

The creature pushed out of the door and took a few steps down the hall. Alan could barely keep himself together. He held on to the broom handle with both hands, gripping it so tight his fingers ached.

'Look,' he muttered. 'Look … food. Go on … take it, you horrible little thing.'

The creature advanced a few more steps, watching

Alan with its nasty little eyes. Its jaw lifted and fell. A cold sweat broke out on Alan's neck as he realised his folly: perhaps it had eaten its fill in the kitchen already. Did these things just kill for the sake of it? Or were they like aquarium sharks, gently swimming among their potential prey until they got hungry?

'Take it, damn you!'

The creature came on again. It was nearly to the bottom of the stairs now, and so far had ignored its dead companion lying just a couple of paces in front. The way it moved made Alan shudder with fear; it was lithe and muscular, springy and deadly. He'd got lucky with the first one, catching it by surprise, his anger fueling him. If the second came at him, he might not even see it coming.

It put one foot on the bottom stair. Its tail swished back and forth like a cat stalking a bird. Only he was the prey now. He knew it. He had made a mistake, and he was about to pay—

The living room door opened suddenly, sharply, striking the creature in the back. Ellis peered out, then quickly slammed the door shut again. The creature, however, surprised, took a few steps back towards the door, almost stepping on the body of its dead companion. Its snout twitched, and it turned, its attention caught.

As it took one more step, over the threshold so that its feet were outside the house, Alan forced himself to move. He reached the bottom of the stairs in two strides, grabbed the edge of the front door, then leaned all his weight on it. The heavy wooden door slammed into the creature's back, knocked it sideways. The gap closed quickly, the door cutting off the outside, about to close—

—and stuck.

The creature wailed, its thin, snakelike tail whipping back and forth like a trapped snake, two feet of it stuck in the door. Alan slammed his foot down, holding the door where it was, but the carpet was loose here—he'd been meaning to have it replaced for the last year—and as the creature pressed, claws appearing as it twisted and tried to push its way back inside, Alan's strength started to fail.

'Just bloody leave!' he shouted. 'Get out of my house, you monster!'

The living room door opened. Ellis peered out, mouth dropping open. 'Mr. Graf, are you all right?'

'Boy—the kitchen. Sometime to cut with. Hurry.'

Ellis stared a moment longer, then, his brain seeming to compute in that childlike way that always felt like an old computer game where there was a frustrating delay between the pressing of the button and the execution of the command, he gave a frantic nod and ran off to the kitchen.

The creature had one claw inside the door and was trying to get at Alan. Its snout was right there, trying to press through the gap.

'Ellis….'

The kitchen door opened and the boy came running. 'Mr. Graf, will this do?' He held up Alan's kitchen scissors, the expensive ones with a serrated middle section he had bought for cutting up his recyclable containers.

'The tail,' Alan said. 'Cut it off.'

'Mr. Graf, I don't think I can—'

'Put your weight on the door, then!'

As Ellis leaned past him, more of a hindrance than a help but at least he was trying, Alan took the scissors out of the boy's hands while still holding the door with his shoulder. The tail, as thick as his big toe, was still whipping back and forth, the edge of the door pressing into the flesh. Alan poked the scissors as close as he could to the trapped part, sliding them up the shaft until the serrated part he used for cutting up plastic containers dug into the flesh. Then, gritting his teeth, he squeezed as hard as he could.

The creature let out a deafening wail. For a moment Alan didn't think he had the strength to cut through the bone, but he did. The tail severed, blood spurted, and the stump softened enough to slip out. Alan leaned on the door, heard it click shut, then turned the latch and slumped down, his back against the door, breathing hard.

The tail twitched for a few seconds before going still. Blood had sprayed up the lovely floral wallpaper that Dad had chosen, and now drippled down in thick streams. Alan wanted the thing out of there, but couldn't bring himself to touch it. He dropped the scissors on the doormat and looked up at Ellis.

The boy, pale faced and wide eyed, looked about to faint.

'Mr. Graf, it's gone now, hasn't it?'

The creature's wailing had faded quickly. Alan hoped it had either run away or bled out. He gave Ellis a tired nod.

'Are we safe now?' Ellis said.

Alan didn't think he'd ever feel safe again, but the boy was watching him, looking up to him as the grown up, the responsible adult, the care giver, the protector.

Knowing it was what the boy needed to hear, he forced himself to nod again.

'Yes,' he grunted, hating himself for the lie. 'We're safe.'

18

OVERCOME

'MUM....'

Kim held her close, trying to concentrate on Emily because it was better than thinking about the throbbing in her leg.

'I'm so scared, Mum. That thing in the kitchen ... it's not natural. I thought it was going to ... and then that man ... I'm so ... scared.'

'So am I. We have to try to stay strong. We've still got each other.'

It was incredible how adversity could bring people together. A day ago, Emily wouldn't have stayed in the same room with her mother unless she'd left her phone somewhere nearby and couldn't find it. Add a healthy dose of apocalypse and suddenly they were best friends.

The man on the floor groaned. He lifted one arm and rubbed the side of his face. One leg twitched, and he jerked from side to side, trying to muster the strength to get up.

Emily tensed, pushing away from Kim.

'I'll kill him, Mum.'

The man gave up his effort to stand and slumped back down, breathing hoarsely into the carpet.

Outside, a group of people ran past, dragging suitcases and children behind them. One woman pushed an old man in a wheelchair who was clinging to the sides like he was facing down a rollercoaster for the first time.

'Perhaps they know somewhere safe,' Emily said. 'Mum, let me help you up. Wait, I have an idea.'

Emily ran off towards the kitchen before Kim could tell her to stop. She was gone a couple of minutes, the bang of cupboards and crash of falling kitchen items animating her passage. Eventually she returned, holding up a broom and a mop.

'Crutches,' she said, smiling, then immediately burst into tears.

'They look pretty sturdy,' Kim said, wiping away a tear of her own.

Emily helped Kim to stand. The broom was a little too short, but the mop was a perfect length, and its bushy head gave some relief to her armpit. Emily peeled a rubber floor protector off the bottom of a chair leg and pulled it over the top of the mop's handle, so that it gave Kim some grip. Then, with Kim hobbling on the makeshift crutch and Emily with a stolen rucksack filled with some pilfered food items and a sealed plastic bag full of ice, they headed for the door.

The man lying on the ground groaned and rolled over.

'Come on, Mum,' Emily said, pushing open the door, but Kim paused, shaking her head.

'We can't just leave him,' she said.

'Yeah, we can. He's lucky he's not dead like his mate. He would have been if you hadn't stopped me.'

'We're not animals, and neither is he,' Kim said. 'He didn't hurt me. We should check he's all right.'

'Mum—'

'Emily, no. Please, do it for me. I can't just walk away from an injured man.'

'I can. Especially one who attacked us.'

Emily started for the door again, but Kim put a hand on her arm. 'Emily, please—'

'Is Graham all right?' the man said, still with his head bowed, but pushing himself up to his knees. 'Please tell me he's all right. I know what you're thinking, but he was good to me.'

'He's dead,' Emily said.

'Ah … fuck.' The man shook his head. 'Goddamn, motherfucker….'

'He got what he deserved,' Emily said. 'Some creature got him, but if it hadn't, I would have.'

Kim glanced at her daughter. It pleased her to see the lack of conviction in Emily's face. The girl was acting tough, that was all.

'Ah, man, Graham,' the man said, shaking his head, running one hand through his hair. His hood fell back and he finally glanced up at them. His eyes were bloodshot, and a line of blood trickled from a gash under his ear. He looked so young, Kim thought. Barely out of school, if that.

'You didn't have to … you didn't have to kill him. He wasn't gonna hurt you. Someone stole our gear when shit went down and we had to scavenge, you know? Everyone for himself.'

Emily looked ready to berate him, so Kim put a hand on her daughter's arm, squeezing in a way that Emily would know meant *relent, back up, calm down.*

'What's your name?' she said, wanting more than anything to humanise him in her daughter's eyes, dim the horrible killing light she saw there.

'Kenny,' he said. 'My name's Kenny Green.'

'Do you go to school, Kenny?'

Kenny shrugged. 'I did, a few times. Mostly Graham just lifted me a few books now and then, and I read them back at the flat sometimes, when we had the power on.'

'How old are you, Kenny?'

Kenny shrugged. 'Eighteen. Maybe nineteen. Thereabouts.'

'You don't know?'

Emily was still staring at Kenny with undisguised hatred, but the hardness in her face had softened just a little.

Kenny shrugged again. 'Didn't really matter, did it? Graham didn't know, either.'

'Was he your … guardian?'

'Kind of, you know. Brought me up and all that. Born in a crack house. Mum was on the pipes. Graham was her dealer. Said he'd look after me.'

'And did he?'

'Never let no one push me around.'

'Kenny, there's some very bad stuff happening right now. We need to go somewhere safe. Do you know anywhere?'

Emily grabbed Kim's arm. 'Mum, we're not going anywhere with this scumbag. He tried to rob us.'

'You killed Graham!'

'I didn't kill him, that fucking *thing* did.'

'Emily, please!'

'Look, I don't need any of this shit,' Kenny said. 'Just let me out.'

Kim put a hand on the door. She knew what Emily was thinking, but neither of them knew anything about survival.

'You owe us. Please. Do you know anywhere nearby? I need to see a doctor. Do you know anyone?'

'There's Marvin.'

'Who?'

'Graham's mate. Got kicked out of the NHS for stealing shit. Got a bit of a problem himself, but Graham used to call him in to deal with overdoses, shit like that.'

'He's a doctor?'

'Yeah.'

'Will he help me?'

'Might.'

'How far?'

Kenny gave another shrug. 'Ten minutes. If he's still there.'

'Take us. Please.'

'Mum, this is crazy,' Emily said. 'We'll just go to a hospital. There'll be one nearby.'

'And it'll be overrun. You have eyes, Emily. You saw what happened in that tunnel. And if that's happening all over London, we'll never find a hospital to take us.'

'She's right,' Kenny said.

'Go fuck off!'

'Emily, *please.*'

'Mum, I can't believe you want this prick to help us.'

Kim held on to Emily's arm, twisting the girl to face her. Emily came reluctantly, as though Kenny might try to rush them.

'And I can't believe this is happening,' she said. 'But it is. It really is. And we have got to get clever, real quick.'

Emily scowled, opened her mouth to protest, then closed it again. It was Kenny, however, who spoke.

'Can I see him?'

'What?'

'Graham. Can I see him? He might have a bit of a … prick, but he was good to me. Never hurt me, like. Please?'

'He's in the kitchen.'

Kenny watched them, nodding. 'Okay.'

'Go on, then.'

Kenny ducked his head, eyeing them warily, then turned and slunk off towards the kitchen. Emily pushed Kim away, and Kim thought she might try to push out through the doors, but instead she headed after Kenny.

'Emily?'

'It's all right, Mum. Don't worry.'

~

He was kneeling beside Graham's body, one hand on Graham's arm, shaking his head back and forth. Emily stepped around him to the block of knives, and pulled out the last two that were left. One was too chunky, but the other was a long, thin fish knife, serrated on one side. Emily turned it over in her hands, letting it linger above Kenny's back for a moment, wondering if she would actually have the nerve to do it. She sighed, stepped back, waiting for him to see her.

When he did look up, he had tears in his eyes. Emily would have felt some sympathy for him, had it not been for the way the man had come at her. Instead, she shook her head.

'You're lucky you're not down there with him.'

'Might as well be.'

'Stay behind if you want. We'll be fine.'

Kenny looked up again. 'I know he was kind of a cunt to people, but he always did right by me. Never hit me, never … touched me. He could have done anything he wanted, but he never did.'

'And that makes him a good person?'

'No, but it makes him better than most.'

'Whatever. That arsehole was going to rape me or beat the crap out of me.'

'He was just trying to scare you. That was his way.'

'Bullshit.'

'You didn't need to kill him.'

'I didn't—'

'Fuck, what the hell…?'

Kenny reached out, touching the long, bony tail protruding out from under Graham's body. He tugged it, and the rest of the bloodied creature appeared, its jaws and eyes wide in a horror show death throe.

Kenny scrambled backwards, almost knocking into Emily.

'What *the fuck* is that?'

'Yeah, don't know. Don't want to know.'

'Jesus fucking Christ. We saw the planes and heard the guns, but … what the fuck?'

'You haven't heard the rumours? Not seen the videos?'

'Don't have a phone, man.' Kenny gave a dry chuckle. 'Graham said they were bad for your focus, said they were full of lies.'

A thunderous boom came from nearby, shaking the kitchen, knocking pots and pans to the floor. A drawer popped open, disgorging dozens of knives and forks in a jarring clatter.

'I don't think it's safe here,' Emily said. 'We have to go. You can come with us, or you can fuck off. Your choice.'

Kenny stared at her. 'Your mum's probably right. Strength in numbers.'

'Lucky us. Is this Marvin guy actually real?'

'Yeah.'

'Will he help us? Mum's leg is really bad.'

'What happened?'

'We were in a tunnel that collapsed.'

'That's fucked.'

'Will this doctor mate of yours help us or not?'

'Might do. Don't know.'

Afraid of the blade's sharpness, Emily wrapped the fish knife in a tea towel and stuffed the whole thing into her belt.

'If you lie to us, or Mum ends up getting hurt, I'll fucking kill you.'

Kenny stood up and looked at her, shaking his head. He glanced down at Graham, then at the remains of the creature lying behind him.

'Rather you killed me than that thing,' he said.

Emily's face was still full of murder when she reemerged from the kitchen with Kenny trailing behind her, but he was at least still alive. It might get harder to read people as time when on, but Kim had seen in his eyes that he was no threat, especially with the other guy out of the picture. Graham had been dangerous. He might have robbed her or worse. But Kenny ... he was just a kid, barely older than Emily. Her daughter trusted no one, but Kim wasn't ready to give up on her humanity just yet.

Kenny barely looked at he as he went to the door, cupping his eyes against the glass to see out.

'Road's empty,' he said. 'You ready?'

'Is it far?'

He gave yet another shrug. 'Not so much. Depends.'

'On what?' Emily said.

'What else is out there.'

Emily helped Kim to stand. Kenny stood a few steps

apart, a look in his eyes that suggested he wanted to help but didn't dare ask. Just as Kim reached the door, though, he stepped back, shaking his head.

'Something I gotta do,' he said, then pulled a tablecloth off the nearest table, knocking salt shakers and a rack of menus to the floor. He frowned at a stain from an overturned chili sauce bottle, roughly folded the tablecloth, then pulled off another, with a similar result.

'What are you doing?' Emily demanded.

Kenny, predictably, shrugged. 'Just a minute,' he said. 'I wanna cover him. That other guy, too. Doesn't seem right leaving them like that.'

He stalked off towards the kitchen, stepping over the overturned chairs. Kim shared a look with Emily, who glared at her.

'I'm not buying his caring guy crap,' she said. 'He's playing us.'

'Says my model pupil daughter,' Kim said, wincing at the relentless ache in her leg. 'What is it about casting the first stone?'

'Yeah, all right. We'll see, won't we?' Emily said.

Kenny came slinking back without the tablecloths. Instead, he had an eco-bag slung over his shoulder with the restaurant's logo on the side. From inside, cans clinked and plastic packets rattled.

'Just in case,' he said. 'Might need something to trade with.'

'I have money,' Kim said. 'I have a … credit card.'

Kenny peered out of the window as another distant boom shook the restaurant.

'Not sure money's gonna be much use from now on,' he said. 'Ready?'

Kim looked at Emily, who nodded.

Kenny opened the door, just as a woman came running

up the street, screaming in terror. Kenny pulled the door shut, holding it closed, as outside a swarm of tiny lizards barely reaching knee-height swarmed around the woman. For a moment they encircled her legs like an army of excited puppies, then they began to pull themselves up, clambering up her clothes. The woman gave one last guttural scream as one climbed onto her face, then she fell forwards, the creatures engulfing her.

'Oh, man, that's fucked,' Kenny said, turning away.

'Emily, please … please don't watch,' Kim said, as inside, everything she had thought she knew about the world began to turn on its head. 'You shouldn't … shouldn't … see … see this.'

Emily, however, stared out through the window, one hand on a bulge at her belt, something wrapped in a tea towel.

'No, Mum,' she said, the other hand cupping her eyes. 'I think I need to see this. I need to know … what this is.'

19

RIVERSIDE

JULIET MADE sure the door through to the utility room was properly closed before she worried about the garage door. She got her bike, checked the tyres had plenty of air, then put it in front of the door, so that she was ready to go.

The electric had gone off in the last few minutes, the lights switching off, even the standby light on the television winking out. The garage door was automatic, but Dad often complained that it didn't work properly and had explained how to open it when the switch wasn't working and she wanted to get her bike out. He had a metal hook thing which she thought was for picking leaves out of drains, and when you hooked it over a wire near the ceiling and pulled, the door would open.

She wasn't quite tall enough, so she fetched a large paint can, set it beneath the wire, and balanced on top. She was just tall enough now to catch the wire with the hook thing. She leaned on it, and the door slid up a couple of feet.

Figuring it was probably best not to open it too much, she let go and climbed back down. She had to tilt her bike to get it underneath the door, and then she found herself standing outside on the driveway, not far from the front door where the little dinosaur had tried to get into the house.

It might still be in the field next door, so Juliet didn't hang about. She climbed on to her bike and pedaled out into the road, standing up to get some momentum going into the shallow hill that isolated their place from the rest of the village. Ordinarily she would have stayed tight to the overgrown verge, Dad's warnings of the crazy drivers who came speeding over the top of the hill close in her mind, but the fear of being ambushed was greater, so she stuck to the middle, trusting her ears to warn her of any oncoming cars.

It was still light, the sky clear, and as she topped the little hill and the village appeared below her, Juliet saw the sun, just above the cliffs to the west. It was approaching midsummer, so there was perhaps an hour of daylight left. She tried to not to think about how Dad wasn't home yet, how he was often home late, but never this late. If the electric and the water were off, there must be something strange going on that was keeping him at the hospital.

She free-wheeled down the other side of the hill, past the first houses, a couple of cul-de-sacs and a couple of narrow farm lanes which she had ridden past a million times but never actually been down. That seemed so funny, now that she thought about it. People were like cats, really. She'd heard that several cats could have territory crossing over each other, perhaps marking trees in the same garden. People were much the same. Her world consisted of her house, the road the led past the shop and the pub to the beach, and the turning on to the estate where her friend Scarlet Adams lived. Perhaps she could try there. Scarlet's mother was a bit strict so they generally played outside, going into the woods or down to the beach, and Scarlet wasn't allowed out on school nights. Today had been a no-school day, though, Juliet remembered. Dad had told her a special announcement had been made on the radio before breakfast. He had also told her not to go out, because she wasn't really allowed to stay home on her own. He had said she would prove she was a really grown-up girl if she just stayed at home, perhaps cleaned a little or did some schoolwork, and watched telly all day, as it was too late for him to take time off work.

And so she had. The day had gone passed pretty comfortably until Uncle Lawrence had shown up.

If Scarlet had been home as well, perhaps she would have done her schoolwork, and be allowed to come to the door. Juliet didn't dare tell Mrs. Adams about Uncle Lawrence, but perhaps if she confided in Scarlet, her friend might get her some water for him or something. She followed the arc of the road around to the left, then pulled into the little parking spot outside the village store. Across the street, cars were parked in the gravel car park outside the village hall, and through the windows came the flicker of torchlight. Normally they had badminton on a Friday night, because Dad sometimes went if he had time. It didn't look like they were playing badminton now, because she couldn't see the set-up nets through the windows. She wondered if she ought to ask them if they knew what was going on. She started to turn her handlebars towards the road, then thought better of it. If there were grownups in there but not playing badminton, they probably had serious things to talk about and wouldn't want her to interrupt.

The shop, however, was locked, even though according to the clock above the counter, which she could see through the window, it was only five to nine. The wooden racks that were usually outside for the vegetables had been pulled inside the door, and one wire rack of postcards had fallen over, its contents scattered across the floor. No way Mrs. Clark would put up with that; it must be one of the other workers who had done it.

Juliet turned her bike around, again wondering if she ought to knock on the door of the village hall. Just as she started to free-wheel her bike out into the road, however, a man came running out of the entrance, jogging down a set of concrete steps and then jumping into a car. The engine roared into life, then squealed as he reversed quickly, heedless of the gravel that sprayed up, hitting an adjacent car. As the car turned, then sped off up the road with another spray of gravel, Mr. Durdent, who owned the petrol station up on the main road, gave her a sour scowl.

That sealed it. Mr. Durdent was always nice when she went in there with Dad. Sometimes he gave her a free packet of Polos. If he wasn't in a good mood, there was no way she was going into the hall.

She turned her bike down the hill again and headed for Scarlet's place. When she stopped outside, though, the driveway was empty. The lights were off, but that was no surprise if the village had a power cut. However, the front door was wide open, as though they had left in a hurry.

Juliet climbed off her bike, but even with the family clearly not home, she still felt too nervous to go inside. Mrs. Adams was a teacher at the local secondary school, and had a sadistic streak. It would be just like her to hide inside, waiting to jump out on any unsuspecting intruder.

After a couple of nervous minutes of deliberation, Juliet decided to try the last place: the pub. It was on the beachfront, separated from the beach itself by a narrow road that crossed the river that flowed down the middle of the beach. Even though she knew she wouldn't be able to go inside, whenever she came to the beach with Dad or Scarlet there were always people sitting outside who looked friendly and approachable. Plus, there was an outside tap with a dog's water dish outside. If someone would lend her a container, she would be able to take some water back for Uncle Lawrence.

She parked her bike on the edge of the car park, next to a couple of mountain bikes chained to the picket fence that separated the car park from the riverbank. There were a handful of cars in the car park, but the lights in the pub were off. She started walking across the car park but was only halfway there when an angry voice came from the raised patio area surrounding the pub. Juliet hurried to the bottom of a set of steps leading up and crouched down beside a pair of rubbish bins.

'Look, just fuck off home, Dave. What did you expect? There's no power here either. All my coolers have gone down, and the last thing I feel like doing is sitting in the dark while punters whine about warm beer and then piss against the wall because there's no light in the toilets.'

'Come on, Bob. Just a quick pint. The real's already warm anyway, isn't it?'

'We're closed, I told you. Unforeseen circumstances.'

'Bob, please, mate. I had a shit day. I just need a pint. Grab me a bottle or something if you want and I'll just drink it out here.'

'Go home, Dave.'

There was the sharp sound of a chair being knocked over.

'Go fuck yourself, Bob. I only want one quick pint. Is that so much to ask?'

'Yeah, right now it is.'

'You're a fucking cunt. Act like a mate when it suits you—'

The man's words were cut off by a dull thud and a scrape of shoes. The two men were out of sight, but the sounds of a scuffle were obvious. A couple more thuds came, along with a grunt of pain and a longer moan. Juliet lifted her head then ducked down again as a figure appeared at the top of the stairs.

Staggering footsteps came on the stairs as the man staggered from side to side. 'You fucking wanker, Bob. I think you broke my nose.'

'You're barred, Dave,' came Bob's hoarse voice from above. 'I don't want to see you around here again.'

'Fuck off,' Dave said, reaching the bottom of the steps. A hand touched the wall just inches above Juliet's face. The knuckles were split and bleeding. He leaned on the wall for a moment, then staggered off across the car park, stopping at a Ford Mondeo parked crookedly across two spaces. He opened the door, leaned on the frame for a moment, then climbed in. There was another long pause during which Juliet didn't dare move in case he could see her in the wing mirrors, then the engine started and the car moved off.

Juliet waited a few minutes until she heard a door close above her, then she crept up the stairs. A picnic table on the patio had overturned, and there were spots of red on the paving stones.

The outside tap used for the dog bowl was across the patio, outside the main doors. Juliet ran across to it, but when she turned the tap, nothing happened.

There was no water here, either.

She looked around, panicking now. *Take a deep breath,* she told herself. That's what Dad would have said if he were here. *Take a step back, take a deep breath, and refresh. Then you can think clearly.*

She had nothing to carry the water in anyway, she realised, when she had calmed herself down. She had been planning to buy something out of the shop, and had the money from Uncle Lawrence's wallet in her pocket. But now she had to think of a new plan.

Trying not to let the panic build up again, she turned around.

Of course.

There was a river right there, next to the car park. You couldn't drink the sea water, but the river was fresh. It might not be so clean, but couldn't you boil it? Dad had a camping stove in the garage which used bottled gas. If she could figure out how to use it, she'd be sorted. She might even be able to cook some beans or instant noodles.

She smiled, proud of herself. Dad's voice came in her head: *See? Just take a deep breath, and things will figure themselves out.*

There was still the problem of the container, but again, Dad's advice was helping. She remembered how she had squatted in the space below the stairs. There had been something down there with her, stacked in the gap, large plastic boxes filled with cardboard and plastic.

Recycling containers.

She went back down the stairs and peered into the nearest box. There were two crushed plastic bottles in there. She took both and pressed them out. Then, to check for leaks, she put each to her lips and blew.

Her cheeks puffed out both times. No leaks.

She hurried across the car park and climbed over the little wooden fence onto the riverbank.

Juliet and Scarlet had come down here to look for frogspawn last spring, scooping up large handfuls of it in the shallows. Now, though, she moved a little upstream from the wide pool to where the water was moving more quickly. That was something she had learned from school, that the faster water was moving, the cleaner it would be.

What was that word? Something to do with deer, she remembered. *Stagnated.* That was it. Standing water stagnated, but flowing water was clean.

She squatted down, dropping the first of her bottles under the water's surface, waiting until it was full, then she removed it and stood it beside the water, leaning against a rock. She had forgotten to check if there were caps in the recycling container, but she could do that after. She took the second bottle and pushed it under the surface.

It was nearly full when she heard a strange, birdlike hiss from the far bank. It sounded like the warning growls that geese made if you got too close, their heads strained forward, beaks open, little tongues waggling about. Juliet looked up, half expecting to see a goose standing there, leaning over the water.

At first she thought it was a crocodile, it was that big. Probably as long as she was tall. But it didn't have a crocodile's head, more of a narrow serpentine face, a long tongue flicking out. It was low to the ground, with powerful shoulders and four huge, meaty legs ending in hooked claws. A thick tail flapped back and forth.

Frozen, Juliet at first thought it was a monitor lizard, like the ones she had seen in Newquay Zoo on a school trip last year. The only difference was that this thing had two bony sails rising out of its back, making a V-shape as it faced her, two crescents that remined her bizarrely of bats' wings with the way the breeze seemed to make them flex.

The river was roughly two metres wide, and not particularly deep. The creature could reach her in a couple of paces, but rather than rushing her, it was simply watching, its head moving back and forth the way she had seen snakes do on the telly.

I am going to die, she thought. Then, more resiliently, *if I die, Uncle Lawrence will die. I have to save him.*

The creature moved, stepping out onto a rock protruding from the water. Juliet let out a cry of fright, and did the only thing she could to defend herself. She pulled the half-filled bottle out of the water, and as she fell back against the bank, she pointed it at the creature and squeezed.

As water splashed its face, it let out a blood-curdling wail, shrank backwards, then turned and fled, climbing quickly through the long grass of the far back, scuttling up into a hedgerow that bordered a garden, and forcing itself way through the bushes. Juliet, waited until the sound of its flight had faded, then grabbed her bottles and ran back to her bike.

By the time she reached it, she was crying.

The creature, or others like the one she had seen at her house, could come back at any time.

The light was starting to fade now, the sun having dipped below the horizon far out to sea. It was only a ten-minute ride back to her house, but she was shaking so much that she didn't trust herself to ride. Instead, she propped the full bottle of water and what was left of the second in her basket, and pushed her bicycle out of the car park and onto the road.

As she started up the gentle hill into the village, she looked around at the houses, their lights all off, seemingly empty. Her heart filled with dread, and she prayed that Uncle Lawrence would still be alive when she got back to the house.

She got the horrible prickly feeling that her father wasn't coming back, and if he wasn't, then Uncle Lawrence was all the family she had left in the world.

She couldn't bear to be alone.

20

DECAY

Collie stuck out his hand. Nikki's eyes involuntarily followed the snake tattoo as it curved around his wrist and up his arm. The crook of his elbow looked red around a fresh needle mark, and she felt her stomach roll with envy.

'Money,' he said. 'How much did you get?'

Nikki reached into the pocket of the jeans that hung off her hips so badly she had tied a thick boot shoelace around them to stop them falling down. 'Three hundred and ten,' she said.

'That it?'

Nikki closed her eyes. 'The last guy stiffed me. Come on, Collie. I did my best.'

Her body was used to rough hands and aggressive, thrusting hips, but it had been a while since anyone had hit her, and her eye still smarted. She hoped it wouldn't close up, or good luck making any money tomorrow.

'Three hundred and ten,' Collie said, sighing as he shook his head. One bony fist clenched and unclenched like he was squeezing out a cloth and she hoped he didn't get punchy. He was too wiry to have much power but he was so bony his hands hurt like stones. 'Three hundred … and ten. What the fuck are you playing at? Were you sat in a café all night?'

'There weren't many johns out last night,' Nikki said, trying to focus, trying not to shut down. 'That was five guys, including the one who stiffed me. The streets were quiet, I don't know why.'

Collie stood up and started pacing around the room. He walked to the door with all the chips in it and the cracks, banged his fists against the frame, then walked across to the kitchen countertop, rapping his knuckles on that, too. Nikki stood beside the bedsit's only sofa, a threadbare thing that used to be red but was more brown grey from sun fading, too scared to sit down. Let him do his show. Maybe she'd get away with it. Maybe it would cost another black eye, but it hadn't been her fault. She'd seen way too many people piling suitcases into cars to know everything was all right. Something fucked up was happening, and it was stopping her getting the money she needed to get her fix.

'Come on, Collie. What about if I do something for you? I'm not tired yet, you know—'

Because you haven't been working!' he shouted, slamming a hand against the countertop. 'You know the rule. Five hundred a night. I give you a place to stay, I give you your shit—'

Some little act of defiance, some tiny artillery battery that sixteen years of being moved from one supposed foster home to another hadn't quite crushed out of her, raised its ugly little guns.

'Hardy much of a place,' she said. 'I can practically touch both walls. And how much am I giving you for what you're giving me, Collie? Five hundred buys a lot of dope.'

He rushed at her, fists raised. Nikki waited for the first

blow, aware there would be many this time. And then, when he was done beating her, he'd push her down and do whatever, and then some more whatever, and then if she was lucky, he'd give her a fix. She could handle everything if she could just get that fix.

The blow never came, even though Nikki found herself thrown off her feet as the bedsit shook. She put a hand against the wall to steady herself as Collie, doing a comical pirouette, punched the wall instead of her face, his fist landing with full force. He howled, clutching his hand to his naked stomach, then fell backwards over the sofa, landing with a thump, one leg twitching up and down, the other hanging over the front.

A distant rumble sounded, and again the bedsit shook. Nikki put a hand on the countertop to steady herself. It sounded like a plane had come past, maybe the sonic boom causing the shaking. It happened sometimes when they were having one of their fucking military flybys or whatever. This was going on and on, though.

'Collie? Collie, get up. I need my shit. Seriously. I'd make it up tomorrow night, I mean it. I'll wander up Clifton, see if I can hook some rich bastard. Come on, man.'

He didn't move. The foot that had been twitching had stopped.

'Collie?'

Nikki pushed away from the countertop. She was starting to get hot flushes mixed with shivers. She could probably only hold on another twenty minutes until the convulsions started, and she'd start clawing up the walls. Collie never kept the shit from her too long because he didn't want her going through withdrawal and making a mess of the flat. He just liked to fuck around with her a bit, maybe give her a smack or two. Whatever made him feel better.

'*Collie?*'

Afraid he might jump up and grab her—it wouldn't be the first time—Nikki crept closer, leaning forwards. If he came at her she might still be able to dodge out of range, but a couple more inches and her mop of crimson hair would make her easy to grab. She was sick of his games—

Then she noticed the dark patch on the wall. It looked like something had splashed there, water or something. Except it was thicker, clumpy dribbles that didn't want to fall, shiny like paint.

'Collie, man, what have you done?'

He was already pale, but now his legs looked paler. He was only wearing a pair of boxer shorts and a dirty Hawaiian shirt that he never buttoned up. As she leaned forwards, she looked up his hairless navel, past a chest cavity that was almost concave, to his chin with that ugly wisp of beard, his head, tilted sideways.

And broken glass, spread out around him.

'Fuck. What have you done?'

He wasn't moving. Nikki reached out and gave his knee a prod with a long, fake-nailed finger. When he didn't react, she plucked up the courage to lay her hand over it.

He was already starting to cool, his skin soft and flexible like uncooked chicken flesh. Nikki leaned down and pulled the sofa away from the wall. Collie's body slumped, one leg thumping hard to the floor, while the other stayed hooked over the sofa's back, toes with filthy nails and the dozens of needle marks in between each pointing to the ceiling.

He'd landed on one of his cigarette glasses, a pilfered pint glass filled almost to the rim. Or it had been, until the glass had shattered over the back of his neck. Now a plume of red was spreading out into the frayed, worn-out carpet. It looked like he'd hit his head on the skirting board as he came down, knocking him out while he bled to death.

'Ah, Collie.'

Nikki watched him for a moment longer, then reached down and pulled a packet of cigarettes out of his jeans. She opened it, pulled out the two crooked cigs forced inside and found his stash hidden at the bottom.

It wasn't much, but it would sort her for now. He would have more hidden around the bedsit, and if he was going to go and die on her she would have time later to find it. For now, though she really needed her fix.

She sat on the floor opposite him as she cooked and shot up, watching his foot, afraid he might wait just until she was feeling better and then come back to life, just to ruin her mood. He stayed dead, though, and soon Nikki no longer cared as the stuff raced through her. In her desperation she'd done a little too much, and for a few minutes she struggled to stay conscious. Once the dizziness had passed, she felt that warm, numbing sensation, that no matter what life threw at her—and it had really gone shit for balls in the sledging contest—she had a coat of armour now that would protect her.

After a while, she got up and switched off the lights and went to the sliding doors that led out onto their tiny balcony. It was barely big enough to hold a couple of shrivelled and dead pot plants, but she had put a deckchair out here to sit when Collie was either off his tits on some rage or she was feeling like jumping again. She'd never quite plucked up the courage, not even in the worst of moments, when she'd come home from a rough night on the streets only for Collie to start throwing his fists about, or like that time when she'd taken the money off one john only to show up at his flat and find he had four of his mates round, and they were all goddamn having some, whether she liked it or not, but she liked to sit anyway, staring out at what lights of Bristol she could see, dreaming perhaps of a better life. Pretty much anything would do; she wasn't all that fussy. The only good thing about selling herself was the money and Collie took all of that. A simple life, that would work, but you couldn't just go and swipe cans on a checkout after a life like hers. It didn't work that way.

Tonight, the sirens were out in full force. The kind of discordant orchestra of emergency vehicles that was usually only applicable to Saturday nights, it was really going off out there. She heard a couple of gunshots ring out too, usually something that predated the sirens.

Something bad was going down. She suddenly felt like another fix, one that would put her out of the picture. If Collie was dead and something bad was happening out across the city, there wouldn't be much room left in the world for her.

I want to live.

The thought was like a bucket of iced water. Nikki sat up, craning herself forwards, feeling almost sober as she watched the flashing lights of the sirens.

Something had changed, but in her daze, she had failed to notice it at first. Then, with a sudden jolt of shock, she realised.

She was watching the lights of the sirens, because that was all that there was to watch.

The city had gone dark.

She glanced over her shoulder, her worst fears materialising.

The bedsit had gone dark too.

Alfred
Lammonby

21

READINESS

Lilian was stacking tins in the pantry when a knock came on the door. She immediately tensed, her fingers trembling, gripping the tin of soup too tight. Then, overcoming her initial panic, she let herself relax.

'Excuse me, Ms. Weekes?'

She stood up and turned around. Dave Brussells, the groundskeeper, stood in the doorway, one hand holding his Wellington boots, pinched between his thumb and forefinger, his thick trekking socks ruffled at the ends as though they had slipped down while he walked. He still wore his overcoat and cap, as though he didn't have enough hands to deal with everything.

Lilian liked Dave. She guessed he was about fifty, but the greying beard that covered pretty much everything bar steel blue eyes disguised him somewhat. He lived in a tiny cottage in the trees beside the main gates, and almost never came into the main house. Unlike the rest of the staff, Richard seemed to like him, because Dave had a couple of shotguns and had shown Richard how to shoot rabbits. Most of the time, Dave patrolled the grounds, filling in holes in the hedges, doing a little of the gardening the mostly-absent gardener was supposed to do.

Lilian smiled. 'Dave, you can call me Lilian. I've told you about fifteen times.'

Dave nodded over his shoulder. 'Yeah, but his lordship's out of bed, judging by the banging around through there. Thought it best to keep things formal.'

'Did you find that man?'

'The ruffian?' Dave chuckled. 'I tracked him across the garden, then out through the fence. He wasn't exactly disguising himself.'

'And he's gone?'

Dave glanced back over his shoulder, then took a step further into the pantry. 'Do you mind if I close the door a moment? I'm sorry to impose on your space in the state I'm in, but I'd rather we weren't overheard. Mr. and Mrs. Lammonby … you know, I worry.'

Lilian nodded. 'Please.'

Dave came inside and closed the door. With both of them in the small room, the space felt overly cramped, the forest scent of Dave's clothes pervading everything.

'I took the bike out, went looking for him,' Dave said. 'Found him up on the main road, heading for Exeter. Lad was about at the end of his strength, so I set him down, gave him some sandwiches.'

The simple humanity in Dave's words brought tears to Lilian's eyes. She looked away, wiping them quickly with a tissue.

'That was kind of you,' she said.

Dave shrugged. 'The right thing to do, was all. Plus, I had my reasons. I asked him a little about what had got him in such a state.'

'And?'

'Once he'd calmed down, had a bite to eat, he started

making a little more sense.' Dave shrugged. 'Well, as much as could be made of such things.'

'So there really is trouble in Marshdown?'

Dave nodded. 'From what I can gather, there was some kind of coordinated uprising.' He shook his head, giving a little shiver. 'And all these years I've thought England was at peace. Seems not. Seems there was something underground, just waiting to bubble over. And now it has.'

'Dave, you're not making much sense.'

'That's because I'm struggling to make sense of things myself. It all happened through those horrid little lumps of plastic we carry in our pockets. From what this lad told me, there was a message came through, and one lot rose up to take control. In reaction, another lot rose up to oppose it. And then there were the authorities, who had to try to talk both down. And that didn't happen.'

Lilian put a hand over her mouth. 'So some kind of civil war has broken out?'

Dave frowned. 'I'm very sorry to say that it looks that way.' He paused rubbing his lips with a finger, staring off into space. 'Something else, too. Something that makes even less sense than the rest.'

'What?'

'He said something else … about some kind of animals roaming about.'

'Animals? Like stray dogs or something.'

Dave looked even more pained than before. 'A little bigger than that,' he said. 'I'm sorry but I'm not repeating word for word what he said because it sounded like the talk of a madman. We need to be careful, that's all. I wished him well, gave him what money I had, and off he went towards Exeter, hoping to find somewhere safe.'

'We should have taken him in.'

Dave tilted his head in a gesture that could have meant

anything. He was silent for a few seconds, then he looked up.

'Ms. Weekes? I mean, Lilian? There's something I'd like to ask of you.'

'What is it?'

Dave looked down. He reached up and took off his hat, and for one absurd moment Lilian thought Dave might propose. Then he put his hat back on and looked up, his eyes hard.

'I have a couple of guns over at the cottage,' he said. 'They're all currently locked up nice and safe. But I think we might be needing them before too long. If you don't mind, I'd like you to come over and let me show you how to use them.'

~

Dave's words lingered long after the man himself had gone. Lilian tried to concentrate on her work, but it was impossible. That Richard seemed to have predicted things in ordering the bunker to be fully stocked only made her more uncomfortable. Grandfather had often talked about how Lord Evans had been into his conspiracies, convinced the sky was set to fall and crush everything his family had built over generations, but now that didn't feel so far off. More than anything she felt an all-encompassing sense of dread. It was as bad, even worse, maybe, than those nights she had lain in bed long after midnight, waiting for Harry to come home, not knowing whether he would climb into the bed and simply fall asleep, or whether he would drag her out from beneath the covers and proceed to relieve himself of whatever stresses the day had caused.

It was that feeling that eventually the bad thing would happen. Not if, but when. With Harry, if she got away with it one night, it only increased the chances that it would happen the next, or the one after that. Because you could bet your whole forsaken life that it was coming, sooner or later. And it always, always did.

That evening, after clearing the dinner things away, she snuck out of the house and went up the driveway to Dave's cottage.

Alfred strained as he lifted the last of the grain sacks into the storeroom. He had done nine this load, and his back was screaming. He needed just a few minutes to rest, but just as he sat down on the arm of a sofa to catch a couple of minutes, he heard footfalls on the ladder.

Fearful it was Lord Richard, he stood up. To his surprise and relief, it was Lilian.

'Grandfather? Are you all right? I'm sorry, I didn't know you were out here.'

Alfred smiled. 'It's not a problem, my dear. Everything is under control.'

'You're pushing yourself too hard. From tomorrow, I'll do all the stocking up.'

Alfred shook his head. 'This is my work,' he said. 'The master's orders.'

Lilian looked for a moment as though she might say something disrespectful, but then she just nodded.

'At least let me help you take them down the ladder.'

Alfred opened his mouth to protest, but he knew she was right. The strength he had once had was a fading memory, and he wasn't far short of straining or pulling something, and then he'd be useless. Lord Richard was tiring of him, that much was obvious. If he had no value to the young lord he feared being dismissed. What would he do then?

'If you could just help with that, I can manage the organisation,' he said. 'I hate to ask such a thing of you, dear, but these sacks are so very heavy.'

'I could call Mr. Brussells,' Lilian said. 'I'm sure he would be happy to help.'

Alfred shook his head. 'Then who would be looking after the grounds?'

Lilian said nothing. Alfred could tell she found his sense of duty a little frustrating, but she didn't understand. He had spent his life in the service of the lords of Carlton Manor. His position and his honour defined him. If he gave that up, he was … nothing.

'Right,' he said, rubbing his hands together. 'Let's get to it. This is the last load of grain. After that it's mostly perishables. I'll be able to manage those myself.'

They headed back to the upstairs bunker where Alfred had left the last sack of grain. Lilian went first, supporting the bag on her shoulder, Alfred coming second, helping where he could. When it was stacked into the storeroom with the others, he turned around and found Lilian standing facing him, arms folded.

'Do you think this is all necessary?' she said. 'I mean, stocking the bunker. Then there was that man that broke into the gardens. I spoke with Dave—Mr. Brussells. He told me that what that man said about Marshdown … it's true.'

Alfred flapped a hand and started to turn away, looking for some little job he could get on with. 'I don't think there's anything too serious to worry about,' he said, at last spotting a box of crockery that needed putting away. 'Everything will blow over if we keep calm and carry on as normal.'

'I don't think it will.'

Alfred paused, one hand on the flap of the box. He turned, looking around at her, and for a moment she looked so much like her mother, his dear, dear Harriet, that it brought a tear to his eye.

'Grandfather, what's wrong?'

He stumbled to a chair and sat down, rubbing his head. 'Nothing, dear. I'm sorry, I just had a funny turn.'

'Perhaps you should rest for a while. I've told you, you're overdoing it.'

'Just give me a minute.'

'I'll get you a drink.'

'No, I'm fine.'

Lilian ignored him, going to the little kitchen unit in the corner and pouring a glass of water. She carried it back over and handed it to him.

'Well, at least it proves that the water works,' she said. 'Lord Richard should be quite cozy in here when the time comes.'

'If it comes, dear,' Alfred said, grateful for the cool taste of the water. 'There's no need for us to worry just yet. We live in a civilised country, after all.'

Lilian was no longer listening. He looked up as she walked up to the TV and took the remote control off the shelf underneath. She took a couple of steps back and held it up.

'What are you doing?' Alfred said. 'I've told you, there's nothing to worry about—'

'We'll see,' Lilian said.

As the TV came to life, however, there was nothing but a blank screen with NO SIGNAL written across the middle.

'It's just the connection, I imagine,' Alfred said.

'Mr. Brussells told me his television is down too,' Lilian

said. 'It has been the last couple of days. I think things are a lot more serious than you realise, Grandfather.'

'Lilian—'

She switched off the TV and turned to him. 'I know you're trying to protect me, Grandfather, but you *are* protecting me by having me here. What's going on in Marshdown and elsewhere is not your fault, or mine, but whatever it is, it's coming, and we need to be ready when it does.'

'The bunker's preparation is nearly complete—'

'For Lord Richard. But what about us?'

'Lord Richard's safety is our priority—'

'Lord Richard is an abusive prick!' Lilian shouted, throwing the TV remote down. It struck the edge of the sofa, and bounced against the floor, the back compartment popping open and the batteries spilling out.

'Lilian!' Alfred said. 'Such outbursts … you have to … you should….'

He couldn't bring himself to finish. He had never been the best with words, not when faced by a robust woman. Harriet had been fiery at times, too. Often the best way to diffuse an aggressive outburst was to say nothing, let it dissipate on its own. Giving her one last regretful look, he squatted down on the floor and began gathering up the batteries.

'Grandfather, I'm sorry,' Lilian said, and he felt her hand on his shoulder. 'Please forgive me.'

One of the batteries had rolled under the sofa. Alfred stretched his hand underneath, dragging it back with his fingers. Clutching it in his fist, he stood up.

Lilian had tears in her eyes. Without a word, she pulled him into a hug.

'It'll be all right,' he said, offering as much conviction as he could muster. 'Lord Richard needs us, after all.'

Lilian pulled away. 'I'd better get back to the house,' she said. 'Will you be all right down here?'

'I just have a few things to finish off,' Alfred said. 'Tell your grandmother I'll be up there in half an hour.'

Lilian nodded and went out.

Alfred sat back down on the sofa. With tired, shaking fingers, he pushed the batteries back into the remote's rear cavity. Luckily the fastening piece hadn't broken, so he clipped it back together and held it up to test it.

The TV came back on, the NO SIGNAL message appearing in confirmation. Alfred watched it for a long time.

Everything would be all right. He was sure of it.

22

SAFEHOUSE

THE PUB WAS a large two-storey white-walled building with a chimney stack at either end. At the front was a low stone wall along the road with a colourful flowerbed along the top. The entrance from the road led into an empty carpark to the front and side. To the rear, enjoying panoramic views of the Shropshire Hills, was a beer garden and a children's playground, separated from the wild moorland by a waist-high wooden slat fence. The grass had been cut in the last few days; mounds of drying cuttings lay waiting to be raked.

Ordinarily, after a long day of dealing with teenagers and their various issues, Claire might have gone running for the pub with open arms. In the light of what had happened over the last couple of hours, even the most banal of situations became threatening, potentially deadly. With the children crowding behind her, she went first across the car park, past the parked cars, to the pub entrance.

She expected to find the doors locked, and had already

been running through her mind what she might say to gain entry, what might be considered the least absurd.

Our bus driver got shot by bandits disguised as soldiers just outside of Clent. Several of our group got eaten by flying dinosaurs up on the hill there, just after we'd finished our picnic. It appears that Birmingham is being bombed, so please let us in. Mine will be a pint.

Tears filled her eyes as she lifted a hand to knock, but the door wasn't even closed. She nudged it inwards with her foot, exposing a musty hallway with the dark red and black patterned carpet that all older pubs seemed to have, perhaps as a stain defense against spillage. A few framed prints of game birds hung on the walls. One near the door hung off-straight, as though someone had knocked it in their hurry to leave. She felt stupid as she reached up to adjust it before stepping inside, but it seemed right, the normal thing to do.

'Hello?'

Her voice sounded hoarse. The pub gave no answer. She waved to the kids to stay by the door.

'Is anyone there? Can you help us, please? We had some … some … some trouble.'

The corridor ended in a wooden door with an ornate sign fixed to it indicating Main Bar. It was closed, but had no handle, just a big lock. She pushed it and it swung gently inwards, brushing on the carpet. Immediately the welcoming smells of food and booze struck her, and she tried to imagine she was walking into the place on a harmless Sunday afternoon. The sight of a long, curving bar, scored and stained from decades of use, lines of optics, shelves of wines, brandies, whiskies, beer pumps with colourful names like Shropshire Fairy, Undertow, Badger's Tail. Photos over the bar of darts and pool teams, a faded panorama photo of the view with the names of each hill written on peeling labels. Stools standing at the bar, tilted for customers to slide into position, ready to order.

I'll have a carvery, please. I'll be outside, enjoying the view.

The bar was empty. From a handful of uncollected glasses on a table by the window, it hadn't been until recently, but whoever had been here was either hiding or gone. Moving silently, Claire walked through the bar, looking for signs that anyone was still here. There was a bag slung over the back of a chair, a switched off smartphone lying on the floor under a table near a door marked Toilets. But no people.

'Excuse me? Is anyone here?'

There was a bell on the bar, a cardboard sign taped to a wooden figurine of an elephant beside it.

RING FOR ASSISTANCE IF NO ONE'S HERE.

She lifted the bell and gave it a shake. The noise was jarring, like a morning alarm set two hours early. She muted it with her finger, and waited.

The door she had entered by cracked open. Claire let out a gasp at the faces there, but it was only Danny and Ishy, eyes wide, mouths agape.

She let out a breath she didn't realise she had held.

'Come on,' she said. 'I don't think anyone's here.'

They came filing in, one at a time. No one looked willing to make a decision, until Tim Parkson waved Jenny Coates to a bench seat. After that, they all began to sit, taking benches or chairs near each other, as though afraid to be apart. She stared at them, the bedraggled remains of her class, a group of terrified kids, many of whom couldn't stand each other under normal circumstances, now huddled together for comfort.

'Can you stay here?' she asked them. 'I need to check upstairs, to see if anyone's here. Just stay here. If anyone comes, tell them where I am.'

A couple of them muttered affirmative grunts, but most just nodded or continued to stare at her. She watched them a moment longer, then went through a gap near the door to get behind the bar, knocking on a door behind the pumps before letting herself through. As she found herself in a charmless, featureless service corridor with a kitchen on one side and a set of stairs on the other, she wondered what she was doing. There was so much she needed to do: check if anyone was hurt, get them a drink, try to contact their parents. Right now, she just couldn't function on more than one task at a time. The images of those horrific monsters swooping down on her pupils just wouldn't take a step back. Everything she tried to do, every thought she tried to have, it was there, bearing down on her like a great, dark shadow.

The kitchen was empty.

'Hello?' she called up the stairs, then started up, not waiting for an answer, each step creaking beneath her feet.

It appeared the pub doubled as a hotel. Upstairs were three guest bedrooms, made up, untouched, and a small flat which showed more signs of occupation. A bed had been made but poorly, the pillow askew, the duvet not tucked in. A pair of slippers stood by the door, one leaning over the other. The small kitchen, barely wide enough for two people to cross, had an empty coffee cup in the sink, half full of browned water. Beside the sink was a filter, cold, the dregs still in the bottom of the jug. Claire couldn't resist the urge to pick it up, pouring the cold, bitter leftover coffee straight down her throat.

A tiny living room with two armchairs facing inwards at a TV had a window that looked out over the surrounding hills. Suddenly desperate for some air, she opened it, leaning out a little until she could see the corner of the bus parked in the car park to the side. She remembered Pauly's body, still jammed into the space between the driver's seat and the window, and a shudder of horror passed through her. She wanted to lie down and curl up into a ball, calcify, wait for the world to corrode her back into dust. She couldn't do this, she couldn't. But she had to. Those kids downstairs needed her.

There was a small framed photograph in a wire frame on a shelf beside the TV. A man with a strong jaw and a crewcut, a military or sportsman's face, a woman beside him with permed, blonde hair—a military or sportsman's wife—and a young boy, eight or nine, between them, one parent's hand on each shoulder. All three beamed at the camera, happy as shit, not a care in the world.

Claire reached out a shaking hand to pick it up, then stopped, realising someone else had before her: a brownish red patch halfway up that she'd considered dirt or dust was a dried bloody fingerprint.

She dropped her hand. Numb, she turned and headed back downstairs.

The kids were where she had left them, clustered together like penned lambs waiting for slaughter, the gate not fully closed, not even bolted, but all of them resigned to their fate, preparing to die.

Claire wiped tears out of her eyes.

'Miss?' Danny, one arm around Daisy's shoulders with Ishy's arm hooked around his other, started to rise, realised he was entangled, and sat back down. 'Do you think we could call home?'

Claire stared at him. 'Home?' Her voice sounded alien, as though something monstrous had possessed her body, leaving her just a spirit floating nearby, unable to do anything but watch the shit go down.

'Our parents, Miss. And maybe we should call the school? Tell them what happened?'

He was right. Everything he said was so heartbreakingly sensible that Claire felt another artillery barrage begin landing on her senses.

I can't hold out. I can't handle this. I'm a teacher, not a fucking survivor. I only know how to do a fucking fire drill, not save people from the fucking end of the world.

'Miss? Are you all right?'

Tim Parkson had spoken. Claire turned to him, shaking her head a little.

'Miss, can you wake the fuck up? We're in the shit here and we need to fucking get a grip.'

Connie Hart, class bitch. Wealthy, stuck-up parents, too tight to send her off to some big name boarding school but willing to let her do whatever the hell she liked, and she did. Drove Daddy's car to school without a license. Got caught shoplifting, paid her way out of it. Studied whenever the hell she felt like it, and got infamously good coursework grades from any male teacher too young to be her father. Spotted weak kids like a hawk hunting mice, and bullied them mercilessly. Slept around. Lied about who she'd slept with first and watched with amusement as her exes beat the crap out of each other behind the bike sheds after school.

Claire would gladly have dumped Connie in the trash if she could have found a bin large enough, but here, in this place, in time, her words were what Claire needed to hear.

She looked at Connie. 'You're right. We're all still alive. There's that. Is anyone hurt? I mean, really, more than just a few cuts and bruises?'

Lisa lifted a hand. 'I twisted my ankle getting off the bus—'

'Shut up, lesbian,' Connie snapped. 'She said real injures.'

Claire rounded on Connie, enjoying the sudden freedom of power without the politicised walls of the school to control her.

'Shut your mouth, Connie,' she snapped. 'Any injury that slows us down is serious enough. Danny, there's a kitchen through there. See if you can find any ice. Be careful, though. I checked, but I don't know this place. There could still be someone hiding somewhere.'

'I'll go with him, Miss,' Ishy said.

Claire nodded. 'Okay.' Turning to the others, she said, 'Anyone else?'

~

They were lucky. No one had any serious injuries beyond a few bumps, and even though Claire would never say it out loud to Connie, Lisa's sprained ankle was little more than a bruise. The pub's power was still running, and there was an ice machine in the kitchen. Aware they'd had nothing to eat or drink since their escape from the Clent Hills, she found a couple of jugs and filled them with some iced water. After she'd set the first jug down on the table, however, Mick Williams got up and wandered behind the bar, leaning down out of sight. When he reappeared, he was holding a bottle of Coke in his hand.

'I'd rather have one of these, Miss,' he said.

'Mick, that's stealing. Put it back.'

'No one's here.'

'I don't care. Put it back.'

Mick stared at her for a moment, the light fading from his face the way it sometimes did in class when he was asked a difficult question.

'Or what, Miss?'

The question caught her off guard. 'Ah … or you'll … I'll….'

'Will you put me in detention, Miss?'

'Mick, just—'

'Put it back, you fucking wanker!' Tim Parkson shouted.

'Make me.'

'All right.'

Tim, chastened by his bus ride dust up with Danny, looked ready to unleash war. Claire walked in front of him as he headed for the bar.

'Sit back down!'

Tim pushed against her, but Claire shoved him back far harder than she had meant to, sending him staggering into the table where the others sat, almost knocking over the fresh jug of water.

'All right, Miss. Take it easy,' Tim said. 'Williams, you're a fucking wanker.'

'Put it back,' Claire said again, and this time, to her relief, Mick Williams did. 'We have to maintain our respect,' she told him, as he threw her an angry glance and grabbed an empty glass from a shelf behind the bar. 'This isn't an easy situation for any of us—'

'I want to go home,' Lisa said.

'Fucking bird should have eaten you instead of Sy,' Connie said.

'It wasn't a bird,' Danny said. 'It was a pterodactyl.'

'Whatever it was—' Claire began, but Danny was shaking his head.

'It was a pterodactyl. Please hold all the bull about how they aren't supposed to exist. It just fucking ate a bunch of us, and it would have eaten the rest if we hadn't got back to the bus on time.' He started shaking his head back and forth, more and more violently. 'It just ate—'

Danny leaned over and threw up behind his chair. Daisy jumped out of the way, but Ishy patted him on the back as his body heaved. He retched a few more times, then sat up, chin smeared with vomit and with tears in his eyes. Claire was grateful for Ishy comforting him, even though the girl looked no less broken.

The shock's starting to hit them. Just as I'm getting over it, they're starting to get screwed up.

'All right,' she said, sitting up. 'Let's get our shit together. Simon, Andy, Emma, Marco and the rest aren't coming back. And if by some miracle they're still alive, there's nothing we can do. You all saw what happened up on that hill. You saw what was happening over Birmingham. All we can do now is make sure we stay alive. The police—' Even as she said it, she knew it was a lie, '—will find us soon. We can't do anything stupid.'

They continued to protest, but with less conviction than before. They were all scared, traumatised, some hurt, but they understood.

It didn't feel right to openly steal anything from the pub, but Claire reasoned that had she been the owner of the place, she would have offered what hospitality she could for a group of stricken schoolchildren. She took what money she had and put it behind the bar as a token for some drinks she relented and let them have, as well as a couple of boxes of crisps that they shared out, but part of her had a niggling feeling that they might be stuck here for a while, and it could be important to ration whatever food was left.

She put them in pairs and assigned each pair a task. Tim and Jenny she put by the entrance, with instructions to warn her if any cars appeared. Lisa and Mick were to look for bedding and make up enough additional beds for all of them on the floors of the rooms upstairs. Daisy and

Ishy—the two she trusted most to keep their fingers out of the supply—were asked to clean up the vomit then go to the kitchens and take an inventory of all the food. And Danny and Connie—one because she knew he was strong and the other because she wanted to keep an eye on her—she took with her back out to the bus.

She didn't know what to do with Pauly's body, but leaving him lying dead against the bus window to attract flies as he slowly began to decompose was the last thing she wanted. They might need the bus, and she wanted to store his body somewhere more appropriate.

Danny and Connie—one obediently, one reluctantly—fetched some bedsheets from upstairs while Claire went around the side of the pub to a shed filled with gardening and maintenance equipment. She found some black piping tape and some plastic sheeting used for vegetable gardens. It wasn't thick, but wrapped enough times, it would do.

Then, with the kids lagging behind, she went back to the bus.

It felt strange to be wearing a pair of plastic gloves to move a man who a couple of hours before had been alive, but Pauly was already showing the onset of rigor mortis. His face had paled where the blood had drained out, and his body felt heavier in some places more than others where his body fluid had begun to settle.

She couldn't ask the kids to help get him off the bus, so she instructed them to arrange the plastic sheet on the ground with the bedsheets on top while she wrestled with Pauly's body. He hadn't been a big man, but as a dead weight it took all of her strength to maneuvre him out from behind the wheel, down the stairwell and out onto the sheet. Neither of the kids looked keen to help, Connie turning her back, Danny standing off a few paces, a look on his face like he might be sick again.

Once she had Pauly on the sheet, however, they moved in, covering Pauly's body with the bedsheet and then wrapping the plastic sheet around him. Claire taped the sheet shut, then began to drag the body across the car park to the shed. Halfway across, Danny came running to help her, and while Connie refused to help, she at least lingered a little closer, as though to offer moral support.

Along with Danny, Claire laid the plastic-wrapped body of Pauly down on the floor of the shed, then whispered a short apology, before following Danny back outside. Connie was standing a short distance away, her phone held to her ear. As Claire and Danny appeared, she dropped her arm and scowled.

'For fuck's sake, what's wrong with this place?'

None of them had been able to get a signal since the nightmare on the Clent Hills had begun, and the phone inside the pub had been dead. The sense of isolation was suffocating, and Claire only tempered her growing urge to take the bus and go looking for help by insisting to herself that they were still on a school trip, and the children were still in her charge.

'Let's get back inside,' she said, starting across the car park towards the front door, just as Tim came running out.

'Miss!' he shouted. 'Someone's coming!'

Having stored Pauly's body with relative efficiency, Claire had begun to feel like she was recovering a modicum of control. Now, as a powerful car swerved into the car park and skidded to a halt outside the pub, its front seats filled by two big, shaven-headed men, she felt that control slip like spilt milk through her fingers.

'Get inside!' she shouted, as the car doors opened and the men climbed out, making quickly for the pub entrance. One carried a cricket bat, held up over his shoulder like a club, the other something much worse: a gun.

23

PARTING

THERE WAS nothing much left of the woman but a few scattered bones and sinew. The creatures had literally torn her apart, dragging parts of her body far from the rest as they fought each other for the scraps.

'I'm fucking staying in here,' Kenny said.

'You're taking us to your doctor friend,' Emily said, glaring at him.

'We won't get halfway. Why don't I just draw you a map?'

'No.' Emily grabbed the back of a nearby chair and started to lift it. 'You're going to take us.'

Kenny lifted his hands. 'All right, all right.' He glanced at Kim. 'Your daughter's a fucking psychopath. Look, it's a couple of streets from here. Maybe if we use a car—'

'How can we get a car?' Emily snapped.

'Hotwire it.'

'You know how to do that?'

'Yeah, easy.' He shrugged. 'On older cars, like. Newer cars are a bit more difficult.'

The restaurant shuddered as an explosion boomed

nearby, a cacophony of shifting metal coming from the kitchen, a plume of dust and debris speckling the tables and chairs. Emily looked from Kim to Kenny. No one spoke. Emily felt a terrible sense of horror building up inside her. She wanted to scream and cry, to hug her mother, hear that everything would be all right. But it wouldn't. Not ever again.

Her voice was shaking as she said, 'Mum, we have to go.'

'I know.' Kim looked at Kenny. 'Please.'

'Fuck, we're dead either way. Come on. But you have to keep up. If those things come back, I'm gone.'

Emily helped Kim up to her feet, her mother wincing with every movement. Kenny peered out through the window, then went to the door and pulled it wide.

'It looks clear,' he said. 'Come on.'

Kenny went first, Emily supporting Kim with her makeshift crutch. The air was filled with the stench of smoke as a grey cloud rose into the air from behind the buildings along their street. High overhead, a plane roared across the sky. A black dot appeared below it, followed by a flash of light. Then it was gone, streaking down towards the north of the city. Emily counted one-two-three, then heard a muffled boom.

'They're bombing us,' she said. 'Our own army.'

'I don't think it's us they're fucking aiming at,' Kenny said. 'Might be a good idea to shut up, in case there's any more of those lizard things.'

Emily wanted to snap back at him, but he was right. She helped Kim along the debris-strewn pavement, following Kenny, who had made his way to the corner and was peering around.

'Man, shit went down quick,' he said.

'I thought we were supposed to be quiet?'

'Yeah, yeah.'

'Which way, Kenny?' Kim asked.

'Not far.'

Kenny moved on up the street, the women following behind. Emily baulked at the sight of a pile of bones on the pavement, suitcases lying nearby, contents disgorged. She saw a rat trying to drag off a bone, the bloody lump wrapped in a piece of shredded cloth which had caught on a protruding drain cover.

'This way,' Kenny said, turning into a small road with a sign marked PRIVATE, which passed through a short tunnel before reemerging in a Mews, one of the secretive London streets that hid behind the other streets. Emily had always dreamed of living in one of these converted coach houses, in a private little world that was London but not. Even though Kim had often dampened her dream somewhat by telling her she would need a couple of million quid just to start, Emily had still dreamed of one day being an artist or an entrepreneur, living in quiet solitude a stone's throw from one of the country's most famous districts.

'He's a bit posh is he, this Marvin?' Kim said as they hurried up the cobblestone street, past palm trees in pots and painted wagon wheels outside trellised windows.

'Short cut,' Kenny said.

'I doubt those creatures understand the concept of private,' Emily said.

'No, but people do,' Kenny said. 'And I've seen plenty already that says we got to worry about them as much as about those lizard things.'

He looked pointedly at Emily as he spoke. Inside, she bristled with anger, but before she could speak, Kim stumbled, crying out and clutching at her leg.

'Be quiet,' Kenny said.

'How far?'

'Not far.'

A humming sound came from up ahead, and a garage door began to rise. Kenny stopped, putting up a hand as a sleek white car began to back out.

'Could do with one of those,' Kenny said. 'Girl, you got that knife?'

'What are you talking about?'

'Things became a free-for-all the moment the bombs came down,' Kenny said. 'That's what Graham reckoned. You can call it what you want, but I'm calling it how I see it.'

'You're a thug,' Emily snapped.

'Says the girl who smashed me with a chair. Come on, let's go get some wheels.'

He started forwards but Emily reached out and grabbed his arm, pulling him back.

'Get the fuck off me,' he said, shrugging her off.

The car had backed out. Frightened children sat in the back, squeezed in among suitcases. A man was driving, a woman in the passenger seat staring wide-eyed at them as the car slowed, backing up close to a bollard.

'Now's our chance,' Kenny said.

'No!'

Kenny turned. 'What the fuck is wrong with you, woman?'

With a squeal of brakes, the car made a sharp turn and sped up the street, bumping over the cobbles.

'There were kids in that car.'

'It could have been *us* in that car, not them.'

'Let them go. We were out on those roads. That car won't help them much.'

'We won't know now, will we?' Kenny put his foot up on a large ceramic potted plant and shoved. The pot toppled, cracking open, spilling soil and uprooted bushes across the cobbles. 'Fuck this, man.'

He stalked off, Emily and Kim following after as best they could. He reached a turn in the road up ahead and disappeared around the corner, not looking back.

'I told you,' Emily said. 'He's left us behind. We shouldn't have trusted him.'

When they reached the corner, though Kenny was waiting for them, leaning against the wall, a pout on his face.

'Took your time,' he muttered.

He led them down the Mews, through a scene of chaos. Doors had been left open, some cars even abandoned, suitcases lying in the street. And there were bodies too. Some had been partially eaten while others were still intact, the day's warmth making them start to smell, as though they had already been dead a while.

'Fancy living in one of these,' Kenny said, nodding at the terraced Mews as they passed. 'Plenty going spare now. Take your pick.'

'Before it gets looted to shit?' Emily said. 'This'll keep you busy, won't it?'

Kenny just shrugged. 'Might not be here tomorrow.'

'You or these buildings?'

'Both.'

They emerged onto a four-lane road with a wide, leafy park on the other side, surrounded by tall railings. Someone had barricaded the nearest gate with a heap of broken chairs and tables, and inside it was eerily empty of people. The road, as Kim had said, was clogged with abandoned cars. Further up the street, mounted onto the pavement, was the Mercedes they had just seen. The driver had tried to get around the abandoned cars and got trapped on the pavement by a chunk of masonry that had fallen on the front of the car. With tears in their eyes, the children were pulling their cases out of the open rear doors, harried by their hysterical mother. The father, if he lived, was trapped inside the car.

'That's what you get for being rich toffs,' Kenny said, starting across the road towards the park. 'Pricks.'

'What did they do to you?' Emily shouted.

'Nothing *to* me, nothing *for* me,' Kenny said, not looking back. 'You coming or what?'

Emily paused, watching the mother trying to hurry the children up the street as they called for their trapped father. She wanted so much to go and help them, but there was nothing she could do, nothing anyone could do.

Kenny was pulling chairs away from the park entrance.

'Another shortcut?' Kim said.

'Yeah.'

'It's too open.'

'Your choice. Marvin is ten minutes that way across the park, or thirty minutes going around by road.'

'What if those things are in there?'

'They're not gonna be in there, are they? No people. Meat eaters, aren't they?'

'So why the barricade?'

'I don't know. Just help me get a way through, will you?'

Emily left Kim leaning against the wall and joined Kenny in clearing a way. Each time she pulled away a chair or a table or an old bag, she was tempted to smash him around the head with it, leave him for dead.

I have to do this for Mum.

'Right, we can get through there,' Kenny said. 'Come on.'

He went in without waiting for them. Emily helped

Kim up, but her mother, face streaked with sweat, shook her head.

'Leave me here,' she said. 'I can't keep on. It hurts too much.'

'Mum, you need a doctor!'

'I need to rest.'

Two fighter jets streaked across the sky, and moments later a series of pops rose from somewhere to the north.

'Mum, I can't leave you here!'

Kim just shook her head. 'It hurts too much. I can't … can't keep moving.'

'I'll get the doctor and bring him back for you!'

'Just … be safe.'

Emily shook her head. Kim was starting to lose consciousness, but Emily slapped her mother's cheek until her eyes opened. Kim stared at her, eyes starting to roll.

'Mum, move!'

Emily pulled Kim's arm around her shoulder and dragged her through the gap in the gate. She stared across the field. It was so wide, so open, but at the moment it was also empty. If they were quick—

Kim's makeshift crutch clattered to the ground, her arm slumping to her side. Desperately, Emily looked around for anywhere Kim could shelter, but there nothing except a toilet block far across the park.

Too far.

'Wait.'

She lowered Kim down onto the ground and went back out to the street. Cars were packed in, unable to move. Stealing one was pointless; there was nowhere to go.

But if she could find one that was unlocked, it might keep her mother safe. She ran down along the nearest line of cars, cursing the absent drivers for leaving car after car locked, as though they would one day be able to come back. A short distance ahead, she saw a group moving away from theirs, and she shouted at them to wait, but after a single glance back, they moved on, quickening their pace.

She went out into the middle of the road, but found the cars also locked. She was getting too far away now, and wouldn't be able to drag Kim that far. In frustration she went back to the kerb, walking along the pavement until she spotted what she wanted.

A lump of concrete, long ago split, the cracks filed with dirt. When she kicked it, a chunk the size of a rugby ball came loose.

It was almost too heavy to lift, but when she slammed it against the front window of the car nearest to where Kim sat slumped over, it held a satisfying weight, and the window became a spiderweb of cracks. A couple more hits and a hole appeared in the safety glass big enough for her to slip a hand inside and lift the locking mechanism.

It took her a few minutes to lever her mother onto the back seat, too long. Kenny would be long gone, but if she could find a hospital or a doctor's somewhere nearby—

'Stay here,' she said. 'I'll be back as quick as I can. Keep your head down and don't open the door.'

Kim gave a tired nod. As Emily made to close the door, Kim reached up a weak hand.

'My love … I'm sorry if there were times I wasn't … there. Times I … didn't do a good job … I'm sorry—'

'Mum, this isn't the time for this!'

'Emily … my love, I just want you to know how proud I am. I love you … so much.'

'Mum, shut the fuck up.'

'Emily, please don't—'

'I'll be as quick as I can.'

'Emily—'

With tears in her eyes, Emily slammed the door shut and backed away from the car, her footing unsteady. Through the tinted window she saw Kim's hand lift to wave.

I have to stay strong for you. I have to stay strong for both of us.

Turning away was like ripping the bandage off a fresh wound, but Emily had no choice. She hurried to the park entrance and squeezed through the gap, resisting the urge to look back. Kenny had said this Marvin person lived on the other side of the park … it was futile, she would never find him. She was lost, and her mother would die a humiliating, painful death.

She gritted her teeth, struggling to stay on her feet. 'I can't—'

A figure stepped out of the trees a couple of hundred yards away. A hand lifted to wave.

Kenny.

Emily wanted to punch and kick him, but she couldn't do that unless she was closer. She started to run, her legs pumping as hard as they ever had, the grass a blur beneath her feet. Even as planes roared overhead and a line of houses along the park's northern edge exploded, the plume of dust turning the grass inside the fence grey, she didn't stop. She ran and ran and ran, closing the gap between her and Kenny, until the trees came up around her, protecting her with their shadow.

As she fell to her knees, sweat sticking her shirt to her back, panting so hard she could barely speak, she looked up at him, her anger gone, dissipated across the field behind her. He might be a violent thug and a looter, but he hadn't caused this. Like her, all he wanted was to stay alive a few hours more, and if anything, he carried the only hope she had left.

'I thought you weren't coming,' he said. 'Where's your mother?'

'I had to leave her. Where's this doctor?'

Kenny looked past her, back towards the entrance to the park, then gave her a knowing nod.

'This way,' he said. 'It's not far now.'

24

FUGITIVE

MARK WOKE FROM A FITFUL, nightmare-filled sleep to the growl of engines in the street outside. He climbed up from the bed where he had slept and scrambled to the window in time to see a line of military vehicles trundle past in the direction of the prison. He reached up a hand to pull back the curtain and wave, then thought better of it.

I'm a convicted killer.

Maybe such things as prehistoric animals on the loose made his previous status null and void, but he didn't want to take the risk. He stayed still as the convoy moved past, heading into the town. He counted nine vehicles, mostly jeeps and transports, but there was one lorry with a tank resting on its back. Along with them came a couple of dozen soldiers on foot, all armed, guns held across their chests.

It could have been an ordinary military convoy, heading for some base across Dartmoor, but when the last flatbed lorry came past, Mark's stomach lurched at the sight of what had been strapped down, and he knew that the world would never be the same again.

It was huge, the size of a small bus, its hide punctured by some kind of rocket weapon, its skin stained with its own blood. One massive back leg had been blown nearly off, a huge, fleshy rent in its thigh muscle, and part of its jaw had been shot up, leaving it looking like it suffered from cleft palate. It was quite clearly dead, but its huge tail had broken out of the wires that held the rest of it, and now its tip dragged along the road beside the lorry, leaving a trail of dried blood and gore in its wake.

Mark was still trying to process quite what he was seeing when a door opened further up the street on the opposite side. A man stepped out, and the nearest soldier didn't hesitate, raising his gun and spraying the man with a hail of bullets. Blood splattered on the white-washed wall behind as the man jerked about, before collapsing to the ground like a broken puppet. Two soldiers ran across the street, stepped over the fallen man, and moved into the house.

A moment of stillness was followed by a muffled barrage of gunfire. A few seconds later one of the soldiers reemerged, falling back into the column. A minute after, the other reappeared, his gun slung haphazardly over his shoulder as he hurried to catch up.

Mark moved slowly away from the window, backing towards the door. He had left his pipe propped up against the door handle to hold the door shut while he slept, but just as his fingers closed around it, a loud banging came from downstairs.

He cracked open the bedroom door and stepped out on to the landing, peering down the stairs. The banging came again.

'You have ten seconds to open up!'

Although loud, the voice had little urgency about it, as though the speaker already knew the house was empty.

Mark waited as the seconds ticked past. He counted ten, fifteen, twenty. At thirty, he started down the stairs. The soldiers might have moved on for now, but they might be back any time. He had to get out of here.

The back door through the kitchen led out into a small, enclosed garden, but the back wall would give him no trouble. From there he would only have to get across the other fork in the road and he was out on the moor.

Those creatures had come from the moor last night. Right now, he feared the solders more, and hoped the creatures would be sleeping during the day.

He had just reached the bottom of the stairs when a shadow fell over the carpet in front of him.

A soldier stepped into the entranceway from the porch, the sun through the open door at his back.

Evidently there were other ways to get into a house than by kicking down a door.

'What the fuck?' The soldier pulled up his gun.

Prison had taught Mark that to survive you had to strike first. He swung the pipe around, knocking the gun aside, the chunks of broken concrete slamming into the soldier's face. The man howled as he fell back against the wall, his features a bloodied mess. As the man tried to stay on his feet, Mark swung again, this time his weapon glancing off the man's heavy body armour and catching him in the neck.

Blood flowed. Mark reached for the gun, but as the solder slumped, his finger depressed the trigger.

The carpet tore apart at the soldier's feet in a deafening rattle of automatic fire. Mark staggered away, ears ringing. He pushed through the kitchen door and stumbled to the back door, shouldering it open.

He was halfway across the garden before his head

began to clear. He began to run, hurdling over the back wall and landing in the street outside.

Facing the road that headed out across the moors, he was dangerously exposed. The military convoy had gone down the fork that led in front of the houses, but as he looked right into the town, a jeep turned into his road a few hundred yards ahead.

Across the street was a local mechanic's garage, a yard to one side of a large garage filled with cars in various states of dismantlement, among stacks of old bumpers, exhausts, tyres.

Carrying his club, Mark dashed across the road and pushed through a metal gate that stood ajar. The jeep's engine roared. Mark ducked between the old cars, keeping low to the ground. At the back of the mechanic's yard was a low stone wall, beyond it just moorland. The rattle of gunfire sounded, but it was distant. Mark hurdled the wall, coming down in squelchy grass on the other side. Crouching, he looked around for somewhere to hide.

The hillside sloped downwards into a hidden valley, then rose again in the distance to a rocky tor. Mark grimaced. It was suicide, going out there among those animals, but the soldiers, for whatever reason, were clearing out the town. And Mark had the blood of a dead soldier on his hands.

If they caught him, he was worse than dead.

Running in a crouch, he headed out across the moor, angling across the hillside. He got a stand of weather-beaten trees between him and the town, then ran hard for the valley.

Thorny, gnarled trees lined a trickling stream. Mark dropped to his knees and drank the cool water until his insides hurt, realising that he'd had no time to eat anything since last night. He sat down on a rock, the stream rushing beside him, the club propped up against his leg.

Those creatures had come off the moor last night. And that thing on the lorry … what if there were more of them?

He still wore his prison clothes: grey pajamas, a thin undershirt, pants, flat rubber shoes that were good for padding corridors but little else. They were already soaked, and he cursed himself for not taking the chance to change his attire.

The roar of an engine came from over the brow of the hill, quickly approaching. Mark scrambled to his feet, jumped across the river, and clambered over a cluster of boulders, dropping down into a narrow space between them.

Risking a peek out from behind the rock, he saw an all-terrain vehicle appear on the brow of the hill, back in the direction of Princetown. It was mottled green and black and armour-plated, heavy-duty tyres churning through the grass. Around it, a line of soldiers fanned out. One lifted what looked like a pair of binoculars to his eyes, and Mark ducked out of sight, cowering behind the rocks. If they had a heat sensor function, the rock might shield him, but if he moved, he was dead.

He waited, barely daring to breathe. The ATV's engine idled. The incomprehensible shouts of soldiers calling to each other, the static hiss of a walkie talkie. They had come closer, perhaps as far as the river. Mark closed his eyes, gripping the pipe. He would fight them rather than let them take him, let them execute him like a dog.

The ATV's engine revved, the sound fading. Mark let out a held breath, counted to a hundred in his head, then risked another peek out.

The hillside was clear, the soldiers had gone.

He stayed holed up among the rocks as the sun moved overhead, dipping towards the grey-green hills on the horizon. There was little to do other than pray the soldiers didn't come back, and scold himself for being so unprepared. He had survived by the skin of his teeth so far, and would be dead within days if he didn't wise up fast. He had tried to stay out of trouble in prison, but learned quickly that he had the kind of face that attracted it, the look of a fighter, perhaps. He had taken beatings and handed out a few, and learned from each. He had got prison survival down to a fine art, knowing when to be hard as hell, and when to show compassion.

Now he had to start learning all over again.

The long July day began to come to an end. Far out across the moor, a sharp screeching, like a dying crow, was answered by a dozen, two dozen more.

Mark emerged from his hiding place, checked the hillside for soldiers or worse, then made his way down to the river. Farther down the hillside, where the river disappeared into a narrow gorge, he saw something that made his blood chill.

A blur of movement, a shimmering, as though the grass itself had begun to move.

Hundreds and hundreds of little running things, racing across the hill, turning as one like a flock of birds moving through the sky.

Giving no further thought to the soldiers, Mark jumped across the river and ran for the town with all his remaining strength.

The towering walls of the prison rather ironically offered the best protection against both soldiers and deadly creatures alike, but Mark wasn't going back there unless he had no other choice. Reaching the town's outskirts, he moved from cover to cover as he crept slowly closer, the shadows lengthening around him as the sun set.

It didn't take long to find where the soldiers had gone.

The gates to the prison had been closed. Lights flickered in the watchtowers either side, the guards obviously not concerned about their presence being known. Mark crept as close as he dared, noticing something in the square outside that hadn't been there when he had escaped just yesterday afternoon.

A large, uneven mound, shrouded in shadow. As he squinted to make out the detail, he put a hand over his mouth to stifle a cry of horror.

Bodies. Dozens, maybe hundreds of them, all piled in a heap. Many wore the same prison garb as he, but many more wore regular civilian clothes.

He looked away, looked back again. It got worse. A groan. Somewhere else a twitch.

Not all of them were dead.

Mark backed away. He would have been sick had there been anything left in his stomach. He had to get out of here now.

He started to head back up the street, but a rising roar was fast approaching. He backed into an alleyway, pushed between two rubbish bins, then found himself at a dead end, the two buildings joined at the rear by a one-storey slate-roofed extension.

A rustling made him turn. A dozen or so shapes scampered past, heading for the heap of bodies.

No way out that way.

Mark turned to the extension, looking for a way up.

Nearby was a low protrusion in the side of one building, slightly slanted, with a closed and padlocked sheet iron lid, like the opening to a coal scuttle. Mark pushed his club up on to the roof then climbed up after it. Three feet off the ground now, but he was still some way from the rear extension. It was a few feet over his head, and there was a gap between the protrusion he stood on, filled with weeds, overgrown pot plants, and stacked flowerpots.

A drainpipe hung down into the gap, too thin to grip but the metal clasps that held it to the wall might just be wide enough for him to get a foothold. Mark reached for the pipe. As he stretched, a rustling behind him made him turn.

A serpentine face watched him out of the gloom. Little bigger than a chicken, it was lithe and muscular, tufts of feathers protruding from among the scales. Its tail whipped back and forth as its head tilted from side to side.

'Go fuck yourself,' Mark muttered, kicking off from the slanted protrusion, grabbing the drainpipe with one hand and trying to lever himself up using the metal clasp for his foot. As his free hand closed over the roof edge, he tried to jump, but missed, slipping down into the gap. He landed with a hard, jarring thump, the slate tile he had gripped coming with him, breaking on the floor at his feet.

He looked up to see the lizard-like face barely an arms' length from his own. With a hiss, its mouth opened to reveal lines of pointed teeth, and it lunged.

Instinct saved him, one hand coming up with a sliver of slate the length of his forearm. He held it across himself, the other hand bracing it, and the creature's jaw split open, the slate cutting into the soft flesh in the corners of its mouth.

Its nostrils flared, Mark flinching as hot, putrid air doused his face. He pressed harder, the slate cutting deeper, and the creature fell away, twitching and scrabbling in the dirt as it died.

More still ran past the alley's entrance. Mark had got lucky. He climbed to his feet, got up on to the slanted protrusion, and this time was able to jump across to the roof. There, he retrieved his club then made his way along the roof until he came to a railing that separated the roof from a flat balcony. He climbed over, then pushed past a set of overturned plastic patio chairs and made his way to the other end.

The balcony faced east. Mark pulled across the picnic table and climbed on top of it, then hauled himself up onto the house's gently sloping roof, pleased to see there was a chimney stack at one end to give him cover. Staying flat and moving slowly, he climbed the slope of the roof then peered out from behind the chimney stack at the square in front of the prison.

Spotlights from the watchtowers illuminated the ghastly feast. Dozens, if not hundreds of the diminutive but vicious creatures ripped and tore at the heaped pile of human corpses. A couple of larger creatures—the size of horses but walking on two legs—had also appeared, powerful claws ripping flesh, blood staining snapping teeth. Mark wanted to run as fast as he could in the opposite direction, but he was morbidly drawn to the scene, unable to look away.

Why were they feeding them? Some of those people weren't even dead—

A metallic scraping sound came from the watchtowers, then the deafening roar of a dozen machine guns filled the air. Mark clamped hands over his ears as bullets riddled the feasting monsters, shredding sinew and flesh, cutting them apart.

Some creatures continued to feast, others turned to

flee, and then the square erupted with a massive explosion, throwing parts of humans and monsters high into the air. Mark ducked down as lumps of gore landed with wet, meaty thuds on the rooftop around him, some rolling away, others beginning to dribble blood. Another blast came as Mark cowered behind the chimney stack, but as the air settled, a defiant shriek came from somewhere far out across the moor.

Mark understood now. The soldiers, desperate, had made a vain attempt to draw the monsters in, but the monsters, whatever the fuck they were, weren't going to be stopped by any simple trap.

Not all of them any rate.

Mark climbed down the roof to the balcony, then used the club to break through the glass French window. Down on the street below, an armoured vehicle moved past, a machine gun placement rattling, spraying up chunks of broken tarmac. Mark broke away the slivers of glass and climbed into the house.

As the rattle of gunfire continued outside, he reached up and pulled a curtain across to cover the shattered door, as thought that might defy the collapsing world outside. It wasn't much … but it was something.

25

REGRETS

Alan couldn't think of anything to do to settle his nerves other than make a cup of tea. Ellis, he had managed to entertain by hunting out a box of DVDs of films that were just about okay for a kid, and now Alan sat at the kitchen table, his hands shaking, as the sound of an old Star Wars film drifted out of the living room.

After getting the creatures out of his house, he had fetched a box of nails and set himself to secure the front door, before realising his folly and leaving the nails where he had put them on the shelf inside the door. He would need to go out for food sooner or later, and possibly more medical supplies for Dad's wound. He had cleaned it up well and administered antibiotics, but what kind of germs might a bite from a creature like that have brought?

Dad's leg was pretty much all he could think about. That and what to do with Ellis. It shamed him to admit it, but he didn't want to look after the boy. They were familiar only by reputation, and that was all from Alan's side. He could have passed the boy in the street a dozen times without so much as a sideways glance. Now, the boy was holed up in Alan's house, his own family home—and possibly his family with it—reduced to rubble.

How easily the boy had been distracted, Alan thought, by the flashing lights of a decent story. Sooner or later the film would end, though, and Ellis's questions would begin. And Alan had none of the answers.

The landline was still out of order, and he was getting no reception on his mobile. Neither was the television broadcasting any regular channels, but at least for now they still had power. He frowned, wondering if there was any way he could find out what was going on without going outside.

Of course there was, now that he thought about it. His phone wouldn't work because it was all digital and modern, but upstairs somewhere was Dad's simple old radio. Alan downed the rest of his tea then hurried up the stairs to Dad's old bedroom, where he rummaged about under the bed until he found a box containing the radio.

He smiled as he carried it back down the stairs. There was a cassette function that had never worked, but he remembered how dad had used to take a deckchair and sit down at the bottom of the garden under their old crab apple tree and listen to Test Match Special on BBC Radio Four. Alan remembered peaceful days when Mum was sleeping on the sofa and he had played with his Matchbox cars in the grass behind Dad's chair, the posh Oxford accents of the cricket commentators crackling out of the radio as they discussed cakes and local restaurants in between describing the game's action.

If there had been a power cord for the radio, Alan no longer knew where it was, but there was a battery port at the back, and after another few minutes of looking through the kitchen drawers he found enough batteries to get the thing to start.

He turned the volume down low so that Ellis wouldn't overhear, then gently began to turn the tuning knob. He went through FM first, but found nothing, but when he switched over to the shortwave function, he managed to catch a grainy man's voice. Touching the knob gently, he adjusted the station to the clearest possible setting.

'….and we're hearing reports of explosions around New Street Station. Someone has taken out the train line, restricting travel in either direction. This appears to be a deliberate act of sabotage, aimed at preventing people from leaving the city. We repeat that we are yet to hear confirmation that a quarantine zone has been established. We will relay whatever information we have as soon as we can. Repeat: Armed Forces helicopters have been seen flying in formation to the north of the city. We have reports that one was shot down. By whom or how, we have no information, and the report remains unconfirmed. Stay tuned for further news. This is Birmingham City Sky Radio….'

Alan continued to listen for a while, his heart slowly filling with a creeping sense of dread. Yesterday he had gone to work as usual, struggled to find a parking space as usual, despaired at the damn drunks wasting NHS funding as usual….

'Excuse me, Mr. Graf?'

'Huh?'

Ellis was standing in the doorway. 'Mr. Graf, may I use the bathroom?'

'Ah, yes … yes, of course,' Alan said, standing up a little too quickly, his leg catching on the edge of the table, causing the radio to rock back and forth. He grabbed it with one hand, then forced a smile for the boy. 'It's upstairs, the second door on the left. I think it's ajar. You'll see it.'

'Thank you, Mr. Graf,' Ellis said, but continued to stare at him. Alan began to potter back and forth, looking for places to put his hands, searching for something to do, but the boy made no move.

'Upstairs,' Alan said again. 'Second on the left.'

'Mr. Graf … I'm scared,' Ellis said.

'Yes, boy, me too—'

'I mean, to go upstairs alone. There might be … more.'

'There aren't,' Alan said. 'I checked.'

'But what if there is? What if one got in a window or down the chimney or something?'

Alan was about to say that the house didn't have a chimney, when a sudden flashback of himself as a child appeared in his mind, of tugging Dad's trouser leg, asking for an escort to the bathroom, past the living room where Mum had been throwing things. And Dad, who had a smear of blood on his cheek from something Mum had thrown, had scooped him up in his arms and carried him.

'Okay,' Alan said. 'Come on.'

He walked past Ellis into the hall and started up the stairs, the boy trailing a few steps behind. At the top, he held open the bathroom door for Ellis to enter. As the boy got to the door, he stopped.

'You'll be all right in there,' Alan said.

'Can you wait outside the door?'

Alan suppressed a sigh. 'Of course.'

'Thanks, Mr. Graf. You're the best.'

Ellis went inside and shut the door. Alan sighed, leaning back against the wall, wondering what on earth he could do to get out of this situation. He didn't have time to look after a child. With Dad hurt—

The toilet flushed and a moment later the door opened, Ellis drying his hands on a towel. 'Thanks, Mr.

Graf,' he said, giving Alan a smile. 'You can go back to what you were doing now.'

The way the boy spoke broke something in Alan. He reached out and gave Ellis's shoulder a squeeze, then turned without a word and headed down the stairs. At the bottom, he waited while Ellis came down, then waved the boy back into the living room.

'I'll … I'll make some tea in a while,' Alan said. 'You like … spaghetti? I have spaghetti.'

'Do you have meatballs? I like meatballs.'

Alan shook his head. 'Just a jar of pasta sauce. I don't know, there might be some in it.'

'I hope so.'

'You should get back to your film, in case you forget the story,' Alan said, feeling like an idiot, wondering how some people seemed to know exactly how to speak to children. 'I'll call you … when the food's ready.'

Ellis started back towards the sofa where the TV remote lay diagonally across a cushion, then stopped and looked back.

'Mr. Graf … if it's not too much trouble, could we go out and look for my parents after tea? We couldn't find them before, but maybe if we look again? I mean, it's not going to get dark for ages, so maybe if there are none of those things outside—'

Alan put up a hand. 'Ellis … I don't think it's safe. Not right now.'

'But they won't know where I am. What if they're out there looking for me? What if they think I'm under that rubble and they're digging, and one of those things—'

'It's not safe!' Alan snapped, much louder than he had intended. Ellis's eyes filled with tears and he backed away, as though Alan was now the monster. 'It's not … safe,' he repeated, softer this time, then offered a smile, which Ellis returned, although with little conviction.

'Please, Mr. Graf,' he said. 'I just want my mum and dad.'

It was Alan's turn to tear up, although he turned away, hiding it. 'Look, I'll tell you what. After we've had something to eat, I'll go out and have a look. You should stay here, though. It's not safe. I can … take care of myself.'

Never had he said something for which the truth was so different. After all, it had been Ellis who had saved him. The boy seemed convinced, though, giving a frantic nod.

'But how will you know what they look like?'

'I … I'll ask them if they know you,' Alan said.

'Okay.'

'You run along now and finish your film. I'll have some food ready in half an hour or so.'

Ellis nodded again and went back into the living room. Alan gently pulled the door closed, then went to check on Dad. He was still sleeping, but his temperature had risen half a degree, perhaps the sign of a fever. Alan changed his drip and checked the wound's dressing, cursing himself for not checking Dad's room better, for letting down the old man at the last. He leaned over Dad's face, one hand over Dad's listening to the shallow breathing.

He had no choice. Dad needed stronger antibiotics, and there was only once place Alan would find them.

Going outside, though, was suicide.

The building shook as somewhere not distant enough an explosion boomed.

Soon, it might be suicide to stay here.

He made sure Dad was comfortable, then went back to the kitchen and busied himself with preparing food for Ellis and himself. Putting a bowl of spaghetti and meat sauce—but no meatballs, alas—on a tray along with a plate of chopped apple, he carried it through to the living room and pulled a small coffee table out from the wall.

Ellis was curled on the sofa, watching the last few minutes of the film.

'You can eat in here if you like,' Alan said. 'Nothing like a TV dinner, is there?'

Ellis sat up and smiled. 'Thanks, Mr. Graf.'

'Go ahead and put on another film if you like,' Alan said, trying his best to sound hospitable, while sure he sounded anything but. 'Might as well pass the time doing something fun, eh?'

Ellis didn't look convinced, but he nodded anyway. Alan smiled again then went back into the kitchen, where he sat down with his own bowl of spaghetti and switched on the radio again.

'….we're hearing reports of more explosions in Walsall and Wolverhampton. A picket line established along the Wednesbury parallel has been breached. All residents are advised to stay indoors. Random attacks continue from unidentified sources, although the RAF helicopter shot down over Aldridge this morning has been claimed by a militia calling themselves VRS, which we've been led to believe is an acronym for Viper Raid Steel, an online hate group known for canvassing for more autocratic governance … more details as they emerge. And if anyone has anything to report, get in touch. Short and medium wave radio still work, although all cellular networks appear to be currently offline….'

'Mr. Graf?'

Alan jerked, snapping a hand forward to switch off the radio. Ellis, standing in the doorway with his spaghetti bowl in his hands, still half full, flinched as though he had been struck.

'Ellis? Yes? Are you all right?'

'Can I eat with you, Mr. Graf? I'm scared.'

Alan wanted to say no, but couldn't bring himself to say the words. 'Of course,' he said, waving at an empty chair. 'Go and get your tray. I was just trying to figure out what's going on. I thought the noise might bother you, that's all.'

'Thank you, Mr. Graf.'

Alan moved the radio to the side as Ellis went out, coming back a minute later with his tray, the apple slices already eaten. Alan gave a brief smile; he had been just the same once. He would have eaten the pudding while Dad was still cooking if he had been allowed.

They ate in silence for a while, then Ellis said, 'That's a radio, isn't it? My dad had one.'

Alan nodded. 'That's right.'

'My dad said people were too crazy about phones and the internet these days,' Ellis said. 'He said that sooner or later someone would take them away, and we'd all be up the creek without the paddle.' He shrugged. 'Something like that.'

'It sounds like your dad was a wise man.'

Ellis smiled. 'Mum said he was full of hot air. Do you have a phone, Mr. Graf?'

'Yes, I have two. A cellphone and a landline. Unfortunately, neither is currently working, but I'm sure they'll be back on again before long.'

Ellis nodded as he forked a tangle of spaghetti into his mouth. 'Are we up the creek without the paddle, Mr. Graf?'

Alan lifted an eyebrow. 'Did your dad ever tell you not to talk with your mouth full?'

Ellis nodded. 'A couple of times,' he mumbled, chewing down his spaghetti.

'Like I said, a wise man. I think that all we need to do is wait, and things will sort themselves out.'

'Are you sure?'

'Yes, I'm sure.'

'Do you promise?'

One of the unspoken rules among the hospital staff was to never promise a kid everything was going to be all right when their parent was lying in a bed about to go down for surgery. Deflect the question, say what you needed to say, but never make a promise you couldn't keep.

Alan gulped. 'I promise,' he said.

26

REFUGE

THERE WASN'T much daylight left. Juliet pushed her bike up the road from the beach, trying to be careful not to spill the water she had collected for Uncle Lawrence, the last light of the day slipping beneath the horizon at her back, the hedgerows and the houses in front of her slowly losing distinction, becoming indecipherable lumps of black against the grey-blue of the evening sky.

All the lights were still off in the houses, but she heard the distant grumbling of car engines, suggesting there were still some people around.

Far overheard a line of lights appeared, moving quickly towards the north. Juliet paused to watch for them for a few seconds, then shuddered as a rumble filled the air. It was a sonic boom, Dad had told her, meaning those planes were going faster than the speed of sound. She wondered where they were going, so late in the evening, but then remembered that high up where they were, the sun would still be up, so they would be able to see, even if they were going crazy fast.

Something was blocking the road up ahead. Juliet

pushed her bike as close as she dared, then switched on her bike's light to illuminate the red sign at now stood in the middle of the road, a couple of metal barriers on either side. It hadn't been there when she had ridden down, or if it had, she hadn't noticed it. It as surely there now, though:

ROAD CLOSED
Please Use Alternative Route

Juliet paused. There appeared to be no one manning the diversion, and there seemed to be no reason why the road would be closed, but Dad had taught her always to respect the rules. What if there was a hidden camera somewhere, or if the work crew people had just gone for coffee and would be back any moment? If she was delayed, Uncle Lawrence might die. What would she do then?

There were no other roads, except the one going right around the village and up the other side of the valley, out to the main road and along. Even riding, that would take her hours.

Perhaps it was just a short section? Maybe she could go through a field? But peering up ahead, she could see no other sign, so it could mean the whole village was cut off. Luckily, her house was just out of the village on the southern side. Plus, it backed onto a field, so if she went that way, no one would see her.

She stood for a moment, frozen with indecision. Uncle Lawrence would need the water soon.

I have to be strong. How can I get around?

Of course! She clicked her fingers with delight, pleased with herself for remembering. There was the footpath, the one from the beach up through the valley. She had walked it with Dad loads of times. There was a branch that came out on the farm lane below her house, so from there she could easily cut across the field. It would take a lot longer, but much less time than the other road up around the valley.

She climbed onto her bike and turned it around, freewheeling down the gentle slope towards the beach, taking the narrow side road that led up to the cliffs on the south side of the beach, and from there headed onwards down the coast. The footpath began at a farm gate a few hundred metres down the road, but already it was dark and gloomy between the hedgerows, the only light coming from the sky overhead. As she pulled up outside the gate, her heart filled with fear. She had her bike light, but how long would that last? By day it was a pleasant and enjoyable walk, the path wide and flat where it followed this tributary of the river, with only one steeper and narrower section further up, just before it came out on the farm lane below her house.

What about that thing she had seen by the river? What if there were more? What if there were other kinds, like the one by the house, or the one that had bitten Uncle Lawrence?

Her chest heaved, and she squeezed her legs together to stop from wetting herself. Was this really better than just sneaking past the road block and hoping no one saw her?

Dad always told her to be brave when facing a difficult situation. He had to cut people open and then sew them up for a job, so he would know. She remembered one time they'd gone out to the farm park near Launceston, and she'd wanted to go on the drop slide, but once she was up there leaning over the edge, all her nerve had failed. She'd stood there frozen for about ten minutes, while other kids dropped over the edge, screaming with excitement as they plunged down the sheer face towards the curve at the bottom. She had wanted to cry but wanted even less to be seen crying, so had backed away down the steps, only to find Dad waiting halfway up.

'You don't have to do it,' he had told her. 'You could walk away right now. Or you could challenge yourself, push yourself out of your comfort zone. Just look how happy those other kids are. That could be you, too.'

She hadn't really known what "comfort zone" meant, but she had understood about the other kids. It couldn't be that scary, surely?

She'd gone back up, and after another ten minutes of standing there fearfully, she had finally mustered the courage to hook her legs over and take the plunge. She had skinned one of her elbows on the way down, but the fall had been so exhilarating that she'd done it ten more times before Dad had said they ought to go home. And even though her elbow had been scabbed over and sore the next day, the thrill had been so great that she hadn't cared.

She doubted there'd be the same kind of thrill reward now, but the challenge was the same. On the road she was in her comfort zone, able to see all around her, to know if any of those things were nearby. Through that gate and she'd be outside it, walking in the dark beside the river, unable to see anything outside the weak triangle of light given off by her bicycle light.

It's not just about me, she reminded herself. *It's about Uncle Lawrence.*

That did it for her. Gritting her teeth, she pushed down on the balls of her feet and spurred herself forwards, pushing up the gate latch with her shoulder and slipping through the gap into the field before the gate could swing shut again. Inside, she reached through the wooden beams and hooked the latch shut again, not just because that was the rules but because it would make it harder for her to chicken out. Then, steeling herself, she pushed her bike towards the path at the edge of the field, that ran alongside the river.

She was barely halfway across the first field before it was too dark to see without her bicycle light. She switched it on, and in near total darkness it seemed so much brighter than usual. It was enough to see several steps ahead, but the glare left her blind when she looked away. If anything or anyone approached her, she wouldn't see them until they were practically on top of her, so she climbed onto her bike and began to ride as best she could over the uneven, gravelly trail, her light jerking back and forth as potholes and protruding stones pushed her front wheel from side to side.

About halfway, the path got too uneven for her to continue, so she dismounted again and began to push her bike over the rocks and divots of grass and weeds as the path narrowed and steepened. It left the river behind, cutting diagonally across a forested hillside, then flattening out again as it reached the farmland at the top of the valley. By now it was nearly pitch dark, and Juliet's bicycle light was starting to go dim. With the trees closing in above her and cutting off the bright starry sky, Juliet found herself starting to panic, terrified she would get lost, even though the sensible part of her knew exactly where she was.

It's only the dark, she told herself over and over again. *It's only a bit of dark. Nothing to worry about.*

And then a growl came out of the trees behind her, and as Dad might have said, all bets were off.

Juliet dropped her bike to the ground with a clutter. The bottle with the lid rolled out of her basket, and the one without the lid began to slosh water back down the path. The light, knocked sideways, illuminated a leafy triangle of undergrowth, the plants glistening from earlier rain.

The growl came again, from downslope, and something rustled in the undergrowth. Juliet had heard foxes, badgers, even a lost sheep wandering through the trees, but this sounded much, much bigger.

Something shifted in the dark, coming forwards. Juliet pulled up her bike, not to ride it but to use it as a barrier, and shoved it forward just as something broke from the undergrowth. She caught a glimpse of something shiny and serpentine, massive and scaly. The bike struck it and a shriek of anger made Juliet's ears hurt. As the thing thrashed about, trying to throw off the bike that had somehow got caught on its limbs, Juliet turned, grabbed the bottle with the lid, and ran.

Uncle Lawrence no longer mattered, but if the water had scared the other creature, there was a thread of hope it would do the same for this one. Juliet's main hope, however, was to outrun it, so with the bottle clutched against her chest, she bolted up the path, unable to see anything, but trusting her instincts and her memory of its angle. A couple of times she nearly stumbled into the trees, but when undergrowth began to whip at her legs she shifted the other way, hoping she didn't trip or crash into low branches hanging across the path.

And then, to her relief, she broke from the trees, finding the shadowy outline of a stile in front of her. She clambered over it, recognising the familiar farm lane. The farmhouse was a couple of hundred metres ahead; perhaps she could find some way to get inside before the creature caught up with her. As she pushed away from the stile she risked a glance back, but the path was nothing but impenetrable darkness. Then, as she found herself staring, a sharp, earsplitting snarl was quickly followed by a crunch of metal.

Juliet needed to see no more. She turned and bolted up the lane, heading for the black lump of the farmhouse.

She nearly made it. It was practically looming above her when her foot caught on a loose stone and she went sprawling forward, scraping both her hands and knees. She rolled to a stop and pushed herself up, disorientated. The bottle was lost, but as she looked for it, a shape bounded out of the dark, the size of a bear, huge and gangly, claws scraping on the ground.

Juliet was dead. She knew it, and whatever hunted her knew it too. Best to give up and get it over with, but some desperate survival instinct had her rolling sideways as the creature leapt.

The bottle, hidden in the dark, saved her. The creature's front foot must have caught it, for with a snarl it twisted, rolling sideways, giving Juliet vital seconds. She scrambled to her feet and sprinted up the lane, away from the farmhouse, in the direction of the road.

She would never make it, she knew, but better to die on her feet than lying on the ground.

And then she saw a shape materialise out of the dark, large and blocky, taking up half the lane's width.

A van. It was parked against the verge, leaving enough space for another vehicle to pass.

Uncle Lawrence's van. It has to be.

His van was old, that was all she knew. Dad had called it a rust bucket behind Uncle Lawrence's back, claimed it was one loose screw away from falling apart. Dad had a BMW, one that opened with pass codes and voice instructions, but as Juliet crashed against the back of Uncle Lawrence's van, she could only hope it was old enough to still have conventional door handles, and that it was unlocked.

Her fingers hooked beneath something halfway up. She glanced up. A shadow bounded through the dark, barely more than a blur.

She pulled.

The door opened. With a cry that was as much rage as it was joy, she jumped inside and swung the door shut, hearing it slam, the mechanism clicking moments before something huge crashed against it, hard enough to make the van shudder.

Juliet waited in the pitch black, hardly daring to breathe. The creature's low growl sounded almost frustrated, and it continued for a few minutes, coming from different directions, as though it were circling the van. Then, with a sudden snarl, she heard its feet thumping over the ground as it bounded away.

For a long time, Juliet could do nothing other than sit in the dark, listening to the hoarseness of her own breathing. She had somehow managed to not soil herself, but she was desperate to go, and she was soaked in sweat, her hands and knees smarting and sore, her body aching.

She wanted to sleep, but she had never felt so awake.

After a while, she slowly began to feel around her surroundings. The back of the van was pitch black, meaning there perhaps wasn't a way to see through into the front bit where the driver and the passenger sat. The sides weren't smooth, with objects fitted along them, tools, perhaps.

Uncle Lawrence worked for the council as a "handyman", Dad said. He fixed things for people. It would be hard to see in here, though, so somewhere there had to be a light.

In Dad's car, the light was fitted into the ceiling. Juliet

reached up in the dark, feeling around, but aside from a few wires and things there didn't seem to be any kind of light.

Where else might there be one?

In Dad's garage, he had a moveable light which was basically a bulb with a wire frame around it, although that was electric. If Uncle Lawrence had something like that, it would have to be battery-powered, but it would also make sense that it was near the back doors, so he could switch it on when he opened them.

Juliet crawled to the back of the van and began feeling around the sides. She had gone over one side and the roof, and was just about to give up when her fingers closed over something halfway down on the other side. It was conical like a light should be, and had a rounded end, like a bulb. Her fingers tingled with building excitement as the searched for some kind of switch.

When she found it, the sudden light was blinding. She had to cover her eyes for a few seconds while they adjusted. When she slowly opened them again, she found herself holding a large battery torch, the kind that watchmen with dogs seemed to carry, long and heavy enough that it could be used as a club to beat intruders and thieves. It had been fitted into a brace just inside the door.

Able to see the contents of the van for the first time, it surprised her. Uncle Lawrence had never let anyone look into the back of his van, but it was mostly tools hanging from the sides, boxes of wires and bits of metal, things that probably fitted somewhere into doors or windows. There were some tins of paint, a box of brushes, a couple of boxes of rags, and some other things that looked like junk.

To her surprise, though down one side was a narrow mattress, squeezed into a gap alongside several boxes of tools. Perhaps Uncle Lawrence took naps here sometimes when he was working too hard.

There were some other things, too. The top corners of the mattress had holes cut on either side, with a chain threaded through and hooked around. At the end of each chain was what looked like a handcuff.

She hadn't known Uncle Lawrence was in the police, but perhaps as a "handyman" he did some side work for them. The cuffs probably wouldn't hold a big criminal, but if it was a kid stealing things from shops or something, it might be enough.

Alongside it too, was a box of other tools, things Juliet couldn't guess the use of. There were some knives, and kind of plastic brushes, bright pink tubes with wires attached to one end. Juliet frowned, thinking of bright, airy sun lounges. Maybe Uncle Lawrence did work for rich old ladies, fixing up chairs or dressers or … she didn't know.

There was something else, too. Something brown and furry, stuffed into a bucket beside the mattress.

As Juliet tentatively pulled it out, at first she thought it was a soft toy. Then, as it flopped in her hands and she turned it over, she let out a little gasp. It wasn't a soft toy, but a mask, the face that of a bear. And not a cute one, either, but a creepy, snarling one with hard eyes, the kind of thing someone might wear on Halloween.

A little freaked out, she pushed it back into the bucket, turning the eyes away.

Dad had always said Uncle Lawrence was a bit weird. As Juliet regarded the contents of the back of the van, she just felt a little sorry for him. Who kept a mask in their van except someone who really wanted to be invited to a party? Dad had said Uncle Lawrence didn't have any friends.

Juliet gave a sad smile. If he survived, she could be his friend. After all, they had saved each other now. She had saved him from the creature in the field, and his van had now saved her. They owed each other.

She looked up, realising the screen that blocked off the front of the van from the back was just a couple of pieces of plywood that looked like they would slide across. She wanted to see if it was light yet, but she knew she hadn't been here long enough, no matter how long it felt. And there was no way she was going back outside until daylight.

She looked at the mattress again, suddenly feeling weary beyond words. The torch was too bright, but she didn't want to switch it off. She looked at the settings, and found there was a second light halfway along. It was a weird pink light which made her feel like she was inside a bit of bubblegum, but it was much dimmer.

Silently thanking Uncle Lawrence for leaving his van here rather than parking it outside their house, she lay down on the mattress, pushed one of the handcuffs away from her face, and closed her eyes.

27

WITHDRAWAL

The lights had gone off, and they weren't coming on again. For a while, Nikki didn't—couldn't—panic, because the dope was taking care of her, but after a while, as the stuff started to wear off, a fresh wave of paranoid thoughts started to run at her like little goblins with sticks, poking and prodding, teasing, accusing.

Collie might be dead. Collie probably was dead, because he hadn't moved since he had fallen and the flat was now filled with a horrid coppery smell. If he was dead, she couldn't stay here. She didn't so much fear the pigs, but Collie had mates who would come round to buy dope, and Collie almost never went out, and almost never slept. Some she could handle herself, but others would want to come in and hang, to shoot up with Collie.

Perhaps she could hide him? Maybe if she dragged him under the bed or even threw him off the balcony? But no matter what she reasoned, no course of action seemed appropriate.

It was her who would have to leave.

On the dope, it was hard to do anything. She sat in the

chair until she started to feel functional again, then she got up and fumbled her way into the flat.

Where had she left it?

There hadn't been much left, but there had been enough for another hit. Nikki began to fumble around in the gloom, trying to find the cigarette packet with Collie's stash at the bottom. Had she even put it back inside, or was it on the table?

Fuck it, she couldn't see a damn thing. She wondered if the gas hob would still work, whether it would give her enough light to see by, but when she stumbled to the kitchen, she found that didn't work either.

Of course, they had been cut off, hence the stinking heap of LIDL pre-cooked food packages in the corner. In frustration, she kicked out at them, heard rather than saw them scatter across the floor, felt something hard behind them, the actual bin which hadn't been emptied in weeks.

Fuck this life, and fuck you, Collie.

She had to get out, but she wouldn't last long without the dope. She needed light, and she stumbled around the bedsit in the gloom, knocking over chairs and rifling through boxes, trying to figure shit out. Where had he put it? He had to have more somewhere. People came round asking all the time, and he always fixed them up. If nothing else, she had to find where he hid his cash, so she could go and get some more.

She bumped into the low glass-topped coffee table, cutting her shin. As she cried out and stumbled forwards, her hand landed on top of something.

Of course.

She lifted the light, flicking on the little flame. It wasn't enough, and a moment later she hissed as it burnt her finger.

Flicking it off, she looked around, then reached for a

cushion. It was Collie's favourite, some hand-stitched bullshit with an embroidered picture of a harbour that his gran had done as a present for graduating college. He'd done something in fisheries, and she'd hoped he'd work on a ship or something. He'd tried to pawn it for dope a couple of times but no one had wanted it. His gran had arthritis and the seams were a bit wonky, but as Nikki held the lighter to it and flicked on the flame, it began to burn nicely. Dirty plastic fumes filled the air, but the room began to illuminate, so Nikki put it on top of the glass coffee table to burn while she went looking for Collie's dope and cash.

There was nothing in the kitchen, nothing under the sofa cushions. She found his wallet in his pocket, but aside from a faded and creased picture of him, his gran, and some little dog, there were only a couple of fivers and some coins. Nikki pocketed them all, then went to the mattress in the corner that was all that remained of their bed and pushed it aside, wondering if there was anything underneath.

The smell of smoke was cloying, even though she had left the balcony doors open, but the fire was holding, keeping the room bright. That old cushion burned well, and Nikki looked up, wanting to be respectful, say thanks or some bullshit before it was completely reduced to ashes.

And her whole body tightened with fear.

Flames licked across the carpet, up the walls. The sofa—some cheap shit Collie had got off a mate without any of the safety regs of the nice new ones—was smoldering, folding in on itself as the covers and spongy bits melted. Nikki stood up, heart fluttering with panic as she saw flames licking at the door.

She had to get out, and she had to get out now.

There was no time to take anything except the clothes she was wearing. She nearly forgot her shoes, slipping on the fuck-me-sandal-heel things at the last minute. She'd have preferred her trainers, but she didn't know where they were and the flames were spreading.

She pulled open the door, leaving it open as she fled down the corridor, past the lift that had never worked, towards the stairs. The dope was still numbing everything, but sooner or later Nikki would start to come down, and then shit would get *really* bad.

~

The streets weren't entirely dark. Some emergency street lighting had come on, dimmer than the usual ones, more spread out. And there were cars, cars everywhere, lights flickering, horns blaring, everyone trying to go somewhere but seemingly no one knowing where to go. As she hurried up Easton Road, sandal-heels clacking on the pavement, she almost laughed. No way the police would come after her with all this crazy shit going on. And the funniest thing was, she had no idea why.

She would need another hit soon, and she didn't have any more. She started to get antsy, scratching at her arms, rubbing her shoulders, picking at a couple of sores on her face. She tried to remember where Collie's mates lived, the ones he got his dope from, but the truth was, he had kept a tight rein on her. She went out when he said, came back when he said. He didn't even like her going to johns' houses, preferring her to do her work in cars or the park at the top of the road. She sometimes did if they offered her enough, and he never knew as long as they dropped her back on the street, but a couple of times she'd stayed overnight and got back late. He'd given her a black eye or a sore jaw for her trouble, even though she knew he liked the money.

Fuck this life, and fuck you, Collie, you arrogant, controlling prick.

At least he was dead. She felt pleased, then as she thought about it, she began to feel sad, too. He had kind of been her boyfriend, and before the dope took hold, he'd been kind of all right. They'd gone to cafés and shit, the zoo, a water park once. He'd said he'd been an addict in his teens, but he'd got over it, and he was clean now. He wasn't going back.

And then his gran died, and he needed a pick me up. And once he was on the dope, he couldn't work, and one day he'd said, 'Why don't we do it together?', and before she knew it, she was fucking strangers on the street to pay for their habits and he was beating the shit out of her if she didn't earn enough and and *and*—

'You wanker,' she cried, slipping back against the tall stone wall that bordered the pavement, her legs giving way. She started to slide down, tears in her eyes, then shook herself awake, trying to throw off the dope haze.

I can do this—I can't do this—I can do this—

Cars roared past, going nowhere in a hurry. She saw a police car, but it was going the other way, and she wished she could sleep. Usually, she'd sleep after a hit, killing a few hours before she needed another, but now she was starting to get desperate, too wired to sleep, the stress burning through the dope quicker or some shit, making her crave, making her need.

She pushed herself back to her feet, staggering on up the street, the gloom of Eastville Park up ahead.

Once it had been nice, and during the day it was still all right, but for whatever reason the council had stopped giving a shit about it a few years back and now it had gone to hell, the sports courts overgrown, the field a tangle of weeds. There was a toilet block just inside the gates on this side of the park, and sometimes fiends hung out there, doing whatever. The money she had stolen from Collie's corpse might just be enough.

At first she thought it was empty, that the blackout, the wailing sirens might have changed people's priorities, but as she did a circuit of the dark building, a wraith materised out of the gloom, towering over her. She could barely make out his features, didn't know if she knew him, but it was a man, big, muscular, skin-headed.

'Hey,' she said. 'I need a little something. I have some cash.'

'Fifty,' he said.

Nikki shook her head. 'I don't have that much. Come on, that's too expensive.'

The man waved an arm. Flames flickered out of the upstairs window of a distant high-rise, stark against the blackness of the city. For a moment Nikki thought it was her building, but it was too far to the east; her building was west, out of sight from here.

'Didn't you notice, shit's gone down,' the man said. She could hear him grin. 'And as a result, the prices went up.'

'I can't—'

A hand lifted, stroking the underside of her chin. 'Oh, I think you can. Pretty little thing like you.'

It started then, and Nikki was pleased for the dope's numbing effect. He was powerful, strong, rough with her, pressing her down on to the wet grass. One weak slap across her face was enough to show her the strength in those arms, that things would get much, much, worse if she tried to resist, so she let the man do what he wanted, trying to zone out, to forget herself like she so often did, to remember how she had felt two years before, in college training to be a hairdresser, looking forward to owning her own salon one day, before she had met a young man with a nice smile who had volunteered his unruly locks for a bit of practical training, a young man whose name was Peter Collins, who liked everyone to call him Collie—

'Can I have some?' she heard herself muttering weakly as the man finally stood up, aware that her body felt battered and sore, used like old toilet paper. 'Please?'

'I don't have it with me,' the man said, pulling up his jeans. 'I'll bring it in the morning. Stay here and wait for me.'

'I can't wait that long!'

'Yeah, you can. Nice welcoming girl like you.' He chuckled, then his silhouette was gone, and Nikki was alone, sitting on the park's wet grass, her underwear lying somewhere nearby, her blouse ripped open, her body aching from rough hands, strong fingers, muscular hips, fingernails, teeth.

And she was starting to withdraw.

He had taken the money out of her pocket, leaving her with nothing.

She lay down, wanting to die. The grass was her only comfort, soft and damp. 'Collie, I need you,' she whispered to no one, feeling the first cramps in her arms and legs, knowing the dope she had taken from him must have been cut too much, weakened. She was coming down, and soon the really bad pain would begin. She had no money, nowhere to go, no one to turn to.

'Peter,' she whispered, face pressed so hard into the grass that she could feel soil on her tongue. 'Peter, I need you….'

28

COMPANIONS

'No, you've put them back incorrectly,' Alfred scolded, as Lilian stood nearby, head lowered, hands in front of her stomach, one over the other. 'Do it again, please.'

June, watching from a doorway farther down the hall, could sense Lilian's frustration, but to her credit, the girl just nodded.

'Yes, Grandfather.'

'I'd prefer to be called Mr. Lammonby while we are on duty,' Alfred said, and June rolled her eyes, wanting to shake some sense into the old fool. This time, Lilian said nothing, but Alfred gave a stern nod and walked off, turning a corner and heading down a set of stairs to the ground floor.

Lilian stood looking at her hands in front of the dresser, the glass doors still open, a line of ancient vases inside. June watched her for a moment then wandered over.

'What's going on between you two?' she asked.

Lilian looked up, tears in her eyes. 'Nothing,' she said.

'Don't give me that. I've been married to that old fool for forty-seven years. I know when something's up.'

Lilian tried to turn away, but June reached out and took her arm. Lilian visibly flinched. Something in June's heart broke.

'I'm sorry … I didn't mean to—'

'We had words about the Master,' Lilian said, not looking around. 'I said harsh words about him. I spoke out of turn.'

June moved closer. 'None he doesn't deserve.'

'Maybe so, but Grandfather … he … he does his best.'

'I'll talk to him.'

She left Lilian to her cleaning, and headed through the halls of Carlton Manor in pursuit of Alfred, but could find him nowhere. Perhaps he had gone out to the bunker, although supposedly it was now fully stocked and prepared, the generators checked, the water, heating, and electrical systems all fully operational. She peered out of a window into the gardens, but there was no sign of him walking over the grass. Her frustration growing, she headed down a service staircase to the ground floor, finally catching a glimpse of him on the patio outside the back window, where he was talking to Dave, the groundskeeper with a shotgun slung over his shoulder. Alfred's finger was poking and pointing in that accusatory manner, as though ticking Dave off for something. June was about to go outside and find out what was going on, when the service bell rang. Squeezing her eyes closed for a moment, she took a deep breath and headed for Lord Richard's study.

The room stank of alcohol and cigars. One curtain had been pulled open to allow in a little light, but the windows were closed, the room stuffy. Richard was sitting at a desk in the corner, a laptop computer open in front of him. On the screen, two girls groaned and writhed, their tinny moans echoing across the high, elegant ceiling. As June entered, Richard watched her for a couple of long seconds, then turned and slowly lowered the laptop's screen until the picture disappeared.

'You took your time,' he said. 'I expect punctual service. No one is irreplaceable.'

'I'm sorry, sir.'

'Don't let it happen again.' Richard lifted up a dogeared pad of paper. 'I've been doing some assessments,' he said. 'Brussells was good enough to let me know the rumours coming out of Marshdown. I think it might not be long before I need to take to my bunker until the worst is over. I've sent a message to Exeter, requesting that Ms. Melinda join me, but I have received no reply.' He grinned, and June wondered how much he had drunk. 'It sounds like a fucking war out there.'

'I'm sure the situation is under control, sir,' June said, not because she believed it, but because she could see him waiting for some kind of response.

'Bullshit to whether it is or isn't,' Richard said. 'Luckily my father was prepared for everything.' He shifted in his chair, knocking the butt of a cigar on to the floor. Ash spread out in a semi-circle around it before Richard kicked it away with his shoe.

'Will you be moving to your bunker soon, sir?' June asked.

Richard tilted his head. 'Looking to get rid of me?'

June took a step back and lowered her eyes. 'I was just inquiring, sir.'

Richard swiped his hand across the desk, knocking the notebook to the floor. 'Well, don't worry, you'll get your wish soon, *Mrs*. Lammonby. I've made a few decisions. The first is that yourself, your stumbling husband, and Brussells will remain above ground to both maintain the house and keep me updated on the situation beyond the boundaries of Carlton Manor.'

June forced herself to look disappointed. 'As you wish, sir.'

Only as she spoke did she realise what he had not said, and her blood ran cold. He could obviously tell from her expression what she now understood, for a thin, sadistic smile spread across his face.

'I will, however, require someone to assist me in the day to day running of the underground rooms,' he said. 'Ms. Weekes will accompany me into the bunker. I am sure there will be quite enough room for the two of us.' He tilted his head and smiled again. 'Would you like to tell her, or should I?'

Alfred sat on the edge of his bed, watching his hands shaking as they rested on his lap. It had started months ago, but over the last few days it had intensified, perhaps through stress or an excessive amount of hard physical labour. He didn't know what it was, but it wasn't good, and it didn't look like going away. The pains in his chest had been coming more frequently, too: at least once daily, sometimes three times or more, a sharp stabbing pain like someone was pressing needles into his heart and then jostling them around.

He couldn't let June or Lilian know. He had to stay strong for them, particularly if the rumours he was hearing from Dave were true. Dave, who got off the grounds a lot more frequently than the rest of them, had heard all kinds of tales out of Marshdown, and while Alfred suspected a lot of it was tall stories, he couldn't dispute that strange things had been happening.

The lack of television connection. Benjamin not showing up with the food order three times in a row, and not answering the phone on the few occasions when June had managed to get a dialing tone.

And then there was the man who had come out of the hedge.

The most important thing was not to panic. He remembered his old rugby master at school telling the team that most losses were inflicted when a team lost its formation. If you kept your shape, kept your formation, you could absorb most attacks.

It was advice Alfred had held onto for his whole life, and it segued neatly into the life of a butler at Carlton Manor. A butler's job was to maintain shape, keep his formation, no matter what. And that's what they needed to do.

He felt bad about scolding Lilian this morning, but the girl was starting to believe all the hype Dave was telling her. Alfred had seen her going down to Dave's cottage early in the morning, and had followed her once, only to see Dave teaching her how to hold and aim a shotgun. Later that day he had heard shots ring out from the woodland down there where Dave often hunted for game, too many shots to have been fired by one person.

Dave hadn't taken it well this morning when Alfred had told him that Lilian had too much work around the house to be messing about with guns, not to mention that it was dangerous. Dave, usually a mild-mannered man, had been quite rude, which hadn't helped with Alfred's stress levels. He had been thinking over the conversation ever since, and still felt a little upset about it. He did not have his head in the sand, and he was not stuck in the past. He was simply doing what he needed to do to keep Carlton Manor running. Surely Dave could understand that?'

It was nearly lunchtime. He would need to attend to Lord Richard soon, so he got up from the bed and went to the sink, where he washed his hands in cold water, hoping it might freeze the shaking. It didn't, but walking with his hands clasped behind his back made things a little more manageable, or less noticeable at least.

Downstairs, June was in the kitchen preparing the master's lunch, making far more noise than Alfred felt was necessary. As she noticed him standing in the doorway, she let out a little gasp and put a pot down on the stove with a hand clatter.

'There you are.'

'I'm sorry, I had things to attend to upstairs.'

June turned around, banging another pot down, every action it seemed part of an orchestra of discontent.

Alfred took a step forward. 'I know things haven't been easy—'

'That's an understatement.'

June turned around suddenly, walking towards him. She put out her hands and pulled his into hers. Alfred flinched, hoping she wouldn't feel the shaking, but her grip was strong, desperate.

'Alfred, we need to leave. Me, you, and Lilian. As soon as possible.'

'Huh. And go where? All we know is Carlton Manor. And if all these rumours even have a thread of truth, we're safer here than we are out there—'

'Are we, Alfred? Are you sure? All of us?'

'Yes, of course. Dave has a shotgun to scare off any trespassers, and there's Lord Evans's bunker if things get really desperate.'

'Richard has no intention of letting us in there with him,' June said. 'Not all of us at any rate.'

'*Lord* Richard,' Alfred began, as June scoffed and rolled

her eyes. 'It's important to maintain our standards … what do you mean, not all of us?'

'He told me that you, I, and Dave would stay in the house to keep an eye on it. He only wants Lilian to go down there with him.'

'Lilian? Well, that's good, at least that means she'll be safe—'

'Alfred, are you damn well blind?'

'June, please watch your language.'

'He *touches* her!'

Alfred frowned. 'He … what?'

'I've seen him. God knows what else he wants to do with her. You really think she'll be safe in there with him? Do you really? It's like putting a chicken into a fox's den and expecting nothing bad to happen. I won't let him, Alfred. I won't!'

Alfred stepped back, gently pulling his arms away from June's. 'No,' he said, frowning as he shook his head. 'He can't be doing that. We brought her here to protect her, to keep her safe.'

'And we're not doing a very good job, not with that … that *monster*.'

Alfred opened his mouth to protest, to tell June she was mistaken, but the words betrayed him. Deep in his heart he knew what June was telling him was true. He had seen the guarded look in Lilian's eyes, and her outburst the other day had contained more vitriol than he had thought was deserved at the time. She had used vulgar language, her eyes full of hate. Could it be true? Could Lord Richard really be doing that to his granddaughter?

'Alfred, where are you going?'

He continued to back away. 'I need some air, June. And a little time to think.'

The truth was, his hands were shaking worse than ever

before. His heart, too, seemed to be skipping beats, as though a fly had got caught in his chest and was desperately trying to get out. His vision felt blurry, his knees weak.

He managed to get out of the kitchen and out of June's sight just in time. He heard her calling him but managed to get through a side door before she caught up with him. Another couple of turns and he was outside, walking along the paved path behind Carlton Manor, heading for the gardens.

He took the path that led along the garden's edge, beneath the trees, where he would have most cover if June was looking for him. He followed the gentle arc of the main lawns—now worryingly overgrown—until he came to the hedgerow that separated it from the enclosed gardens, a series of smaller lawns on multiple levels, separated by little waist-high hedgerows. Beyond these he came to the meadow where the bunker was, an obvious path to the concrete entrance made in the grass by his feet, the trolley with the punctured tyre, and the wheelbarrow. Now, however, he carried on past, reaching the end of the meadow and climbing labouriously over a stile into the leafy woodland at the very end of the house's grounds.

Here, multiple trails led through the trees. Once, Lord Evans had given them names and coloured labels, in the hope of inviting primary school groups to visit the house and grounds, but he had died before his project got underway, and Lord Richard had let the plan fade. A couple of rotten wooden stakes were all that remained, the embossed markers indicating Rabbit Trail or Mushroom Walk now broken, chipped, or covered with moss and lichen.

Alfred knew them all by heart, though, and didn't need to see them to follow the trail once known as Lookout

Point Way. It meandered through the trees, gradually sloping uphill to the top of the highest point of the property, until it ended in a wide treeless area which had a panoramic view of the surrounding countryside. Once there had been a handful of picnic tables here, but only one remained intact, right by the very edge of the clearing, just before the slope dropped steeply away into thick forest.

Alfred had once lovingly considered this spot to be the edge of his world. The boundary of Carlton Manor's grounds lay one metre in front of him, at the top of the slope, and when he was younger Alfred had often come here to gaze out at the villages of Thistlewell and Dimble West which lay at opposite ends of the patchwork valley spread out before him. Little more than two clusters of houses each surrounding a church, he had often sat and watched the lights coming on in the houses as the sun went down though the trees behind him, thinking how lucky he was to live and work in such a majestic place as Carlton Manor, so elegant, so dignified, so … safe.

Now, as his old eyes looked down through the valley, he began to pick out the differences. A lorry lay overturned on the road that connected the two villages. The spire of Thistlewell's church had collapsed. Two houses in Dimble West were on fire.

Lord Evans had always feared some coming catastrophe. With one ear to the ground and the other in the secretive corridors of government and commerce, he had picked up on rumours that had encouraged him to build the bunker in the garden, even if mentions of his suspicions in Alfred's presence had been rare. It now looked like Lord Evans had been right, but Alfred had always felt that within the boundaries of Carlton Manor, they would be safe from the world's ills.

Until Lord Evans had died, and a devil had taken his place.

Alfred felt a sudden ache in his heart, and gripped the edge of the old table to steady himself. Flakes of wood came off in his fingers. His heart began to flutter, and his hands shook far worse than ever before, until the table was creaking beneath his grip.

Here, in the quiet woodland, where the ills of the world were yet to reach, would be a pleasant place to die. Perhaps to lie down on the earth, feel its coolness beneath him, and slowly fade away. As Alfred felt the shakes slowly subside, he knew his time wasn't quite done; he had one more task he needed to complete.

Taking his time, he climbed back to his feet, holding on to the picnic table to steady him. Then, moving slowly so as not to stumble or trip, he headed back towards the house, his eyes straight ahead, his thoughts on one thing only.

I have to protect my family.

29

CAPTIVES

CLAIRE MADE it to the door just as the two men started to climb out of the car. The heavy pub door opened outwards, and with Tim Parkson's help she was just pulling it closed as the man with the cricket bat looked up and shouted, 'Oi!'

'Pull!' Claire shouted, angry at the warped wood for refusing to close properly. She leaned back, but felt the weight of the man outside forcing his way in, and suddenly he was there, driving himself into the gap, podgy, jowly face contorted into a scowl, his cheeks flushed. For a moment they were face to face, and Claire's eyes traced the line of a snake tattoo that wound from underneath his left eye, back behind his ear, then he was through, forcing her to the ground.

'Miss!'

Tim reached for her, but the man's elbow came up, striking Tim in the face with a sickening blow. He gave a gurgling cry and twisted away, blood from his busted nose spraying across the cigarette-stained wallpaper.

'Who you got in here?' the man snapped, advancing as Claire kicked herself backwards away from him. The other man came in too, gun held across his waist, ignoring a moaning, slumped Tim as he marched down the hall into the bar.

'Get up,' Snake-Tattoo said to Claire, reaching down to grab her wrist and haul her up with one powerful jerk. Without letting go, he turned her around, then pushed her down the hall in front of him. 'Whoever you've got in here, call them together.'

'Please, we weren't stealing anything,' Claire protested as she was shoved hard in the back and found herself stumbling through the door into the bar, where several of the kids had gathered. There were Daisy, Jenny, and Mick, Ishy with her arm around Lisa's shoulders, Lisa who was crying, wiping her eyes with a sleeve. Tim was in the hall, hurt, but Danny and Connie had been with Claire. She had seen Danny go in through the door, but where was he now, and where was Connie?

'What the fuck is going on here?' Snake-Tattoo said, swishing his cricket bat through the air. 'Where is he?'

'We just arrived,' Claire said, pushing herself in front of the kids. 'We got attacked on the Clent Hills by … something.'

'Long way from the Clent Hills,' Snake-Tattoo said. Then, turning to the other man, he said, 'What do you reckon, Clay? Think they've got him hidden here somewhere?'

The man called Clay narrowed his eyes. Skin-headed but with a light beard, he had scars in his cheeks and a metal chain around his neck. He wore a dirty grey polo shirt that was a size too small, revealing bunched, threatening muscles beneath. He walked up to Claire and pushed her aside. Looking from one kid to another, his eyes settled on Mick.

'We're looking for a man called Trousers,' he said. 'So called because he has trouble keeping his on in the presence of other men's wives.'

Of all the kids to have asked, Mick was entirely the wrong one. He let out a brief chortle, before cutting it off. 'Huh, Trousers—'

Clay scowled. He started to turn away, then swung back towards Mick, the gun butt coming around, striking Mick in the stomach. He doubled over, wheezing.

'Think you're funny, cocksucker?' Clay lifted his gun, the butt looming over Mick's head.

'No!' Claire shouted. 'Leave him alone.'

'Why? Looks like you've got yourselves some deadwood here, darling.'

'I'm a school teacher and this is my class. We were in the middle of a school trip when we had some … trouble.'

Clay glared at her, but lowered his gun. Mick scrambled backwards, the side of the booth chair at his back.

'Pretty small class, darling.'

Claire met his eyes. 'That's because half of them are dead.'

Lisa let out a sudden loud sob.

'Shut her up,' Clay said, lifting the butt of his gun again. 'I fucking hate a sniveller. You do it, or I will.'

'Lisa, please, it's all right,' Claire said, putting up a hand, but Lisa was beyond comforting. She tried to cover her face with her hands, but her sobs broke through them, spittle landing on the carpet. Ishy tried to pull her down into a seat, but Lisa began to shake, hands flapping at her sides.

'Fuck this,' Clay said, pointing the butt of his gun like a spear at Lisa's head. Claire imaged her glasses smashing into her eyes, her forehead cracking open like a coconut, and some kind of protective mist came over her. She didn't know if she screamed or even made a sound, but she leapt forwards, grabbing Clay by the shoulder and pulling him back around.

She caught a glimpse of a scowl on his face, then the wind was leaving her and she was doubling over.

'Clay, for fuck's sake!' Snake-Tattoo said. 'We're not here for them.'

He had barely shrugged her off but the power in his arm had been immense. Crouching on the ground, clutching her stomach, Claire could only stare helplessly at her pupils while praying her breath returned.

When it did, she let out a desperate wheeze. 'We … saw … no one else.'

Clay rolled his eyes and stalked away across the room. 'So what next, Stitcher?

Stitcher scratched at the snake tattoo beside his eye, then turned to Claire. 'We're looking for the man who owns this place. You seen him about?'

Claire shook her head. 'We just got here.'

'On that bus out there?'

'Yes.'

'Why here?'

'It was … it seemed … safe.'

Stitcher smiled. 'That view turning on its head, is it?'

'We don't want any trouble.'

'Nor do me and my man Clay here. All we want is good Mr. Trousers, then we'll be on our way. You have a name?'

'Claire. Claire Hopgood.'

'Claire.' He smiled. 'That's nice. And what about that

piece over there?' He nodded towards Ishy. 'What's her name?'

'Please, they're just children.'

Stitcher lifted an eyebrow. 'I hope you're not suggesting that my colleague and I are anything less than honourable men? How dare you.' He said it with a smile on his lips, but the latent threat was obvious. Claire stared at him, not daring to speak.

Clay, spinning his shotgun on a finger like a gunslinger, walked behind the bar. 'Might as well have a drink while we wait,' he said, taking a glass from a shelf above the bar and pouring himself a large brandy. He lifted the bottle and peered at it, then gave an approving nod. 'Trousers got some good stuff. I imagine you get the posh tourist tours up here and all that. All that money floating around. No wonder he's out buying expensive gifts for other people's wives.' He lifted the glass and downed the contents in a single swallow, then poured another.

'So,' Stitcher said, turning to Claire, who was still crouched on the floor. 'We have a little situation here. What do you think we should do about it?'

'Just let us go. We'll get back on the bus and leave.'

Stitcher nodded. 'That's one suggestion. A pretty good one, although most of you look too young to drink, so there's not so much a problem of you getting through our winnings here. What else?'

'I—I—'

'Please just let us go,' Ishy said.

Stitcher stared at her for a long time. Then, eyes not leaving Ishy's face, he walked over to the table where she sat, the cricket bat tapping on the carpet, making a dull, ominous thud.

'Stand up,' he said.

Ishy squeezed Daisy's hand, then slowly got to her feet, eyes on Stitcher's.

'You're a bit of a mess,' Stitcher said. He reached out and tugged at the light sweater Ishy wore, stained with dirt and blood. 'Take it off.'

'Please—' Claire began, but Stitcher turned sharply, pointing the cricket bat at her face. 'Shut *up*.'

Behind the bar, a second glass of brandy in hand, Clay sniggered.

'Off,' Stitcher said to Ishy. 'Off … now.'

Claire stared, horrified. Ishy, face smeared with dirt and hair flecked with twigs, slowly pulled up the sweater and slipped it off, passing it to Daisy. Beneath she wore a GAP t-shirt tight over her attractive figure.

Stitcher gave an approving nod. 'Isn't that better?' He lifted a hand. 'Still a little dirt in your hair, though. How about we go upstairs together and see if the shower's working? Don't worry, I won't hurt you.' He ran a finger down her cheek. Ishy, trembling, stared at him. 'No, I won't hurt you at all. In fact, I'll treat you very, very nicely.'

A single tear ran down Ishy's cheek. Behind her, Daisy and Jenny didn't dare move. Mick stared dumbly at Stitcher from the floor, one hand still clutching his sore stomach. Lisa, sobbing, had her hand over her mouth to stifle the sound.

'Don't worry, your friends will be all right,' Stitcher said. 'My friend Mr. Clay here will look after them. Won't you, Clay?'

A chuckle. A glass lifted in a toast. 'Of course.'

'So, it's all good, isn't it?' Stitcher said. 'You do want to come with me, don't you?'

Ishy, bottom lip trembling, gave a barely perceptible nod.

Stitcher smiled. 'I thought so. Of course, you do. I'll take good care of you, young lady. I can promise you that.'

He reached out a hand. Claire willed Ishy to refuse, but knew in the darkest bottom of her heart that the girl had no choice. Ishy lifted a hand and Stitcher's closed around it. Dying inside as she watched Stitcher lead the child she had failed across the bar towards the hall and the stairs leading up to the guestrooms and the landlord's flat, it was all she could do not to scream. Just as Stitcher and Ishy reached the doorway, however, a loud thump came from beneath their feet.

With a snarl of anger, Clay threw his glass across the bar and stood up. The glass struck a table and shattered, brandy splashing across the carpet.

'That motherfucker's in the beer cellar. Let's go.'

A look of intense frustration passed across Stitcher's face. For a moment Claire thought he would ignore Clay and take Ishy upstairs anyway, then he shoved the girl away, back towards the others.

'None of you *move*.'

The two men went through an archway behind the bar. Clay bent down, lifting up something Claire couldn't see. She had briefly worked in a pub during her late teens, and remembered there being a trapdoor in the floor that led down to a cellar. This pub stood on flat ground, but perhaps there was a rear entrance they hadn't seen.

As Clay went first down a set of steps, Claire turned to the kids. 'Don't anyone do anything stupid,' she hissed.

'Miss, we can't stay here,' Mick said. Jenny, Daisy, and Lisa all nodded. Ishy, tears in her eyes, just stared straight ahead. Claire didn't want to think about what might be going through her mind. As though the horrors of the day hadn't been enough already.

'I know. I just—'

A thumping sound came from beneath their feet. Claire forced herself to stand, to take a couple of steps, to peer over the bar at the hatch. For a moment she thought about rushing around the bar and slamming it shut, dragging a table on top of it, perhaps. But there would be another entrance, outside somewhere, where the beer barrels were brought in.

'We could run for the bus, Miss,' Jenny said.

Claire glanced back at her. She was so pretty, less commercial than Ishy, but more homely, welcoming. Stitcher might have his eyes on Ishy, but if they didn't get out of this situation, sooner or later his eyes or Clay's would turn to Jenny. Lisa and Daisy were plainer and might avoid it, and Connie, wherever she had gone, was out of their firing line, but Ishy and Jenny … Claire had recognised the look in Stitcher's eyes. He might once have been restrained by society's rules, but the lines had been redrawn, and he knew it.

She looked around for something she could use as a weapon. This was a pub, there had to be something.

Of course.

Behind the bar were a line of heavy, potentially skull-breaking objects that would serve perfectly well as weapons.

She chose what was left of Clay's bottle of brandy, because it felt appropriate. As she hefted it in her hand, movement came at her shoulder and she glanced up to see Mick standing there, hands out.

She passed him a bottle of rum.

'Do not hesitate,' she whispered, wondering if she could take her own advice. Then, turning to the four girls, she hissed, 'Go out to the bus. Take Tim with you, and if you find Connie and Danny, take them, too. We'll come as soon as we can.'

'What if you don't, Miss?' Lisa said.

'Have any of you started driving lessons yet?'

'It's a bus, Miss!' Jenny whined.

'But it works the same. The key's in the ignition. If we don't come, or if they do, get away. Anywhere. Just get away.'

Her words sounded weak, insubstantial. If this had been a film there might have been some dramatic music playing, the growing moan of cello, the rising shriek of a violin. In the silence of the bar, she could hear her voice tremble, and no doubt the kids had heard it too.

As they opened the door to the hall, she caught a glimpse of Tim, slumped against the wall, his face crusted with blood. He looked like he was sleeping. As the girls crowded round him, she crept closer to the hatch, positioning herself behind it, ready for whoever came up first, hoping it was Clay with his gun. If she could just hit him then maybe grab it—

Voices were approaching, and almost immediately Claire knew something was very wrong. A shape appeared below her, climbing the stepladder up from the cellar as a torchlight flickered below. She lifted the bottle, ready to strike, then dropped it as the figure came into the light streaming through the bar windows.

Even then, as he turned towards her, it was his figure she recognised more than his face, which was battered and crusted with blood. One eye was closed completely, but in the other she saw a look of hopelessness.

'Why didn't you run?' Danny said, his voice little more than a gargle. 'I thought you'd run.'

Someone pushed him from behind, and he stumbled forwards, almost into Mick's arms. Claire, still holding the bottle above her head, looked down at the muzzle of Clay's shotgun. Above it, his face materialised out of the trapdoor's gloom.

'Well, look what's going on here,' Clay muttered, as Claire, her courage fleeing like rats leaping from a sinking ship into the sea, dropped the bottle. It landed on its neck, breaking off, the brandy spreading out across the floorboards. 'You, darling, just made a very big mistake.'

30

DOCTOR

Kenny had never really known his mother. Graham had told him a few things, mostly bitter anecdotes which had done nothing but paint a dark, grey-smeared picture to accompany the few memories Kenny still had. None of them were good. None. There hadn't been a time before, when she'd held him in her arms and cooed softly, told him she loved him before the shit took her over, she'd been a fucking bitch from the moment he was born, as far as he could tell. He had one dark memory of standing in the middle of a circle of leering, scowling people while smoke clouded about the ceiling above them. One had been his mother, the others people he didn't recognise. They had been laughing, pushing him back and forth, telling him to dance, making him repeat things, vile things. Then one man, fleshless, all bones and skin so white it was like he'd been carved out of ivory, pulled his dick out, this dirty, throbbing thing. He'd handed something to Kenny's mother, then stood up, taken Kenny's hand, and led Kenny out of the room.

What had happened after that, Kenny didn't know. It

was like a veil had gone down. His mind had blocked it so entirely he felt sure he was safe from it.

But there was worse.

The one that hurt more than the rest, the one that broke him, had been the day he had been whining for food, or toilet, or something he no longer remembered clearly. He had been perhaps four. His mother had screamed at him, tried to strike him with her weak, druggy flails like she always did, then got up and shooed him out of the room. When he had come back, desperation forcing him, she had taken a black bin liner off a roll, ripped a hole in it and pulled it over his head, covering him like a sleek, shiny dress. Then she had pushed him to the front door, opened it, and shoved him outside.

For a while he had beaten at the door, wanting to get let back in. A while after that, he had begun to wonder why he wanted to go back inside, and had simply sat on the step and cried, waiting for salvation.

And it had come.

He didn't know how long he had sat there. Hours, maybe. Graham had arrived with something for his mother and her friends, and seen him outside. He had asked Kenny what he was doing. Just waiting, Kenny had told him. Graham had nodded, then gone inside.

Twenty minutes later he had emerged, held his hand out for Kenny, and taken him away.

For reasons Kenny couldn't understand, for a while he had cried for his mother. Then, over time, with Graham offering food, comfort, and a soft, warm bed all of his own, he had started to forget her.

Graham hadn't been kind. There had been no bedtime stories or hugs when Kenny cried. But there had been safety, and over time, Kenny had begun to look on

Graham as something in a similar but different mould to that of a parent: as a mentor.

Not once had Graham ever lifted a hand to Kenny, but he had taught Kenny when he might need to raise a hand to someone else, when it was better to fight, or better to run. He had shown Kenny how to live when there was no money to buy what you needed, how to read someone's face to decide whether to trust or hold suspicion. Kenny could only read what he needed to, could only understand rudimentary maths. He knew nothing of history or geography, could name no more than twenty foreign countries. There might as well be nowhere beyond London.

But he knew survival. And right now, he wanted to survive.

The girl, Emily, she was one of those entitled look-at-me types, the kind that threw tantrums and got in trouble at school without realising how lucky they were just to go to school in the first place. The kind who wore stupid clothes because they wanted to *make a point*, rather than wearing clothes because that's all they had, all they could steal, all they could find. The kind of girl who had been mollycoddled her entire life and learned no discernible life skills, yet thought she knew everything. The kind who could step in front of a train and have the gall to expect the train to stop.

Yet still, he kind of liked her. She had fought for her mother, and that was something he could respect. And being near her, it was filling a void. For years, it had been Graham and him, together against the world. He knew Graham had had other friends, because Graham had often gone out, coming back sometimes with goods, or money, or even bruises, but he kept Kenny out of it. Kenny was his secret, his thing to protect.

Now Graham was gone, and Kenny felt a loneliness like nothing else in the world. It was like a knife stuck in his back, twisting back and forth, one he couldn't reach to pull out. And the girl, in a way, was helping to ease it.

'It's not far,' he said, not knowing what else to say.

The girl had also run out of things to say and just followed behind him, puffing, out of breath, like she'd never so much as ran to cross the street. She wasn't fat like many of the greasy, overfed elephants he saw walking around these days, but she had a roll around her belly underneath the dumb clothes she wore, a roll she'd probably earned while bitching on her phone to her weirdo friends.

The street was a fucking mess. Cars blocked all the roads, like people had suddenly forgotten how to drive straight. In a few places there was evidence of explosions: craters in the road, a building on fire, another with a semi-circle of masonry carved out. But much of it looked like disorganised chaos, like people had all got up and once and decided to run in different directions.

From time to time they saw people too, in the distance, running between cars, some even peering out of windows, too afraid to leave. There were plenty of dead. Some had been killed by cars or bombs, their bodies twisted, limbs ripped off. Others had been partially eaten, their bodies opened up, clothes ripped away, faces reduced to bare skulls. Some just lay there, dead for no clear reason, arms spread out as though they'd given up.

Graham had always said in any adversarial situation you had to identify your enemy. You couldn't fight unless you knew who you needed to fight, and in a situation where that enemy was undefined, you played it safe: everyone was the enemy. Who had dropped the bombs, who had let the animals out, and whether or not the answer to that was the same, it didn't matter. They had to avoid both.

A terrific boom came from a couple of streets away, and above them, windows blew out of a block of flats. Kenny grabbed Emily and pulled her into the building's lobby as deadly shards of glass rained down, shattering on the pavement. Further up the street, someone screamed, revolved in a bloody, sparkling pirouette, and collapsed out of sight between two jammed cars.

Emily shrugged off Kenny's hand, but her eyes thanked him.

'It's not far,' he said again.

They waited until the cascade of debris had stopped, then Kenny led Emily farther up the street, pausing at the next corner beneath the overhang of a shop front with its windows blown out. Dusty mannequins, their display clothing shredded, hung out into the street.

Marvin's building was down here, an abandoned tenement, the front boarded up, set for demolition on some unconfirmed future date. There was an alley alongside, clogged with bins. Kenny pointed, then reached for Emily's arm. She pulled it away, but nodded.

At the far end of the street, something the size of a bus broke from a gap between buildings, leaned its sofa-sized head forward, and scooped a running man up between two rows of swordlike teeth. Kenny held his breath, held his bladder, as the man was split soundlessly into two. As the monster leaned down to collect the pieces, he forced jelly-like legs to move, not daring to look back, trusting that Emily had followed.

As he reached the alley, she bumped into him. This time, it was her hands clutching his arm.

'It's … not … far,' Kenny said.

The entrance was at the end of the alley, a metal

service door that slid back, but only if you know at what point to lift it a little, to take its weight. Kenny stepped back, waving Emily into the dark opening.

Marvin lived on something like the fifteenth floor, but Kenny couldn't be sure because on the handful of occasions Graham had brought him here, he always miscounted as they climbed the concrete steps, the lifts long out of use. And Marvin tended to move around, too, perhaps when one place got too trashed, or a gang moved in and took over another. The last time Kenny had been here, after contracting some kind of infection, he had found Marvin had newly moved, most of his stuff in boxes. Graham had paid, though, and Marvin had found what he needed.

Now, though, as they climbed up through the dusty, piss-smelling spine of the building, Kenny's doubts started to creep in. What if Marvin was gone? Or worse, what if Marvin was dead? The girl was trusting him. It felt weird, but he liked it. And he didn't want to let her down.

And then, he turned a corner to see a landing through a doorless entrance, strewn with rubbish and junk. A cat, thin, uncared for but tame, looked at him with disdain for a moment, then wandered off between two boxes. Kenny let out a sigh of relief. Marvin liked cats. He was still here.

Kenny looked back. Emily was a few steps below him, giving herself room to run. It was all right; he would have likely acted the same.

'You can wait here if you like,' he said. 'But he's here. I know it.'

'Are you sure this guy can help my mother?'

There was no point in lying to her. 'He might. He might not. But we're here now so let's find out.'

The girl looked about to say something, but he could tell from the way her jaw went hard that she was biting her tongue, holding back the barbs she wanted to spit at him. Her mother meant too much to blow this chance, slim though it might be. Kenny churned inside; he was terrified too, of proving a disappointment.

Turning away, he headed up the corridor. A cat scampered out from a pile of rubbish and danced across his path; for a moment his heart lurched, thinking it was one of those creatures. He walked past closed doors, past heaps of rubbish piled up for seemingly no reason. Perhaps to make the place look abandoned. Perhaps not.

'Doctor?' he called as he reached the first open door. 'Doctor? Are you there? It's Kenny. Graham's boy.'

There was nothing but the distant rumble of exploding bombs to answer him. He walked on, to the next open door. This time he peered through into a cluttered apartment, a series of small rooms connected by corridors so full of junk you could barely squeeze through. He peered into a bedroom, then pulled away, wishing he hadn't. Something had been lying on the bed, something that had been cut open. Something that might have once been alive but had died, something human-shaped. As Emily came in behind him, he put up her hands, shaking his head.

'He's not here,' he said, unable to meet her eyes.

He herded her out into the corridor and carried on, picking his way through the rubbish as the occasional cat hissed at him or leapt out of nowhere to run into an open doorway or some cavity behind a pile of boxes. Shaken by what he had seen, he could only force it out of his mind when a voice frighteningly close said, 'What do you want?'

He stopped. It had come from a doorway to his right. Kenny froze as the crunch of footsteps over something hard but brittle came closer. A shadow fell over the corridor and then Marvin stood there, Doctor Marvin, as Graham had always called him.

Marvin wore a faded black rock band t-shirt that struggled to contain his gut. His hair and beard had grown out, his beard patchy from scars along his jaw. Tattoos of snakes and strange symbols smudged podgy forearms. His belly overflowed jeans belted too tight, and dark stains covered the thighs. He watched Kenny out of beady eyes, mouth chewing on something. One hand reached up as his mouth opened and pulled out a bone which he tossed to the ground.

'Kenny,' he said. 'I remember you. What do you want?'

Kenny waved at Emily, who stared at Marvin with a look of horror. 'This is my friend. Her mother got hurt. It's bad. We need your help. Please, Doctor.'

Marvin nodded. He looked Emily up and down. 'What kind of injury?'

'It's a—'

'I'm asking her.'

Kenny shut up. Emily glanced at him, then opened her mouth awkwardly, as though not expecting to have to speak.

'It's … a … some kind of impact wound. Her leg. We were in a tunnel when the roof collapsed on our car.'

'Where is she? I don't see her here. What do you expect me to do?'

'She couldn't make it. She's outside, on the other side of the park.'

'Are you fucking serious?'

Emily began to tear up. Kenny looked away, playing with his hands.

'She couldn't make it any further,' Emily said. 'But she's safe. We locked her inside a car. Please. Please help her.'

'If she can walk at all, it might not be too serious,' Marvin said, still staring at Emily. 'I have a set of braces, some antibiotics. Painkillers.' He shrugged. 'The best you can do right now.'

'Anything you can do until we can get her to a proper hospital—'

'Ha.' Marvin's severed laugh was like a knife blade cutting through the air. 'You think there's even such a thing anymore?'

Kenny glanced at Emily. She had tears in her eyes. He quickly looked away.

'Anything you can do,' she repeated.

Marvin nodded. He reached out and drummed his fingers against the doorframe. 'Yeah. Might help. Might do for now.'

'Thank you so much. Can I take you to her?'

'How are you gonna pay?'

Kenny looked up. Emily had already gone a couple of steps, as though the rescue mission was already underway. She turned back, lowering her head like kid caught shoplifting. After a pause, she said, 'My mother has a credit card—'

'You think money's much use to me?'

'I—I—'

'The world has changed, young lady,' Marvin said, eyes not leaving hers. He waved his loose hand around. 'Things seem to have regressed, rather more quickly than anyone might have expected. We've gone back in time, quite literally, by the look of things. Money ain't a thing anymore. All that matters now is goods and services. An exchange of skills, so to speak. And I ask you again: how are you gonna pay?'

Emily's mouth worked soundlessly. Kenny watched her, too afraid to speak. Marvin smiled, then stepped back. He kicked out, pushed away some of the rubbish that was holding the door open.

'Come in for a bit,' he said. 'And we can discuss things in a little more detail.'

For a long time, Kenny didn't think Emily would move. She stared at the scuffed shoes Marvin wore, arms folded protectively across her chest. Part of Kenny was willing her to refuse, to stay out here with him. Then, with a slumped step forward like she was pulling herself out of glue, she walked forwards, not looking up, into the bowels of Marvin's flat. Marvin smiled. Kenny started to follow her, but Marvin stood up, blocking him, shaking his head.

'You stay here,' he said, smile dropping, eyes heavy with menace, and Kenny could do nothing but stand and watch as Marvin, smile returning now, stepped inside, and pulled the door shut behind him. The lock clicked, and Kenny, standing alone in the corridor except for a couple of wandering cats, felt something in his heart crack.

Alan
Graf

31

VIGILANTES

ALAN CRACKED OPEN the door and peered outside. It had been a couple of hours since the last explosion, and the city had fallen quiet. In this part of the city, many of the street lights were solar powered, leaving the streets illuminated by a dim glow, but the lack of lights in the houses up and down the street was stark. At the far end of the street, flames flickered in the windows of an upstairs flat, but across the street from Alan the long terrace was a dark, silent sentinel.

Ellis was sleeping upstairs in Dad's old bedroom. Alan had been reluctant to let the boy use Dad's bed, but his attempts to get Ellis to sleep on the sofa had failed, the boy complaining of nervousness so close to the front door. Alan had given him a rubber door stop to push under the foot of the bedroom door, and then dug out an old music box from a cupboard and given it to the boy. The gentle twinkling music had brought bittersweet tears to his eyes, reminding him as it did of his early childhood, and of Mum tucking him into bed, before the drink and the depression had turned her bad, but it had calmed Ellis enough that he had wished Alan goodnight and taken himself to bed.

Downstairs, Alan had checked on Dad, doing what he could to keep the old man comfortable, before returning to the kitchen to drink tea and listen to the radio.

Now, nearing midnight, he thought he might never sleep again.

He closed the door behind him, pocketing the key. As though afraid of snipers, their crosshairs zoning in on his forehead, he shifted from side to side as he took one tentative step, then another, slowly making his way down the steps from his front door to the pavement. Twenty feet from his front door he had a sudden panic attack, and nearly bolted back up the steps. He was a professional nurse; he understood the difference between caution and recklessness, and after what he had witnessed today his actions were firmly in the latter. He had tried—and tried to convince himself that he wanted—to stay in the house, keeping an ear to whatever developments were unfolding, ready to act when the situation required it, but found it impossible to sit still. When an emergency situation arose in the hospital, you acted, decisively and immediately. Sitting back, waiting for things to happen, left people dead.

He couldn't bring himself to cross the street, so stayed close to the line of garden walls along his side, most of them above his head, ducking into the alcoves of other stairways at the slightest sound.

Alan had always kept himself to himself, and his interactions with his neighbours had been rare. The electricity had gone off on his side of the street shortly after Ellis had gone to bed. Now, with the power out, he spotted the odd flickering light in other windows, from fires or gas lamps, perhaps. Most houses looked deserted—some even had doors standing wide open—but it gave him some comfort to know that he and Ellis weren't alone, despite the collapsed buildings just past the junction, and the car pile-ups that had blocked whole lines of traffic.

Eventually he reached the street corner. The tyrannosaur—for that had surely been what it was, despite all his years of logic telling him it should be otherwise—had come from that way, and now he crouched down beside a low, curving corner wall, fearful that another might appear.

The street, though, remained dark and silent, so after a couple of minutes of barely allowing himself to breathe, he hurried across the road to the ruins of Ellis's family's building.

There was barely anything left to prove it had once been somewhere filled with life. Whatever had struck it had barely left two bricks together. The nearest streetlight was across the road, so Alan wasn't about to go clambering over the rubble. Somewhere up there Ellis had pulled a severed human arm out of the debris, but after seeing the dinosaur Ellis had never mentioned it again, as though one shock had been overwhelmed by another. Ellis had only asked Alan to find his parents, so Alan had let the boy hold on to the comforting blanket of hope, even while it flamed in his hands.

Now though, hollow as his promise had been, he hoped in part to keep it. He pulled a sheet of paper out of his pocket and slid it into a clear plastic file. He couldn't read it in the dark but he remembered exactly what it said: *To the parents of Ellis Webster: if you're looking for your boy, he's safe. He's at my house.* Then he had added his address, and before realising the phones were out, his number too. Then he had signed it *Alan Graf.*

He pulled a claw hammer from a belt loop on his side and a nail from his pocket. He walked up to the sturdiest looking peace of masonry, found a crack, then positioned the nail over the middle of the paper and gave it a tap. The nail slid into the crack, holding the paper in place. The sound, light as it was, echoed up the empty street.

Not wanting to overstay his welcome, Alan retreated back across the road, crouching down by the wall as he had before. Now he was over his initial terror, an old, childlike curiosity began to take hold, a need to know what was going on. Instead of going back up Porter Street to his house, he headed west down Abbot Street, in the direction of Edgbaston Cricket Ground.

He was barely out of sight of Porter Street, however, when he heard voices from up ahead.

Instinctively he lifted the latch of the nearest gate and made to slip through, but the hinge gave an alarming creak, making Alan jump back. He was still standing with one hand on the gate when a group of men appeared from out of a junction a couple of doors down.

Some carried large, powerful torches. One near the back held up a gas lamp on a stick, like something out of Victorian Britain. Several had crude weapons: knives, broken table legs, cricket bats. One carried a garden fork over his shoulder like a Legionary's spear.

They turned Alan's way, a couple spreading out into the street as though to block the way through. One thumped an arm on the driver's window of a car parked at an angle across the street as though to wake a sleeping driver. With so much light, there was no way Alan could hide, and he wasn't so young that if he ran they couldn't chase him down. He was left with no choice but to make his presence known.

He lifted a hand. 'A good evening to you all.'

Those at the front of the group stopped. A murmur passed through them, and for a moment Alan wondered if they might flee. Then, a tall, overweight man took a few steps forward. His hair had receded back to the top of his head, and couple of days of stubble spotted a jowly neck. He had forearms thicker than his biceps, the kind of man who trucked for a living, hauling heavy pallets from Plymouth up to Glasgow.

'You're brave to be out here alone,' the man said. He had a hint of a Brummie accent, a man who had perhaps grown up on one of the estates.

'I wondered what was going on,' Alan said.

'You and us both,' the man said. 'You see anything untoward?'

Alan thought of terrifying monsters both large and small, of demolished houses, of severed limbs. He could bring himself to speak of none of it.

'Some,' he said.

The man nodded. 'There's some shit going down. We've taken it upon ourselves to keep our streets safe.'

'Thank you,' Alan said. He took a couple of steps back. 'I'd better get back to my … father.'

The man clearly read something in Alan's words. 'He's old? You're a carer?'

Alan nodded. 'Yes.'

Another man stepped up beside the ringleader. He was younger and much thinner, but no less haggard, a man from the construction sites, wiry, tough.

'What's wrong with him then?'

Alan picked his words carefully. 'Dementia. And respiratory issues.'

'You got gear?' the second man said.

'Gear?'

'Yeah, gear.'

'He means medical supplies,' the first man said. 'They

hit the hospital, blew the shit out of it. No one knows why, but we're gonna have to make do with what we can find.'

Alan's heart sank. 'It was destroyed?'

'You might have heard rumours that there's crazy things roaming the streets,' the first man said. 'But we seen men fighting men. Tanks pointing at other tanks.'

'Where have people been going?' Alan said.

'The net said south was safety, before it went down. Most people heading that way. The cities are choked, though. Out on the motorways they're walking thirty wide. Never seen anything like it.'

'Like a fucking buffet,' a third man said as he pushed through a gate and headed up a path to a nearby front door that stood ajar. He nudged it with the handle of a garden fork. The light of the gas lamp held above their heads illuminated several knives hanging from his belt. One glistened with something fresh and wet that left a brownish stain on his jeans.

'So, you got gear or what?' the second man said. 'Wanna show us? We're gonna need to start stockpiling, bringing our resources together, especially if we ain't gonna leave.'

'We've decided to stay in the city,' the first man said. 'This is our city, and we want it back. Are you with us?'

'I'm going nowhere,' Alan said. 'Even if I wanted to, my father—'

'You live nearby?' the second man said.

'Not far,' Alan said, starting to feel a little nervous, wishing he'd gone straight back after all.

'Wanna poke around in here?' the third man said from the doorway, kicking the door open and shining a torch into a tidy hallway with a pale green carpet and floral wallpaper. 'Mrs. Tressick,' he added, nudging a letter lying just inside the door. 'NHS logo. Might have some antibiotics or something.'

'I'll go with this guy,' the second man said, patting Alan on the shoulder a little harder than was comfortable.

'Lee, leave him,' the first man said. 'We'll go door to door tomorrow.'

'If there is a tomorrow,' Lee said. 'I say we go now.'

'Get to cover!' someone at the back of the group suddenly shouted. 'There's one coming!'

Alan didn't know what the "one" in question might be, but as several men dived behind parked cars, and others ran into gardens, a couple even following the third man into Mrs. Tressick's house, he took the chance to get away. He turned and bolted up the street, not pausing nor looking back until he reached the corner of Porter Road and Abbott Street. There, he leaned on a wall and paused to take a breath. It had been years since he'd run so fast, and was so out of breath that he didn't hear the running footsteps until they were nearly upon him.

There was nowhere to hide. He looked up, saw a bobbing torch, caught a glimpse of Lee's face behind the glare. Lee came up behind him, stopped and grabbed Alan by the shoulder, grinning into his face.

'Hey there, friend,' he said. 'What made you leave so fast? Nothing to be afraid of, you know. We've got it under control. But since we're here, I'm guessing you live nearby? How's about we go and check out your stash? We're gonna need everything we can if things keep getting worse. You can't be keeping things to yourself.'

Alan thought of Dad, lying inert, the wound on his leg. If it was true the hospital had been bombed, it might be more difficult to get stronger antibiotics than he had hoped.

Everything was uncertain, but one thing he knew for

sure was that he was not letting this man over the threshold of his house.

'It's this way,' he said, pointing across the road, further up Abbott Street, past Ellis's demolished terrace. His heart was thundering as hard as it ever had in any emergency situation, but like he did when assisting in the operating theatre, Alan felt wired, alert. He needed to buy himself time, so he started across the street, Lee beside him, still holding on to his shoulder, strong, wiry fingers digging through Alan's sweater.

'Caring is sharing,' Lee said. 'You're a good man. What's your name?'

Alan hesitated. Lee's fingers squeezed tighter. Creativity wasn't Alan's strong point. He thought of the film Ellis had been watching.

'Ha … ha … Harold,' he said.

'Well, *Harold*, let's hope we're nearly there.'

'Yes.'

At the end of Abbott Street there was a small park. Alan wondered if he could give Lee the slip there. Lee was faster, stronger, and tuned for the situation. Alan could only keep walking forwards, hoping for an opportunity to present itself.

Somewhere in the distance a flash of light lit up the nearby rooftops. A moment later a massive boom rattled windows and shook trees.

'Here they go again,' Lee said. 'I think I might need to crash at yours tonight.' His fingers gave another threatening squeeze. 'That cool?'

Alan stumbled as Lee pushed a little too hard, and put out a hand to steady himself against the front wall of the adjacent garden. A piece of paving that topped the wall felt loose in his hand.

When called to action in the operating room, to

hesitate meant a critical patient might die. Alan saw his opportunity. He slipped a finger under the bottom edge of the piece of slab and pulled it upwards, aiming over his shoulder, for Lee's face.

It was heavier than he had expected, and the speed he might have needed to make a decisive blow wasn't there. The chunk of paving slab, about the size of a dinner plate, caught Lee across the side of the face, but its momentum took it out of Alan's hands. It fell to the pavement and broke in two.

Lee cried out and stumbled away, clutching his face. When he pulled his hand away it was slick with blood. He groaned in pain and shook his hand, blood splattering the pavement.

'You old fucking prick.'

Lee reached under his belt and pulled out a knife. Alan backed away, bumping against the wall behind, and something pressed into his hip.

The claw hammer. In his panic he had forgotten it was even there. As Lee came forwards quickly, far too quickly, Alan reached for it, struggling to pull it free. Lee's hands came up with the knife angled sideways, as though to cut through Alan's throat, and Alan swung his arm up in a desperate arc, the hammer building momentum and speed.

It struck the side of Lee's forehead with a hollow crack. Lee barely even cried out, just let out a dull grunt and sunk to his knees, the knife falling out of his hands. As Lee knelt at his feet, Alan lifted the hammer again to deliver another blow, but Lee, staring straight ahead, was defenseless now, and Alan could only watch as the hammer fell from his shaking fingers. As Lee, one hand clutching the side of his head, slumped forwards, Alan turned and ran.

He cleaned the blood off himself as best he could. Then, after locking and bolting the door, he sat in the kitchen with a cup of tea, three extra sugars for his nerves, and tried to clear what had happened out of his mind.

Dad was stable. And upstairs, Ellis was still asleep.

He had done what he had to do, but the memory of it, of the feeling of necessity, of the weight of first the piece of paving and then the claw hammer in his hands, the thud as the blows struck, it would haunt him.

He was still sitting at the table, sometime long after midnight, when a muffled shriek came from the street outside.

Alan crept to the living room window, cracked open the curtain and peered out.

Porter Road was gloomy, only a couple of solar street lights working, but after a moment the figure stumbled into view. He was staggering, pushing himself back and forth between parked cars, as though he were drunk. His face was a sheen of crimson, that in the gloom looked black, just one eye peering out.

'Harold?' he screamed, his voice slurring. 'Harold! Where are you? I'll find you, you bastard!'

He staggered across the street, and banged on a door, then stumbled back out, walked a few metres, picked another door at random, and this time rattled the handle.

'Harold, where are you?'

Alan gently lowered the curtain, his heart thundering. Then he crept back through his dark house, into his utility room at the rear, wondering if he had some boards he could nail up over the windows.

32

BIGGER

After the slaughter, the town went quiet for a while. Mark waited until he felt sure the last of the dinosaurs was dead or fled back out on to the moor, then he crept from house to house, finding clothes that would fit: jeans, a shirt, a decent thick outdoor sweater. He found a small rucksack and filled it with anything useful he could scavenge, a pen knife, a Zippo lighter with a phoenix design which felt somehow appropriate, even a compass. He took a solid, serrated garden knife with its own case, climber's fingerless gloves, a collapsible runner's water pouch. He stuffed some spare clothes into a rucksack, then as much dried food as he could carry.

As dawn light began to stream through the windows of a cottage where he found a bagged rain jacket and a small gas camping stove, he crawled into a narrow loft space, rolled a blanket up under his head, and slept.

When he woke up sometime in midmorning and crept outside, he found the soldiers had gone.

Was it worth checking the prison buildings for any real weapons? Perhaps the soldiers had left something behind, or he could scavenge some batons or pepper spray off the bodies of the guards.

In his cell he had kept a picture of his family. Amanda, his wife, his children Hannah and Evan. In the picture the kids were younger, still in primary school. Amanda was yet to get grey strands in her hair.

It was more important to him than any weapon, but still, he couldn't bring himself to go back in there.

Better would be to find them, in case what had happened around here spread.

A sudden flush of panic struck him. What if what was happening had *spread here* … from somewhere else? Dartmoor was isolated, a wilderness; if there had been an outbreak of some kind, a quarantine situation, it would be logical to have happened here.

They had lived in a quiet village outside of Exeter before what had happened. Mark knew the way, if he could find transport. He could be there in an hour.

But what if he was safer here than there? What if, beyond Dartmoor, the world had already gone to shit?

He held onto a doorframe, leaning over, waiting until his heart slowed. The thought of finding a world beyond this hell had kept him focused, but the thought of finding nothing but more devastation … he almost couldn't bear it.

Focus, focus, focus….

He would find them, and if they were alive—*they have to be they have to be they have to be*—he would keep them safe.

The solders had made a mess of the town, looting and pillaging. Most cars had gone, taken by their fleeing owners, and many of those that remained had been torched or battered into uselessness by passing tanks. Certain that he was the last living person in Princetown, Mark wandered the streets, checking whatever cars he could find for keys or simple enough mechanisms that he could hotwire. After an hour, though, he had found nothing, and was beginning to despair that his only method of transport would be a bicycle.

Then, as he approached the end of a narrow street that led out on to the moor, he came to the wide red door of a closed garage. The lock had been bashed in an attempt at entry, but for whatever reason the soldiers had been distracted before the job had been completed. Mark lowered his bag, lifted his club, and stuck the lock with all his might.

An almighty clang echoed out across the street. Mark paused, looking around, watching for any sign of movement. When none came, he turned back to the door.

It had shifted slightly, dipping forwards. Mark leaned down and pulled it up.

At first he was disappointed. An old Ford Escort, tires a little soft, sat on one side of the garage, footprints in the dust space around it to show it was used regularly. He might be able to get it to go, but it wouldn't get far. The first roadblock and he'd be stuck.

There was something else, though, hidden under a thick blanket sheet to the car's left. The floor around it had been swept, the work surfaces tidied, a whole other level of care. Mark left his club propped up by the door and walked over, hauling back the sheet.

He couldn't help but smile.

A heavy-duty three-wheeler, tall handlebars, thick, powerful off-road tyres, amped up suspension for bouncing over rough terrain.

It was a moor-rider's dream, the kind of machine that

would devour the bumps and troughs of Dartmoor like a hungry dragon. The key, fitted with a jeweled snake keyring, hung in the ignition. Mark gave it a twist, and the powerful engine roared into life. The fuel gauge pointed to full. Mark retrieved his club, threw his bag into a rack at the back, and climbed on board.

The seat fitted him perfectly. It felt like fate.

~

He took a road leading northeast out of Princetown, heading across Dartmoor towards Moretonhampstead. He had gone no more than a couple of miles when he found the road blocked by overturned military vehicles, and brought the trike to a stop. There was no sign of any life, but a couple of mangled bodies lay in the road. Mark, club over his shoulder, walked closer.

Scorch marks covered the men's shredded clothes; bullet marks punctured their bodies. Mark nodded. Killed by men, eaten by monsters. The enemy took many forms.

He walked among the wreckage, collecting a handful of weapons and ammo, throwing it into the back of the trike.

The front lorry had been blown onto its side, its flatbed buckled, the result of a missile strike. Whatever nightmare was unfolding, it was as much man against man as man against beast. Afraid of being so near the target, Mark headed back to the trike.

From here, the road angled down across the rolling hills of Dartmoor, grey-green, bleak, punctured by rocky tors. As he turned the trike off the road to get around the ruined vehicles, he saw something that made his throat tighten, his heart lurch.

Far across the valley, a group of massive, long-necked

animals moved among the rocks. One lowered its head to drink from a stream, its tail rising as though to balance it. As it swung, it knocked against a stack of rocks, one boulder the size of a small car breaking away to bounce into the water.

This is a hallucination. This cannot be real.

One of the creatures lifted its head and bellowed at up at the sky. The sound was loud enough to rattle through the damaged vehicles. Mark moved the trike forwards, back onto the road. He wanted to leave, to get out of this place, but a childlike wonder filled him, and he couldn't draw his eyes away.

He had been a kid once. He had read books about prehistoric monsters just like all his schoolmates, played with plastic models. He'd had them eat toy soldiers, then be crushed by falling rocks. He'd picked up rocks at the bottom of the garden, scraped lines on them and tried to convince his parents they were fossils. And like all his school friends, he had seen Jurassic Park, marvelled at the CGI, wondered how it would feel to see such things in front of him in the flesh, wondered whether he would experience the same jaw-dropping wonder that the scientists had.

Now, seeing them down there at the bottom of the hill, all he felt was a dark, nagging terror. It wasn't just that they shouldn't be here, that these were things from another time and place, that they couldn't, shouldn't exist. It was far worse. He'd seen the scale models, the skeletons.

These things were *much bigger* than they ought to be. Much bigger than any scientist or museum had ever claimed.

As he watched one take hold of a gnarled tree trunk and rip the thing out of the earth with a shower of rocks and mud, he understood why.

These weren't ancient prehistoric beasts brought back to life. These were lab-designed, lab-made, lab-born.

These monsters were the creation of the worst monsters of all: humans.

And now they had been unleased upon the world.

Mark's hands shook as he climbed back on to the trike. He gunned the engine, the vehicle taking him away from them, towards what, only the devil himself might know.

33

STRANGER

JULIET WOKE to find natural light creeping in through cracks in the plywood partition wall that separated the back of Uncle Lawrence's van from the seats. She blinked, rolling over on the mattress, rubbing her arms against the numbing cold. Sitting up, she reached out for something made of material that was folded up in a corner. She hoped it was a blanket, but it was just an old curtain, crusted with patches of dried paint. Still, wrapping it around her shoulders, it kept the heat in, and slowly she began to warm up.

Having dealt with the cold, she found she really needed to pee. Remembering how she had ended up here last night, she didn't dare go outside, but the feeling was almost crippling, twisting in her gut.

There was no way she could go outside, because what if that thing was still there, but she couldn't just go in her knickers. That was what babies did.

She crept forwards, and slid one of the plywood boards back just a crack, until light stretched back into the van's corners. There was a pile of buckets in one corner, stacked one inside the other. It made Juliet squirm to think of herself peeing like that, but she was so desperate, it was either a bucket or wetting herself.

Pulling one free from the stack, she pulled her knickers down. The feeling of relief made her close her eyes with satisfaction.

When she was done, she pushed the bucket to the far back of the space and crept forwards again, sliding back the plywood and climbing into the front seats.

Uncle Lawrence's van was cramped, dirty, and smelled bad, but behind the windscreen glass she felt safe as she looked out at the lane ahead. It wound up between overgrown verges, arcing out of sight around a corner before it reached the road. Left, out of the passenger windows, her house was visible on the other side of the field that sloped down and then rose again, only a couple of hundred metres as the crow flew, but Uncle Lawrence had been attacked in there, so that way was out. She would have to go by the road, which would take much longer.

She peered out of the driver's window, towards the farmhouse. It had been empty for years, Dad said, but it was barely a stone's throw away. Juliet shook her head. The front door was closed, probably locked and bolted, the family who had lived here securing it before they moved away.

Having a sudden idea, she felt around the side of the steering wheel to see if Uncle Lawrence's keys were in the ignition. She'd never driven a car, but she'd watched Dad do it. If she could get the van to start—

No keys.

Juliet gave a quick shake of her head. She had no choice. She had to go outside.

She climbed back into the van's rear and began to poke around, looking for something to use as a weapon. She hadn't got a good look at the thing that had chased her, but it had been massive, the size of a bear or more. A stick or a knife wouldn't do much good; it would run right through either.

She found a bag of hammers, but most were too heavy even for her to swing. The best she could do was a small pickaxe with a single spike on each side, perhaps used for breaking up rocks. It was a little lighter than the rest. She wanted something more, though, and continued rummaging through Uncle Lawrence's things, no longer caring about leaving them out of place or not putting them back.

Hanging in one corner, she found what looked like a bottle with a tube thing attached to the top, and a trigger on one side. There was a twistable knob just above the bottle part, and when she gave it a twist, she almost dropped the thing in fright when a blue flame appeared at the other end of the tube. Some kind of blowtorch or firelighter. When she squeezed the trigger the flame lengthened and intensified, so she switched it off and hooked it into a belt loop on her jeans.

Outside, it began to rain, fat drops streaking the windscreen, obscuring her view of the world. She knew she couldn't stay here forever, because Uncle Lawrence needed her, but it took her several minutes to build up the nerve to finally open the van's side door.

At least the rain might cover any sounds she made, or her scent, if that was how these creatures hunted. With the pickaxe in her hands and the blowtorch weighing down on her jeans, she crept along the side of the van, peering around the corner at the rear doors.

There was no sign of the creature, but there were scuff marks on the ground and dents in the back doors, scratches in the paint that must have been done by claws. Juliet stared, imagining what such power could do to her. Lowering herself to the ground, she first peered underneath the van for anything hiding there, then scanned the lane and the hedgerows. Apart from a bird fluttering between tree branches in a heartbreaking mockery of normality, she saw nothing.

She had no choice but to head for the road so started to walk that way, clutching the remaining bottle of water in one hand, keeping the other on the handle of the pickaxe. Every ditch, every break in the bushes along the hedgerow was a threat, but she reached the road without incident. She wished she still had her bike, but there was nothing to be done, so she walked down the centre of the road, preferring to see anything coming rather than be ambushed by something hiding in the verge. The fear was starting to get to her, the constant thumping of her heart an irritation, every creak and groan of the trees, every rustle of a bird in the hedgerow, every gust of the wind another heart-in-mouth moment. Her hands trembled, and she clutched the water bottle to her chest just to keep it still.

Then, in the distance, the sound of an approaching car.

Juliet froze. She was still standing in the middle of the road as it came around the corner, moving much too fast for the road's blind curves, swerving from side to side, a bright red family wagon, as her Dad might have said.

For a moment she thought it would run right through her, dispersing her as though she no longer existed. Then, with a screech of brakes, it slid to a halt barely five metres in front of her. There was a pause for the collection of breath, then the driver's door opened and a tall, overweight man with a moustache half climbed out, keeping one foot inside the car as if to leave it entirely would make it too difficult to squeeze himself back inside.

'Get the fuck out of the way,' he shouted, his voice a little ragged, as though he had spent most of last night screaming. 'I nearly fucking ran you over.'

Dad said anyone who used the F-word in front of a child was common, and not the kind of person to associate with, but this man didn't seem to care. He swore a couple more times, then punched the roof of the car.

'Look, aren't you the Fields girl? James Fields' lass? What is it, Julie? Jessie?'

Juliet stared at him, wondering whether this man was dangerous. She didn't recognise him, but her dad must have a lot of friends she didn't know.

'Juliet,' she said quietly, and the man frowned.

'What? Juliet?'

'Yes.'

'Well, what the fuck are you doing out here? Don't you know what's going on?'

Juliet shook her head. 'No.' She wanted to tell him about Dad, that he hadn't come back, but then the man would know no one was home, and Dad said you shouldn't trust strangers.

'You'd better ask your dad. You're leaving, right? Heading for Plymouth? To the ships?'

'Yes,' Juliet lied.

'How are you getting there? Where's your dad?'

'He's … he's—' The man had just driven this way. He would have passed her house, and had he looked closely he would have seen Dad's car was gone. 'He's working,' she said at last. 'He's coming back soon.'

The man took a couple of steps closer. 'He works down in Bodmin, right? The new hospital there? When did he leave? The A39 now from Camelford down is jammed.

The only way is going through Egloskerry, and once word of that gets out, you'll never get down there. If he's not back by now—'

The man's words were a jumble of information Juliet didn't need. 'He's on his way back,' she said.

The man was right in front of her now, making his way towards her step by laboured step.

'Look, if he's still down at the hospital, there's no way back up here except maybe the coast road, and there were a bunch of sightings out that way before they shut down the Net and the phones. Everyone's gone, the village is emptied out. I can't just leave you behind. It's too dangerous.'

He was reaching for her. His eyes said he wanted to help her, but he was a stranger, and he was too close. Dad said sometimes that you couldn't trust anyone but your family, and even though he said not to trust Uncle Lawrence, he was still family, and he was hurt. This man, he was a stranger. If he got hold of her, he might never let go.

'Come on, Juliet,' I'll take you as far as we can go. I can't leave you here—'

He lunged, one hand reaching for her shoulder. Juliet twisted, trying to break free. The blowtorch bumped against one hand and the other reached for the starter knob. She pulled it free from her jeans, squeezing the trigger as she twisted it in towards the man's stomach.

'Hey, what—'

The screaming, when it started, was like nothing Juliet had ever heard. It was more animal than human, and the shock of it made her only more scared, made her hold the handle tighter, the blowtorch searing up the man's front as he tried to bat it away.

Then she was free, the man dropping to his knees

and rolling on to his side, hugging himself like a child as he wailed and howled. Juliet released the blowtorch's trigger, almost dropping it as the flame cut out. The man rolled across the road, gasping and moaning, curling up like a caterpillar burned by the sun. Juliet stared at him for a few seconds, then took her chance and bolted up the road, running as fast as she could, the hammer bumping against her side, the water bottle clutched against her chest, the blowtorch held like an awkward, unwieldy gun.

The man's screaming died away as the road arced out of sight. Her own house had just appeared up ahead when from behind her came a single bloodcurdling scream, followed by a series of loud snarls. Juliet closed her eyes, leaned forwards, and raced for home.

The garage door was still partly raised. Juliet ducked inside, glanced around for any intruders, dinosaur or human, then lowered the door and locked it from the inside.

Only then, safely home, would she let herself relax.

Was the man dead? Had she or something else killed him?

Dad told her it was wrong to kill someone, but she had been protecting herself. He had tried to grab her. Wasn't that different?

In her relief at making it back, she had almost forgotten the reason for her quest in the first place. Uncle Lawrence. Was he still alive?

She put her hammer and blowtorch down by the entrance into the house, then took off her shoes. She carried the bottle of water, the miraculous, life-giving bottle of water, into the house, down the hall, into the kitchen. Uncle Lawrence lay where she had left him on the floor, his eyes closed. There was a pool of something beside his face, a yellowish slime. He had been sick, but that was good, wasn't it? It meant he was alive.

His cheeks were pale, his forehead lined with a kind of white powder. Salt, maybe. Dad said you sweated out salt sometimes, if you sweated too much. But if he had a fever, wasn't it good to sweat?

'Uncle Lawrence?' He didn't move. She reached out a hand and touched his shoulder, depressing it slightly. 'Uncle Lawrence? Are you all right?' She shook him a little harder. 'Uncle—'

His eyes opened. For a moment his eyelids flickered, then his head turned slightly, angling towards her. His mouth moved, his breath rasping.

'Jul … Juliet?'

His voice was so gravelly that she could barely tell he had said her name. When she recognised it, tears sprung to her eyes.

'I brought you some water.'

He smiled. 'Thank you.'

She remembered it then, and brought the bottle to his mouth, removing the cap and pouring a little between his lips. He gasped for more, and by the time he gave a little shake of his head, almost half the bottle was gone.

'Thank you,' he said again, his voice a little smoother now.

'How are you feeling? Are you going to be all right?'

He sighed, his eyes meeting hers. 'I think I'm all right,' he said. 'I think I'm going to be just fine. And that … that's thanks to you, Juliet.'

The feeling of pride that came over her was like nothing else she had ever felt. Uncle Lawrence was okay, and that was down to her. She had looked after him, and she had been brave. What had happened outside … none of that mattered. Uncle Lawrence was alive. Dad might not be home yet, but Uncle Lawrence was family, and together, somehow, they would get through this. And when Dad got home and found them both here, he would be so happy.

Uncle Lawrence was still looking at her, a thin smile on his face. Juliet met his eyes, felt her cheeks flush with pride, and smiled back.

34

PROTECTOR

I'm DEAD. *And if I'm not dead, I'm going to die.*

Nikki rolled across the grass, the wetness of the dew soaking her. Once, as a child, she had done it across the front lawn of her mother's house and the smell and feel of the grass and the water had been worth the bollocking she'd got for getting stains on her clothes. She searched for that same sensation now, craving it, anything to break through the plastic wrapping of nothing that was squeezing her tighter and tighter, crushing her insides, bending and moulding and realigning her body until it was poured *(drip drip drip)* into a petri-dish where it lay in a slowly growing circle of grey nothingness—

Nikki opened her eyes.

It was day. The sun shone high overhead, making it eleven, twelve o'clock.

Her body—every last inch of it—ached.

She was soaked from head to toe, but she felt warm all over, almost feverish. She gripped handfuls of grass with her hands, her fingertips working their way down through the fronds to the thicker stems and into the soil below, sampling every sensation.

Very slowly, dizziness coming with every movement, she sat up.

Her stomach felt hollow, her throat dry. But after a moment of waiting for the dizziness to subside, she looked around. The grass field of the park, the line of trees along the bottom of the sloping edge, the roofs of the terraces in the valley beyond, the lines of the houses rising up on the opposite hill … it all seemed so … clear.

Nikki wrapped her arms around her herself, like a protective cocoon.

She was clean.

As the realisation dawned, the suspicions took over. She shouldn't still be here. Withdrawal took her into the darkest places, and only chains would have kept her in place. She would have run and run and run until she either found a fix or found something strong enough to stop her, like a brick wall, a cage.

Unless of course, she'd done all that, and ended up back here.

Then she noticed a figure standing beneath a line of nearby trees.

A man.

Her eyes took in details that the drug haze would have ignored. He wore a red sweater with a zip up the middle, one of those stupid rich boy cardigans. His shoes were brown dress shoes, and shone with polish. He wore black jeans, one knee scuffed. Light, pine-coloured hair was brushed over the top of his head, lifting in the breeze, and it marked him as young, maybe as young as her. Glasses. A face that was square, almost as wide as it was long.

His arms were folded. Now he unfolded them, and lifted a hand to wave.

He started walking towards her, still waving. Nikki tried to get up, but her feet—bare feet—slipped on the wet grass and she sat back down again as he stood over her.

'Ah, you're awake. Do you feel capable of eating anything?'

In the distance, an enormous boom made the leaves of the trees rustle. Nikki felt a sudden warm wind on her face and flinched, but the man didn't so much as look up. In fact, he even smiled. Then he squatted down and pulled a rucksack off his back, one Nikki hadn't noticed because the straps were the same colour as his sweater. Up close he looked strangely bland, like a cardboard cutout of a man. She could imagine him sitting in an office all day, chewing the end of a pencil, staring out of the window at a pub across the way to which he was never invited.

'Who are you?'

'Mitchell,' he said. 'My name's Mitchell. Mitchell Egglesfield. I know it's a mouthful.' He gave a smile as uninspiring as his voice. 'You can call me Mitchell Egg. Or just ... Egg. Others ... do.'

His eyes looked up and down her body. Used by more men than she could remember, and abused by enough substances for a lifetime, it was nevertheless still worthy of a man's eyes. Mitchell, though, looked at her like a postman assessing the quality of a package's wrapping.

'I brought you some clothes,' he said, unzipping the bag and pulling out a thin, grey sweater. It was better quality than anything she had ever owned and bore the label of a high street brand, some of the cardboard inserts to keep its shape tucked in among the folds. As he held it up, one of them fell to the ground. Nikki watched as the wind caught it, sending it tumbling away across the grass, picking up beads of dew as it went.

'And I have these, too,' Mitchell said, pulling out a pair

of jeans. 'They should fit. There's some underwear, but I'll let you sort through that yourself.' He gave another bland smile. 'Your clothes have … seen better days.'

She watched him, saying nothing. He looked like he expected thanks or at least some positive response, but when Nikki said nothing, he gave a brief grimace that suggested frustration, then squatted down. He pulled a plastic bag out of his pocket, smoothed it out on the grass, then piled the clothes he had brought neatly on top. Then, standing up again, he turned around.

'You can change,' he said. 'I won't look.'

Nikki found it hard to bring herself to move, but after more than a minute of staring at the back of Mitchell's jeans with no sign that he was losing patience, she climbed unsteadily to her feet and began to undress.

At first she tried to hide herself, but when she glanced around, she found the park empty, only herself and Mitchell standing together in the middle of the playing field, so she pulled off her clothing once piece at a time, letting them drop to the floor, until she was standing naked behind Mitchell's back.

The wind, cool again, chilled her, making her shiver. She looked down at her body, bruised and scarred, her breasts deflated, her stomach hollow. Track marks in every nook, elbows, knees, toes, like a hideous children's song.

Can I come back from this?

The grass was wet. So, she now realised, were the shredded remains of her clothes.

She felt clean, and she also felt *clean*.

Mitchell still hadn't moved, but he was now humming quietly to himself as though enjoying the day.

Nikki reached down and began to pull on the clothes. The material, brand new and dry, felt strange on her skin. Not uncomfortable, but unfamiliar.

Undeserved.

It was all a little loose, sized for how she might have been, were she not so underweight.

She got the uncanny feeling that Mitchell somehow knew her.

'Are you ready?' he said at last. 'There are shoes in the bag, too. I'm sorry, I had to guess your size. A five, isn't it?'

'Yes,' Nikki said. 'How did you know?'

'May I turn around now?' Mitchell asked, ignoring her question.

'Yes,' Nikki said again. 'Thank you.'

Mitchell turned. Again, he looked her up and down, the barest hint of a smile on his face. 'Much better,' he said.

'Thank you.'

'My pleasure.' Mitchell pulled off his rucksack, reached inside and withdrew a shoe box. Nikki blinked at the brand name emblazoned across the top.

'You shouldn't have—'

'You're right, I shouldn't,' Mitchell agreed. 'But things have changed a little over the last few hours. A lot of doors are being left open.'

Nikki took the shoes out the box, a pair of neat trainers. She wiped her feet on the shredded remains of her old clothes, then slipped them on.

They fit perfectly.

'You must be hungry,' Mitchell said. 'You look like you are.'

Nikki nodded. When she was using, food never mattered. It kept her alive, kept her on her feet as she walked to the next corner, climbed into the next car. Now, her blood clean for the first time in how long, she understood what hunger felt like.

'Come with me,' Mitchell said. 'I need to show you something. Then I'll take you somewhere to eat.'

Nikki nodded. Mitchell shouldered his rucksack again and headed away across the field, heading downslope, towards the bottom of the park, where it ended by a large roundabout feeding on to the motorway. For the first time, Nikki noticed the lines of cars blocking the roads, as though everyone had tried to leave at the same time, and as a result, no one had. Of the people who had left them, though, there was no sign.

'It's just over here,' Mitchell said, angling towards a stand of trees. 'It'll only take a minute, then we'll get on.'

He stepped onto a path, then headed around behind the trees, coming to a stop beside a path of undergrowth. Something lay among the tall weeds, crushing them down. Flies buzzed overhead.

Nikki's temples pulsed with blood. Her hands shook.

A body. Lying face down, head twisted to the side, flies dancing around an open mouth, glassy eyes staring at nothing, his collar caked with dried blood.

She hadn't clearly seen the man who had raped her, only remembered the size and shape of him. This man would fit.

'I watched him,' Mitchell said, in the same bland tone that he said everything. 'I watched him … fucking you. I couldn't condone such an act, so when he was done, I followed him. I cut his throat with chicken wire and left him here, out of harm's way.' He turned to look at her, his face still horrifyingly devoid of any emotion, as though someone had pulled a suit of human skin over a robotic frame.

'I apologise for not returning sooner,' he continued, as Nikki stared at him, heart thundering. 'But I had to go home and change.' Finally, a flicker of a real smile, but one not aimed at her, but beamed off into the air. 'Appearances maketh the man, do they not?'

Nikki could only give a dumb nod.

'You don't have to worry anymore,' Mitchell said, looking back at the body. He kicked a stone that had rolled out onto the path back into the verge. 'I'm going to protect you from now on.'

35

RESCUE

WHEN EMILY DIDN'T COME BACK OUT after a couple of minutes, Kenny got restless. He picked at his fingernails, then started to wander up and down the corridor, kicking past piled boxes and heaps of rubbish, Marvin's cats scattering out of the way.

She was tough. She'd be all right.

He went back and listened at the door. Nothing.

Marvin was a proper doctor. He'd helped Kenny out in the past, and Graham had returned with cuts stitched and bandaged. Marvin would help her. She just had to pay, that was all.

Kenny stuffed a hand into his pocket and pulled out a scattering of coins. A few pounds in loose change. Nothing. Not enough to pay for anything. He could barely buy a coffee with that.

But he didn't need money anymore, Marvin was right. Shops and houses were abandoned; they could take what they liked. No one to stop them, no gatekeepers, no police. A free-for-all, one giant fucking party.

You have to pay.

Kenny kicked an old porcelain plant pot, its only contents a sandy bowl of soil and a few wispy brown sticks that might once have been a proud houseplant. It split neatly in two, the dried soil filtering out and making pyramids on the floor, the sands of time slipping away. Emily was still in there. She hadn't come out.

Kenny, head shaking back and forth with nervousness, pushed against one of the other flat doors. It was heavy, that kind of metal-framed chipboard wood with a plastic veneer and solid locks. Even if he got angry and kicked out, he'd never get through one. He probably couldn't do it with a sledgehammer.

'Emily,' he muttered under his breath, then gave the door a weak punch.

She still hadn't come out. Kenny looked down at a bone lying on the ground as a cat came over and gave it a sniff. It was too long to be a chicken bone, and something about it repulsed him. The cat started to chew the end. Kenny turned away.

Emily still hadn't come out. Kenny clenched and unclenched his fists, pacing the corridor. Emily … where was she?

(you have to pay)

(I'd never get through that door)

The doors were solid *(solid solid)* and Emily was on the inside with Marvin. What was she doing? What was he doing with *(to to to)* her?'

Further up the corridor, he pushed against one of the doors in frustration. It gave a little, and his curiosity took him inside. A ransacked apartment, a few pieces of furniture—a sofa, table, old sideboard—but everything of value had gone. Kenny wandered through, finding himself at a pair of doors that opened out onto a wide balcony.

Several floors up, he had a good view of London from

here. It took his mind off things, so he went outside, gasping in dismay at the columns of smoke rising all across the city. In the far distance, between two other high-rises, he caught a glimpse of the Thames. A bridge—he didn't know the name—had collapsed in the middle, and colourful cars, like little rectangles of candy, lay piled in the water or pressed together along the sections that hadn't yet given way.

Shit was going down. He started to turn away, saw the balcony was separated from the next only by a flimsy partition wall just above head height.

He stared at it for a long time.

Numbers buzzed in his head like flies. He counted doors, estimating.

Three down from Marvin's.

It wasn't hard to get over. He just needed a chair and a bit of balls. On the next, though, there was no chair, so after a minute of shitting himself, he climbed up, feet on the railing, facing in towards the flat with his back to the sky and a murderous drop to the ground, and shimmied around the partition wall. As he briefly hung out over the void, his stomach seemed to lurch, as though it knew what one missed step would feel like. And then he was down, moving across the balcony.

The next, the same. And the one after was Marvin's.

He didn't let himself think. Nor consider what might happen if the glass doors were locked from the inside. A dumb spectator to whatever horror was going on, but they were open, slid wide to let out a charring, barbeque smell.

The inside of Marvin's flat was as chaotic as the corridor outside. The carcass of a cat lay on a sofa cushion, half skinned, pieces missing. Kenny remembered the bones in the corridor and put one hand over his stomach as though to hold the contents in.

He peered through an open doorway into a narrow hall. The smell of a kitchen came from one side, so he guessed a bedroom was on the other. The door was closed.

No one was in the kitchen. Kenny picked up a knife with one shaking hand and turned towards the bedroom door.

(walk away walk away walk away)

(How are you gonna pay?)

Kenny nudged the door with his foot. It slid open with a vicious, rusty creak, and Marvin, leaning over an operating table, looked up from where Emily lay, naked, seemingly unconscious, her face and chest covered in black lines. Nearby were two low tables, one containing shiny knives and other surgical tools, the other with several plastic bags. On the floor at Marvin's feet was a large blue cooler box, its lid open. Chunks of dry ice released a cloud of steam into the air.

Kenny stared at the lines crossing Emily's body, like she was a giant embroidery project.

'What the fuck?' Marvin said.

He reached out to close the door. Kenny let out a gasp and swung the knife, embedding it in Marvin's forearm. As Marvin howled and stumbled backwards, the knife still sticking out of his flesh, Kenny rushed forwards and grabbed Emily's arm.

Still warm. She was alive.

'I'm sorry,' he whispered, pulling her upright. Her head lolled, eyelids flickered. She let out a groan.

'You little fucker!' Marvin shouted. He jerked the knife free from his arm, then let out a howl of pain before collapsing to the ground.

'Come on,' Kenny muttered, pulling Emily's arm over his shoulder. She was slick with blood, oil, and stinking disinfectant, and he nearly dropped her, but she was slender, not as heavy as he had feared. He dragged her out of the room, into the hall.

The front door was just in front. A cat pawed at it to get out. Kenny tried to turn the latch but Emily slipped out of his hands. The cat scattered out of the way as Kenny stepped over Emily, and this time managed to get the door open.

Kenny smelled rather than saw Marvin come up behind him, and he had no other way to defend himself than to throw himself backwards and hope Marvin didn't have a weapon. His back hit Marvin in the chest, and they both fell, Kenny landing on top of Marvin. Kenny twisted away as Marvin tried to grab him, aiming a weak punch that made a brief indent in Marvin's spongey stomach, but as Marvin's fingers closed over Kenny's arm, Kenny flapped his free hand at Marvin's knife wound, fingers digging into the bleeding flesh. Marvin howled and let go. Kenny dragged himself up to his feet, then aimed the sole of his boot at Marvin's face and kicked out hard. He felt Marvin's nose crunch, then blood was splattering over Marvin's mouth and chin. Kenny kicked out again, this time only connecting with Marvin's shoulder, pushing the big man down.

Emily was stirring. Kenny reached her, pulling her up. She groaned, her legs unsteady, but leaning on Kenny's shoulder she was able to walk. Together they staggered out of the flat and up the corridor.

If Marvin came after them, they wouldn't get far, Kenny knew. Emily could barely walk. She managed to make it down one flight of stairs, but instead of continuing down, Kenny pushed through the double doors onto the next landing. Leaving Emily slumped against a wall, he tried the flat doors until he found one that was open, then went back to Emily and helped her inside.

There was no bed, but there was an old mattress in one room. Kenny laid Emily down, then turned the lock on the inside.

Emily had leaned her head to the side and appeared to be sleeping. Kenny found himself looking at her naked body, despite hating himself for doing it. In the end, he went into the flat's living room, pulled down a threadbare curtain, and laid it on top of her. Then, unsure what else he could do, he went into the living room, opened the doors, and stepped out onto the balcony.

His mind was spinning. He stared out at London as blood burned in his ears and his heart thundered in his chest. This was all his fault. He had brought her here, to Marvin. He had let Marvin do horrible things to her.

He leaned over the balcony edge and wondered if it would hurt. Would he know much about it? Would it be easier if he went backwards, or if he shut his eyes?

Then, just as he wondering if he really had the nerve, he heard a weak voice from inside the flat.

'Kenny?'

36

RESISTANCE

Dave Brussells was brooding over a cup of coffee in the staff kitchen. June, standing by the sink, where the dishes from Lord Richard's evening meal waited to be washed, watched the groundskeeper with nervous eyes.

'And you don't know what it was?'

Dave shook his head. 'No idea. Nothing I've ever seen in this lifetime, that's for sure. Might have taken a shot had it come at me, but it was heading away, so didn't want to attract its attention.' He sighed, slumping down over the drink as though trying to disappear. 'You know what it reminded me of? Those monitor lizards they used to have in Paignton Zoo. Only double, three times the size.'

June said nothing. She held on to the edge of the worktop with both hands, fingers clenched tight to stop them shaking.

'You know,' Dave continued, 'not sure it would have made any difference anyway, if I had taken a pop at it. Animals take more killing than you'd think, you know? You can take out a fox or a pheasant with a single shot, but an animal like that, unless you get a kill shot first up, he's still coming on. And moving low like that, it's all legs and tail. Nothing sizeable to aim at.'

June suspected Dave was no longer talking to her but to himself, reliving the encounter in his mind, going over what he might have done differently. She could tell how shaken he was from his colourless cheeks, even when her initial instinct had been to deny it, to claim he had seen something else, that he'd been spooked by nothing more than the evening's shadows.

And not by a monster roaming around outside.

'Have you told Lord Richard?' she asked, finding her voice at last.

Dave shook his head. 'Don't want to worry him. As I said, it was heading away. It went into Randall Flower's fields to the west of here. I'll walk over in the morning to let him know, tell him to keep an eye out.'

The reluctance in his voice was obvious. June said, 'It might be good if you stayed the night in the house, just in case it shows up again.'

Dave nodded, and June understood. She had saved his pride, saved him having to ask, even to beg to bed down in one of the back porches to avoid having to walk back to his cottage in the dusk.

'You're probably right,' he said, feigning a sigh. 'Just to be on the safe side.'

June got back to the dishes, aware she needed to finish them in time to help Lilian with the preparation of Lord Richard's bedroom. While Lilian could deal with it alone, of course, it had been Lord Richard's request to have Lilian come to his room each night for the simple purpose of plumping his pillows and drawing his curtains. She shivered at the thought of the young lord anywhere near her granddaughter, but a lifetime of servitude had left June unable to speak out. Instead, the best she could do was station herself outside the door to ensure Lilian reappeared promptly.

Dave stood up. 'Thanks for the coffee,' he said. 'I'll just take a look around downstairs while I'm here, make sure the place is secure.'

June nodded. It was technically Alfred's job, but Dave was again covering for his reluctance to go back outside.

'Thank you, Dave.'

He shuffled off. June finished the washing up as quickly as she could, then headed upstairs. To her surprise, though, Lilian was alone in Lord Richard's bedroom, the young lord nowhere to be found.

'His lordship desired to stay in the drawing room,' Lilian said, giving June a sideways look while maintaining her professional airs as though Lord Richard might have been playing a prank on the both of them. 'He said he had urgent matters to attend to.'

June waited anyway, and together they went back downstairs. Safely in the servants' quarters, Lilian leaned close.

'He found an old radio,' she said. 'I heard him listening to a news broadcast.'

'Did you hear what it said?'

'He dismissed me from waiting table after he had set it up,' Lilian said. 'I couldn't hear much but it said something about an uprising. I'm afraid that's all I heard. I think he plans to enter his bunker in the next couple of days.'

The fear in her voice was obvious. Lilian's darted back and forth, and her lower lip trembled. June knew what the bunker meant. It was a safe bolt hole for Lord Richard, a hellhole in waiting for Lilian.

And there was nothing either of them could do.

'I thought I might leave tonight,' Lilian said suddenly. 'I … I already packed a bag.'

'No! You can't!'

Lilian leaned close. Her eyes were watery, desperate. 'I'd rather take my chance outside than go in there with … him.'

'We can talk to him again. Maybe convince him to take me in your place, after all, I'm an experienced housekeeper….'

June trailed off. Lilian shook her head.

'Help me get away. Get me the keys to one of the cars—'

Lord Richard had several vehicles, lined up in a multi-berthed garage along the side of the house. The keys for each were kept in a safety box for which Alfred had the master key.

'You know I'd have to steal it—'

'Then do it. I can't stay here. I'll walk if I have to.'

'Let me go and talk to your grandfather. I might be able to convince him. I'd rather you didn't go, though. I'm hearing terrible things about outside. Things about monsters—'

Lilian stared at her. 'The worst monsters are the ones behind closed doors,' she said softly. 'I know, Grandmother.'

'I'll talk to your grandfather.'

She found Alfred checking windows and closing curtains on the second floor.

'She means to leave,' she said.

Alfred shook his head. 'She can't. It's too dangerous outside. I have just spoken with Dave. He told me what he claimed to have seen—'

'Did you believe him?'

'Dave Brussells is a man of his word,' Alfred said. 'I believe that he believes in the truth of what he saw. I don't think any of us can doubt that strange occurrences are going on. I've … seen things myself.'

'What things?'

Alfred turned away, making a show of closing a stuck window and pulling a lock bolt across. 'Things that … alarm me. However, I do believe we will be safer here.'

'Alfred, look at me.'

She had to pull his arm before he would turn and meet her eyes. Even then he seemed reluctant, his gaze flickering from meeting her eyes to the floor and back again.

'I told you before that we need to leave.'

'Mrs. Lammonby—'

'My name is June, you old fool.'

Alfred looked at her. His eyes were red, as though he hadn't slept in a couple of days. 'June … I don't know … leave it with me. I'll think about it for a while, and decide what to do.'

She watched as he walked away up the corridor, feeling all hope draining out of her. As he reached the bottom of the stairs leading up to the third floor, he tripped slightly, catching the banister for support. He paused for a moment and then started up.

June wiped a tear out of her eye.

~

A bright and sunny morning defied any of Alfred's fears, but the bell calling him to attention seemed to come with an urgency that made him nervous. He headed downstairs, making sure to keep hold of the stair banister as he descended. He had found simple tasks difficult of late; he was sure it was down to worry. He had neither been eating nor sleeping well; it didn't bode for a healthy constitution, but once things settled down, he would be all right.

Lord Richard's study stank of cigar smoke and whiskey. Lord Richard himself was slumped in a chair facing the only open curtains in the room. Alfred greeted his master, then made to open a window, only for Lord Richard to put up a hand.

'Lammonby, there you are. What took you so long?' His voice was slurred as though he had been drinking all night and was yet to go to bed. Alfred took note of the glass on the tabletop nearby, half filled with amber liquid. It was likely his estimation was correct.

'Good morning, sir,' Alfred said. 'Would you like me to call Mrs. Lammonby and have your breakfast brought here?'

'Never mind that,' Lord Richard slurred. 'There's no time. I have decided I will enter my bunker today. Have that slut of a granddaughter of yours prepare a bag. As I told you, I will need someone to assist me. You and your wife will remain in the house to ensure its smooth running.'

Alfred closed his eyes, clenching his fists at his sides. 'As you request, sir.'

'Get to it. There's no time like the present. Did you know we are in the middle of a civil war? Three different factions, would you believe? Slaughtering each other like dogs. My dad was right all along.'

'I'm sure things will settle down soon,' Alfred said.

'Huh. You're as stupid as you are formal. I will meet you at the bunker in thirty minutes.'

'Lord Richard wishes to enter his bunker this morning,' Alfred said to June's back. 'Prepare him a small packed meal. Lilian can assist him from then on. And instruct Dave to do a circuit of the grounds, just to make sure everything is secure. I will speak to Lilian beforehand. She will understand.'

June said nothing. Her shoulders shook with her crying. Alfred lifted a hand, wanting to touch her, but withdrew it and turned away. He needed to speak with his granddaughter.

~

At just after half past ten, Alfred stood beside June next to the concrete bunker's open door as they watched Lord Richard stumbling across the gardens towards them. At times he looked certain to fall into a nearby flowerbed, only to right himself at the last moment. As he reached them, Alfred saw his face was puffy, his hair dishevelled and his clothes stained, one shoelace undone.

Alfred closed his eyes briefly before Richard reached them. He remembered the boy's birth like it was yesterday, a joyous day for Lord and Lady Evans as they welcomed a bouncing baby into their lives. At first, he had seemed like a good little boy, his care entrusted almost entirely to Alfred and June while Lord and Lady Evans fulfilled their professional duties. At some point, however, the trappings of wealth had spoiled him. By his teenage years Alfred was already pining for the rose-coloured days of Richard's early childhood, when a butterfly or a frog would have been held gently between podgy fingers rather than being crushed to a lifeless pulp.

'When he sees she's not here, he'll go wild,' June said.

'I've told you. I've spoken to her. She understands the situation. Her duty must come first.'

'Damn you, Alfred.'

Lord Richard came to a stop in front of them. 'Everything all right?'

Alfred took hold of the door and held it open. 'I have made personally sure that everything is ready,' Alfred said. 'You will not want for anything. Now, if you would like to go down, I will come down with you and remind you of how everything operates.'

Lord Richard looked at him, then turned slowly on his heels. 'Where is she?' he said. 'I told you I wanted her here.'

'Oh, do you mean Ms. Weekes?'

'Of course I fucking mean Ms. Weekes, you old toad. Who else would I mean?'

June's head was lowered, her body shaking with uncontrollable sobbing, the sound of which she was struggling to contain.

'She's already inside,' Alfred said, holding Lord Richard's glowering stare. She's been preparing for your arrival since you made your announcement.'

'Already?'

'Yes, look. She's right down there, waiting for you.'

Alfred lifted a hand, shaking more than ever, and pointed into the gloomy stairwell. Lord Richard leaned forwards, peering down into the dark.

'Where? I don't see her.'

Alfred shifted his hands, holding them out behind Lord Richard's back. He remembered the time he had caught the little boy in his arms when Richard had been chased by a cow in one of the neighbouring fields. He had held the boy close while he cried, then taken him to the kitchen where June had prepared a plaster for a grazed knee.

He closed his eyes and forcing his hands forwards with all the strength he could muster. His anguished cry covered the first crunching bump as Richard fell face first down into the gloom, but as the cry cut off, others came *thud-thud-thud* as Lord Richard tumbled over and over.

Tears filled Alfred's eyes, to the point that he couldn't even see the shape lying in the gloom at the bottom of the steps. June was crying beside him but he didn't look at her. He stepped back, pulled the door closed and twisted a key in the lock.

'Alfred!'

'I think we should go back to the house.'

'What have you done?'

Alfred turned away from her. In the shadows by the back porch he saw Lilian standing, arms folded tightly around herself, and he let himself smile, even as his own strength started to fail. He didn't really feel the ground as it came up to meet him, but the grass was cool and damp with morning dew, and that was all the comfort he needed.

June was calling his name, crying for him. Alfred opened his mouth to speak, but was unsure whether what came out were words, or merely traces on the air.

I did what had to be done.

37

FRACTURING

MICK HAD BEEN PUSHED BACK into the nearest booth, Danny slumped on top of him. Stitcher grabbed Claire by the hair and turned her towards the hall.

'Get those kids back here,' he snarled at her, shoving her in front of him, forcing her to stoop. 'Where the fuck have they gone? Clay, watch those. Kill them if they move.'

'Sure.'

'If they've run off, you're dead,' Stitcher said, warm breath close to Claire's ear. 'But I'll make it slow, got it? Make sure you enjoy it first.'

'Why can't you just leave us alone?' Claire sobbed, the fight gone. 'We did nothing to you.'

'Someone's always done something to someone,' Stitcher said. 'Way of the world, ain't it? Now open that door.'

Claire fumbled with the latch. The door was old, the latch ill-fitting. The lock scraped, and only as she pulled the door back, letting in the wind, did she hear the roar of a bus engine. Some crazy fight-or-flight reaction bit down on her, and she dashed out into the car park, slipping out of

Stitcher's grasp. Her momentum sent her tumbling, and she fell forwards, rolling over, her back slamming hard against the tarmac, knocking the wind out of her.

'Hey, come back here—what the fuck?'

Claire, winded, could only look up as the bus sped across the car park. Tim Parkson sat in the front seat, face bloodied, jaw set hard. Behind him, Ishy, Daisy, and Lisa leaned over the front seats. Stitcher, running out into the car park after Claire, barely had time to turn before the bus hit him, slamming him into the pub's outer wall, sliding him along the stonework until the bus came to a grinding stop.

The front door opened. Daisy and Lisa climbed down and ran over to Claire, helping her to her feet. Ishy helped an obviously hurt Tim get down, but instead of letting her help him over to Claire, Tim pushed her away. He staggered over to Stitcher's mangled body and leaned over him.

'Got what you deserved, you fucking prick,' he said, then hawked and spat on the dead man's face.

Claire, only just able to breathe again, felt words of admonishment pulling at her tongue, but she pushed them away. After all, the lines had been redrawn.

'There's still the man with the shotgun,' she said, the words barely out of her mouth before a thundering boom came from inside the pub.

The girls screamed. Lisa ran back on to the bus. Daisy knelt down on the ground with her hands cupping her face, while Ishy helped Claire to her feet. Tim, face caked with blood, stood on shaky legs by the corner of the bus, peering over Stitcher's body at the pub's entrance.

'Who's in there?' he asked.

'That man Clay had Danny and Mick,' Claire said. 'And maybe Connie's in there, too.'

'I'm going in.'

'Wait!'

As Tim limped towards the door, Claire hurried to overtake him. Despite everything, she was still their teacher; she had to put herself in the way of danger, had to protect them. With Tim behind her and Ishy behind him, she leaned through the pub doorway.

The hallway was empty.

'Here, Miss,' Tim whispered, pushing something into her hand. A lump of slate, a piece of broken window ledge. It had nice, sharp edges.

One step at a time, she moved down the hallway. The bus's engine still turned over, making it difficult to hear anything. There was a sound, though, a rasping, throaty sound, like something being dragged over a rusty fence.

Claire stepped into the doorway.

Danny lay on the ground, his eyes closed, shirt soaked in blood. A few feet away lay Clay, the gun still in his outstretched hand. Between them stood Mick, holding a bottle, a crack running down the side of the glass. And in the corner, at the bottom of the stairs, Connie crouched, arms pulling her knees up to her chest. She stared at Danny, unblinking.

'What happened?' Claire asked, mouth dry.

Mick stared at her. 'He shot Danny,' he said, in a weak, quiet voice, so unlike Mick it was as though layers had been stripped away to reveal the soft underbelly beneath. 'He was gonna shoot me too, then *she* came down the stairs. When he turned away, I hit him.'

'Respect, man,' Tim said. 'Is that fucker dead?'

Mick's fingers opened, and the bottle dropped. Where Clay's skull had failed, the carpet succeeded, and it broke, making a spongy circle of dark navy rum on the pile.

'He shot Danny,' Mick said again.

They're looking at me again, Claire thought. *They're looking at me for answers. Not all of the lines have been redrawn, not yet.*

Clay's foot twitched, and he let out a low, weak groan. 'Look in the cupboards, Claire said to Ishy. 'I need a medical kit. Anything you can find. Connie, get up and help her.' She turned to Tim, then looked at Mick. 'Get that gun away from him and tie him up. Tape, rope, whatever you can find. Make it tight. Hands behind his back, and tie him to something.'

'Let's just bash his fucking head in,' Tim said.

'We're not killers,' Claire said, looking at Tim, who, after the bus incident, was exactly that. 'And he might know something that can help us.'

'If you say so.'

'I do. Do it now. Please.'

As the boys reluctantly went to follow her instructions, she staggered over to Danny. By the time she had reached him, however, she knew it was too late. The blood had drained out of his face, and his body was already cooling down, the blood starting to congeal. She pulled back the shredded remains of his shirt to reveal a ragged, bloody hole in the centre of his chest. She closed her eyes, struggling with a feeling of utter despair. Good, good Danny. At least it had probably been quick, but right now her heart felt like it was bleeding too.

For Danny, there was nothing she could do, but while Claire wanted to slip away into a pit of self-loathing and despair, she had to focus on the living. With Clay secured to a foot rail below the bar with duct tape and some cable ties Tim had found, Claire recruited Mick to help carry Danny out into the shed, where she wrapped him and laid him down beside Pauly. Then, heart heavy but mind fizzing so badly she thought she might never sleep again, she called the surviving kids into the bar, gathering them at the far end, away from the slowly waking Clay.

'I feel like I'm in fucking Battle Royale,' Tim muttered, holding an ice-pack to his busted nose. 'Any other cunt want to come and take a pot shot, or can we take a rest for a bit?'

Claire felt the urge to scold him for his language, but something in his eyes had changed. Tim had always acted the tough guy around the schoolyard, ready with his fists to down any challengers or suitors to his endless string of girlfriends. With his dad as a doctor and his mother as a newspaper reporter, however, he was from the sort of well-off, cared for background that had always made her think his stance was a well-cultivated act, one that would fade as he grew up. Now, though, dark wings had closed around him, and the look she saw in his eyes suggested that Stitcher's brutal death might have opened a floodgate, one that would become increasingly difficult to close.

Mick, sat quietly by himself, his eyes down, hands on his lap, fingers carefully avoiding the stains left by Danny's blood. Connie stood by herself near one wall, arms folded, mouth in a petulant pout as though her father had just refused her the use of the car rather than anything much worse. Ishy, Daisy, and Lisa sat together, arms around each other, quickly forming a bond Claire hoped might help them cope with everything. They were all—

'Where's Jenny?' Tim said. 'She was on the bus. Where is she now?'

The others looked around. 'She was on the bus,' Ishy echoed.

'I'll go and look for her,' Tim said.

'Not on your own, you won't,' Claire said quickly, the

teacher part of her still there, despite everything. 'Ishy … you, Connie, and Mick stay here to watch that man. If he wakes up, do nothing that he says, don't answer his questions. If he looks like he's going to break out—'

Ishy, staring at her, gave a short nod. Connie rolled her eyes and sighed. Mick didn't look up.

'Daisy and Lisa, you two come with me and Tim to look for Jenny.'

She sent the girls to search the flat upstairs while she and Tim went out to the bus. There was no sign of Jenny either on the bus or in the luggage compartments underneath, so they began to make a circle of the pub, first checking the car park, then the beer garden behind. Claire forced herself not to look at the shed where the bodies of Pauly and Danny now lay.

'If she's done a runner, she could be anywhere,' Tim said. 'This whole thing is fucked up.'

'I wouldn't blame her if she did,' Claire said quietly.

'I mean, what the fuck? We go on a goddamn school trip, and—'

'Tim, what is it?'

They were standing at the back fence of the beer garden, above a gentle moorland slope that led down into a distant river valley. Aside from a few rocks jutting out of the grass and the occasional wind-harassed tree, it was almost entirely featureless until it reached a shallow gorge at the bottom through which a stream ran.

'There. Something's lying on the grass down there.'

He was over the fence before she could stop him, running down the slope. Claire followed, taking more heed of her step, reaching him only after he had retrieved the item from the ground and turned around to hold it up with a look of horror on his face.

The blood dried around his nose and mouth only made

him look paler as he held up the old trainer, part of the upper layer ripped away, clean lines cut through the cloth as though cut by razor blades.

Claire didn't have to ask if the shoe belonged to Jenny.

'Miss,' Tim said, eyes wide, voice hollow. 'Where is she?'

Claire looked around. The hillside, and the skies above them, were empty. There was nowhere for Jenny to hide, and if someone

(something something come on, Claire, say it)

had taken her, they were long gone too.

All she could do was look back at Tim and shake her head.

'I don't know,' she said.

38

HOPELESSNESS

All Emily remembered was Marvin offering her a drink. He had twisted the top off the plastic bottle himself, handed it to her. Even as a whisper at the back of her head told her to say no, her aching, sweaty body craved it and her resistance had collapsed. The next thing she knew, she was lying on an old mattress, staring at Kenny sitting on the floor nearby, nervously playing with his hands.

Her head ached like hell. Her body felt worse. As she shifted she felt tight and sore where she hadn't felt that way before.

'You want water?' Kenny said, jumping up. 'Sorry. I'll get water.'

'Where's Marvin? Where's … my mother?'

Kenny pointed at the ceiling. 'Upstairs. Marvin, he's upstairs. Your mother … back there.'

Emily started to sit up, but as the curtain slipped off her body, she realised she was naked, and quickly snatched it, holding it up over her breasts.

'Jesus, fuck, where are my clothes?'

Kenny reappeared. He walked with a stoop, ducking his head, as though she were a dog who might bite.

'Ah … Marvin. They're in his place.'

'What the fuck?'

And then she realised. But the pain wasn't what she might have expected if he had raped her. Instead, there were sore lines across her body, and when she rubbed her skin, her fingers came away with a black, inklike substance.

'Kenny … what the fuck did he do to me?'

Kenny gave a frantic shake of his head. 'I don't know. He had a bunch of knives, and a cooler—'

Emily started to stand up, the horror that she might have narrowly escaped being harvested for her organs overshadowed only by the thought that her mother was still out there, hurt and needing help.

'I'll get you some clothes. I was looking around—'

A sudden tempest of rage rose up inside of her. She looked at the young man who had brought her here, led her to the mouth of the lion's den and then left her to be consumed, and all she wanted to do was kill him.

'Don't you do a fucking thing!'

She pushed past him, running for the door. The curtain fell away, and for a moment her dirty, soiled modesty bothered her, then it became an afterthought. She saw Kenny's eyes run down her body, his mouth agape, staring at her as though he'd neither seen a naked girl nor anything so hideous before.

'Wait, Emily—'

She ran for the door, twisting the lock and pulling it wide, revealing a rubbish-strewn hallway. Kenny was lingering somewhere behind her, useless, helpless, and she tried to slam the door on him, to shut him in. The door, on an irritating safety hinge, resisted, but Emily didn't care. She ran down the hallway, dodging between piles of discarded furniture, suitcases stacked ready for escape then abandoned and looted, climbing over a sofa someone had left jammed through an open doorway, and made it to the stairs.

She took them two at a time, swinging around corners, heedless of debris under her bare feet, the sharp prick of broken masonry, shattered glass.

By the time she burst out onto the street, it had begun to rain, big, splashing drops puddling together on the pavements. Emily took stock of her surroundings, trying to remember which way they had come, then chose the best option, running across the street, around a corner she thought she remembered, praying she would see the park they had come through.

It stood at the end of the road, behind a tall railing fence. With a sigh of relief, she sprinted for it, pushed through a gate and raced out across the soaking field in the direction of the far gate beside which she had left her mother. The rain was teeming now, and she slipped more than once, the rain and the sodden grass combining to wash the sweat and filth and blood and ink from her body. Over the roar of the rain, it was impossible to hear anything, but in the trees far to her left massive creatures moved, their features hidden, their presence announced only by the rough shake and shudder of the branches in a way no wind could do.

Heart thundering in her mouth, Emily reached the far gate and pushed her way through. Exhausted, she staggered along the pavement, trying to recall which of the sodden cars her mother was hidden within.

'Mum?' she called, voice growing increasingly desperate as she walked up and down, searching for the car. 'Mum? Where are you?'

It had to be here, but it was gone. Emily, desperate,

wiped raindrops away to peer in through windows, but nothing.

She was crying now. She staggered up and down the street in an increasingly wide zigzag, desperately searching. Then, just as she was about to give up she saw it, a car with a broken front window, some way ahead, and realised to her shock that she had come out of a gate further along the park by mistake. Barely keeping her feet, she ran through the blocked lines of cars until she reached the one with her mother inside.

Kim, having shifted herself for comfort, lay across the back seat, her head against the passenger side rear window. Her eyes were closed.

'Mum?'

Kim didn't move. Emily reached in through the broken window and lifted the lock to the rear door. As she opened it, her heart began to flutter, and when she reached out to touch her mother's hand, she let out an anguished wail.

Kim's hand was stone cold. Sometime in the hours since they had parted, her mother had died.

Emily could only scream, for as long as it took to let the anger out. She no longer cared who—or what—heard her; part of her wanted to lie down and die here alongside her mother. She wanted to blame everyone, in particular Kenny and that sick bastard masquerading as a doctor, but in her heart she knew it had been a vain gesture; the rockfall had done for her mother long before, it had only been a matter of time.

She wanted to give her mother one last hug, but this cold, lifeless thing was no longer Kim. Her mother was long gone, departed from this place, somewhere better. Instead, Emily leaned inside, just to touch her mother's face.

Kim had scratched something on the plastic cover

along the bottom of the car window. A piece of broken glass lay nearby.

Emily began to sob as she read the jagged, uneven words.

I love you. I always will. Stay alive for me. Mum x.

Emily backed away, leaving Kim to her tomb. Her whole body shuddered with misery, even as the rain teemed down. Somewhere through the grey skies overhead, a plane flew, and over the downpour a muffled explosion sounded. And something, somewhere not so far away, gave a thundering roar.

She turned away, and found Kenny standing a short distance behind her, equally sodden. He held up a canvas bag.

'I found you some clothes,' he said.

Mark
Raine

39

CONVERGENCE

MARK REMEMBERED the day he and Amanda had got the keys to their first house together. At the time his career had been taking off, and they'd found a bargain right when the housing slump was at its worst—or best, from the view of a buyer. They'd found a lovely little cottage tucked away on the outskirts of a quiet town, in an idyllic middle of nowhere. They had a big garden made cozy by fruit trees, stone-walled flowerbeds, and hedgerows of flowering shrubs, and views from their upstairs windows out towards the coast. On a clear day, the Atlantic was visible glittering between distant hills.

Cows and sheep were a constant audio accompaniment. In spring, the birds sang in bright voices from the towering beech trees at the end of their drive. In late summer, nut shells came cascading down, discarded by squirrels high in the branches. In winter the same trees swayed and shook as the winds pulled them back and forth.

A small primary school was just a mile up the road, perfect for the kids. There was a post office and village store run by an eccentric old man with a long beard whom everyone called Mr. Gonstable, regardless of whether that was in fact his name. The was even a pub, the Honest Pound, homey and quiet, with hearty food served all day long.

Everything could have, should have been perfect.

And for a while, it was.

Prison was what finally helped Mark control the impulsive anger that had got him banged up. In prison you couldn't lash out, because there were always consequences, times when the warders' backs were turned, quiet moments which could turn bloody in an instant. In prison, you had to pick your battles carefully, time them even better.

He'd always been a fighter, right from playground onwards, his fists answering questions that his mouth had no time for. Other kids quickly came to understand him, and while there was always the odd tough guy who wanted to take him on, a few Saturday night after-club brawls, by his twenties the fights were rare. His friends were long-term, understanding. And Amanda, whom he had met at university, had started there, too. A couple of years they had known each other before they got involved, but soon things escalated, and they were married soon after graduating.

The house, the kids, better jobs and cars came, and life was good.

And then someone collided with Amanda's car as she pulled out of the supermarket.

She was a terrible backseat driver, so Mark always let her drive. A rare day off together, the kids were in school. Just a few groceries to get, then they were off for a nice pub lunch together.

Amanda was going a little fast out of the turning, that was true. But the man—an off-duty fireman called Gerald

Wilson—a name Mark would come to loathe—was going ten over the speed limit.

It was a minor knock. No one was hurt and neither car would have even been written off. A couple of hundred pounds of damage, a little inconvenience.

And then Mr. Wilson had decided to refer to Mrs. Laine as *a fucking bitch*.

No one called Mark's wife *a fucking bitch*, and Mr. Wilson certainly wouldn't be calling anyone that again.

Amanda must have seen the signs, because she got between them far quicker than Mark could have believed.

Not quickly enough, however, for Mr. Wilson.

~

It was a relief to leave Dartmoor behind, even if the narrow roads with their tall hedgerows and overhanging trees offered their own kind of threat. Mark had hoped to take one of the major roads to save a little time, but found it blocked with abandoned cars. Of the people, he saw little sign other than a few distant corpses lying among the cars, but he kept away so was unable to tell how they had died. In some areas, however, craters punctured the roads and groups of cars had been blown apart, as though aerial bombing or shelling had taken place. In others, they had been turned sideways to create channels of space as though moved by gigantic beasts.

It wasn't until he reached the outskirts of Marshtown, the nearest town to where he had lived, that he saw signs of people who had stayed in their homes.

Pulling up his trike by a field gate that overlooked the main part of the town nestled over two valleys, he killed the engine and was met by the crack of distant gunfire. He pulled a pair of binoculars out of the trike's rear compartment and held them to his eyes.

There were people down there, moving among the buildings. He saw guns, saw what looked like a crude, homemade armoured car, basically an open-backed Land Rover with sheets of corrugated iron bolted to its side, and a gun emplacement fixed to the top of the cab. A handful of ragged-looking men in the back were pulling other men off the street into the back behind them. With black smoke puffing out of the exhaust, it reached a street corner, where a sudden rattle of gunfire left a line of holes along its side. A tyre deflated. One man screamed and fell out of the back as the others squatted to take cover.

Mark lowered the binoculars and turned the bike around.

He could only hope the war, such as it was, had not yet reached his family.

Most local roads passed through Marshtown, and many of those that didn't were blocked, so it took Mark a while to find a way around, onto the road on which he had once lived. As he passed familiar landmarks—an old church, a large oak leaning out over the road, a white-walled farmhouse with a spread of mould on its sun-shy side he'd always wished they would paint over—he found himself smiling on the outside while his gut twisted and wrenched.

And then, finally, in front of him was the old wooden gate that led down the tree-lined drive to the Laine cottage. Mark had tears in his eyes as he turned the trike off the road.

~

Mark only hit him twice, but they were both hard, clean

shots. Gerald Wilson was badly overweight and that helped him ride the first punch, but the second put him down, and here his weight betrayed him, taking him down quicker than another man might fallen, unbalancing him, his fat, flabby neck swinging his balding head into the tarmac like an egg against the side of a frying pan.

Mark's lawyers had argued self-defense, but Mr. Wilson had no history of violence, and it was only the word of Mark and Amanda to say he had insulted her. Even then, a few words hardly constituted a threat, and Mark found himself lucky to get away with manslaughter. Still, eleven years meant the end of their idyllic rural dream.

~

Amanda, taking an extra job, had managed to keep the house. As Mark drove down the lane, however, he found she had let the garden go, the grass far longer than she might once have allowed, the bushes and hedges growing wild. The house itself looked much the same, but as Mark pulled up outside, he saw that the front door hung loose on its hinges. A couple of the downstairs windows had been shattered, one left as little more than a gaping hole.

He was off the trike and running inside in an instant. The place had been trashed, but nothing much seemed to have been taken until he reached the kitchen and found all the cupboards open, discarded food packets, tins, and cartons strewn across the floor.

He went from room to room, expecting the worst. But while he found his wife's and children's things disturbed and upended, he didn't find what he feared most: their bodies, nor any sign they had been hurt. Soon, the closer he looked, the more apparent it became that they had somehow got away.

The shoes Hannah had been wearing after Christmas when they visited him in prison, they were missing. As was the bag Evan had brought in which he'd kept the schoolwork he'd wanted to show his father. And in the bedroom he had once shared with Amanda, the cupboard where they had kept their holiday suitcases was empty.

Downstairs, in the garage, the car was missing. Mark breathed a sigh of relief, then went back into the house, looking for some indication of where they might have gone.

The living room, perhaps for its absence of anything worth stealing, was the most orderly room of the house. Mark went inside, hardly daring to touch anything, looking along the shelves and on the tabletops, praying there was something. A map maybe, a jotter pad, anything on which Amanda might have made a note.

Then, on the mantelpiece above the stone fireplace, he noticed something. Stood central was the last picture they had taken as a family before his incarceration: on a family zoo trip. In front of a blurry lion sleeping in the background, Mark had an arm around Amanda, who held Evan in her arms. Hannah, already a beanpole at six, leaned in against her father's side.

There was a clear line in the dust around the framed picture. Someone had moved it, then attempted to put it back in the same place.

Not looters. Who would have cared about something like that?

Mark snatched it up, and a small envelope hidden behind it dropped away, falling into the grate. Mark caught sight of his own name scrawled on one side, but as he reached for it, the window behind him exploded in a cacophony of breaking glass. He dived away from the fireplace, which lay in the direct line of sight of the window, pushing behind the sofa. Glancing back, he saw the letter lying among the ashes, but had no way to reach it without exposing himself. Instead, he pushed forwards, using the sofa as cover, then scrambled through the door into the hall.

Through a narrow side window, he risked a glance out. Two motorbikes stood in the driveway. Electric, which was why he hadn't heard them. His own trike was around the side of the house, out of sight, so perhaps the gunfire had just been a warning. Ducking low, he ran through the hall and into the kitchen.

He had brought the club, leaving it inside the kitchen door. He reached for it and squatted down beside a cabinet inside the door. Across from him, the world outside was reflected in the glass of the oven. Mark waited until a sepia-tinted man appeared, a gun slung across his chest, peered into the doorway.

Mark didn't dare breathe.

Hands closed over the club's cloth handle, gripping tight.

The man stepped inside, looking left first, which was a mistake.

Mark stood, the club swinging up with all his might, into the man's face.

The blow crushed the man's nose and sent his teeth spraying across the floor. As he staggered back, too shocked even to scream, a second blow split his skull.

Mark, panting, crept to the doorway. The second man stood by his bike, holding a walkie-talkie to his ear.

Mark stood up, took a step forward to get his aim, then sent his club spinning through the air.

He had aimed for the man's back, but the adrenaline rush had given him a buzz that outweighed his skill, and the club instead struck the handlebars of the bike with a metallic scrape. As it deflected, the handle hit the man in the jaw, but it was a weak blow, only enough to cause a little disorientation. However, it gave Mark a couple of vital seconds to get close.

He balled a fist as the man lifted his gun, expecting a wild haymaker, but Mark dropped at the last moment, barrelling into the bike instead as the *rat-tat-tat* of bullets passed over his head.

He hit the ground, kicking out at the bike, knocking it into the second man. It was lightweight, not like the heavy street bikes of old, but it was enough to trip the man and send him sprawling onto the gravel. Mark, anger flooding through him, was on his feet in an instant. He kicked the man once in the head then once in the stomach, then leaned down, fingers squeezing over the man's jaw as blood dripped out of his mouth.

'What the fuck is going on?' he hissed.

The man just stared at him. 'Who the fuck are you?' he groaned.

'Why did you come here? What happened to my family?'

Movement rather than sound made Mark turn. Three more electric bikes were gliding down his driveway. With a scowl he jerked the man's head around, snapping his neck, then grabbed his club and ran for the side of the house.

With his surprise lost, he had no choice but to flee. He climbed onto the trike and gunned the engine, throttling the vehicle and racing forwards, straight across the back lawn as an angry shout came from behind him.

Thankfully Amanda hadn't changed the layout of the garden. Mark cut around bushes and flowerbeds, using them for cover, heading for a back gate that led out onto a farm lane at their property's rear. The gate had slipped its hinges, and Mark sped straight out into the road.

As he drove, the unseen contents of the letter haunted him. He would go back for it—he had no choice—but for now, he needed to find cover.

Up on the main road, he saw more electric vehicles in the distance, so he cut off the road again, down a narrow lane that led deep into the valley. It wound downhill, hedgerows towering over him on either side. There was a place up ahead, somewhere he hoped he might be able to hide for a while, but as he turned a corner, he saw a tree had come down.

Pulling up, he climbed off the trike, then climbed up on to the hedge, looking to see if he could move it. It wasn't a big tree, but its branches were bushy and thick. To his surprise, however, he found the trunk had been cut through with a chainsaw, the tree left as a deliberate deterrent.

He climbed back down and went to investigate the branches. Near one side, they had been partially cut through close to the trunk, easily movable. Lifting them up and hooking them over others, he made enough space for the trike, then carefully drove it under the space. As an afterthought, he got back off on the other side and pulled the branches back down into place.

He carried on down the lane, passing another tree similarly left across the lane, until he arrived at a pair of heavily bolted wrought iron gates.

There was no way past for the trike, so Mark climbed off, went to the gates and inspected the padlock. He had taken a pair of bolt cutters from Princetown which would deal with it, but he liked the idea of being able to lock the gates again once he was inside.

Taking a deep breath, he peered through the bars at the sign by the road just inside the gates.

Carlton Manor
PRIVATE PROPERTY

Hidden away from the world, it was only visible at a distance from a couple of spots along surrounding public footpaths. Amanda and Mark had often joked about what kind of crazy lord must live inside, while idly wondering how it would feel to be that person, living inside a vast manor house tucked away behind a screen of trees deep in the Devon countryside.

With a grim smile, Mark started looking for a way to climb up over the gates.

It was time to find out.

40

SURVIVORS

'THANK you to everyone who's managed to get in touch,' the man on the radio said. 'We've received multiple new reports this morning. Sadly, few of them are verifiable. A unit of the Armed Forces has created a battle line north of Wolverhampton. In Plymouth, we hear that a ferry carrying people seeking asylum in France has returned, and remains at anchor offshore. We're yet to establish any kind of radio contact with the ship, nor anyone on the European side of the Channel. At this point, the fear that what we are experiencing here in the UK is in fact a worldwide event remains unconfirmed. We pray that it isn't so.'

Alan sipped his tea as the news reports continued. A pad of paper beside him was lined with an inventory of what food and provisions remained in the house. *Two tins of beans. Half a lettuce. Three packs of frozen*—now defrosted—*cut chicken.*

It was scant, and it was worrying. Alan had never kept much in the house, preferring to shop fresh from the Morrisons he passed on the way home from work. There were a few dried packets of pasta, but that was it. Nothing much else that would keep for long.

Dad, for the moment, was stable, that was the most important thing. His medication would last no longer than another week, though.

You and me, son. It's not going to be easy, but we can do it together, if we help each other. We can make it through this. We'll grow together, and we'll be stronger.

Alan closed his eyes. Every word Dad had said had come true. They'd kept the house Mum had done her best to destroy, and Alan, eventually, had qualified as a nurse. The smile on Dad's face the day he received his diploma was one Alan would never forget.

A knock came on the kitchen door and Alan's eyes snapped open. Ellis stood by the door, wearing an oversized sweater Alan had found for him to sleep in. His hair was dishevelled, but his eyes were bright. It looked like one of them had had a good night's sleep at least.

'I'm sorry to bother you, Mr. Graf,' Ellis said, as Alan reached over to switch off the radio. 'I don't suppose you have a spare toothbrush? I mean, I haven't brushed my teeth since yesterday morning. I thought to go back and look, but, you know….'

Ellis looked down at his feet.

'In the cupboard under the sink,' Alan said quickly. 'There might be one or two. You can use anything you can find.'

'Thank you, Mr. Graf.'

Ellis started to turn away, but Alan slid back his chair and stood up. 'Ah, Ellis … if you want to wait a minute, I can prepare you some breakfast.'

Ellis's eyes lit up. 'Ah, sure. Thank you, Mr. Graf.'

Alan swept a hand towards the cupboards. 'There's

some cornflakes, a box of Weetabix, I think.' He forced a smile. 'We'd better use up the milk, hadn't we?'

'Yes, thank you.'

Alan watched Ellis as he moved into the kitchen, following Alan's instructions to find cereal packets, bowls, and cutlery. He poured himself a politely small bowl of cornflakes, then barely enough milk to even wet them.

'Go on, take a little more,' Alan said. 'We might as well use it up.'

'Oh, sure. Thank you.'

Ellis topped the milk up a fraction before putting the carton back into the fridge, a pointless gesture now that the power was out.

Alan watched the boy eat. Leaning low to the bowl like a cat, Ellis ate the cornflakes in near silence with slow, carefully measured spoonfuls, the only sound the quiet crunching of the flakes in his mouth. Ellis didn't look at him, just stared straight ahead at the light brown wood of the tabletop, his eyes clearly on other things. All things considered, the boy looked in good health. Alan wanted to smile, but too much had happened since yesterday to allow him to give one up so easily.

As Ellis scraped the last of the cornflakes into his mouth and set the bowl down, he finally looked up.

'Thank you, Mr. Graf.'

'You're welcome. You can have more if you like.'

'No, thank you. I think we'd better … you know, save some.'

Alan briefly closed his eyes. He could try to force a sense of normality, but the boy was no fool. Beyond his front door the world was no long the same, and they both had to get used to it.

'I'll go and get dressed,' Ellis said, standing up. 'Is it all right to wash in the bathroom? I see that the water's still on. That's good, isn't it?'

'Yes,' Alan said. 'It is.'

'If there's time later, perhaps we could go over to my house and see if we can find a few more of my clothes,' Ellis said. 'Do you think we'll have time?'

Alan thought of piles of rubble, giant beasts, tanks, and severed arms. He thought of how it had felt in his hands and arms to slam a piece of rock and then a hammer into someone's face. He thought of how it had felt in his heart.

And his hands began to tremble.

'Are you all right, Mr. Graf?'

Alan lifted a hand to cover his eyes. 'Yes … Ellis … I'm fine. How about you go and have that wash? I'll … I'll clean up down here, and … I'll….'

He squeezed his eyes shut, wishing there were things he could forget. He thought of Dad lying in the bed, and how he had wanted Ellis to leave, to give him space to concentrate.

I don't need this complication in my life. I have to keep Dad safe.

(I'll look after you. I'll keep you safe. Whatever happened before, it's over. It's just you and me now, Alan.)

'Mr. Graf?'

'Go and take that wash, Ellis. Please.'

He waited, trying to keep himself together, but it was no good. The sobs came hard and fast, great shuddering things that made his chest shake. He clapped one hand over his eyes as though to disguise himself, and one hand over his mouth to hold the misery inside. As his body gave itself over, he tried to shrink down, to curl into a ball, to hide himself, protect himself from the world. He couldn't face this. He couldn't handle what he was being forced to take on. He had no strength or energy left.

And then he felt something touch him, a soft patting feeling on his shoulder, rising slowly up and down.

'It's all right, Mr. Graf,' Ellis said. 'Don't worry. It's all right.'

A wave of shame washed over Alan so strong that for a moment he wasn't sure he could continue even to breathe. This boy—this *little* boy—was comforting him, a man, a man who should be standing up to protect him. Ellis's home was a heap of rubble, his family perhaps crushed underneath, and here he was, stronger than anyone, in the circumstances, should be.

Alan forced himself to wipe his eyes and look up. Ellis's eyes were wet with tears. Alan gave a slow nod, then put a hand out and braced himself on the edge of the table before forcing himself back to his feet, a boxer down for a nine-count climbing up to make one last stand. He wiped his eyes again, then reached out and put a hand on Ellis's shoulder. The boy melted against his side, arms wrapping around Alan's waist.

'Thank you,' Alan said quietly, one arm around the boy's shoulders. 'Thank you for not … giving up.'

'What are we going to do, Mr. Graf?' came Ellis's muffled voice, his face pressed into Alan's sweater.

Alan shook his head. 'I'm not sure,' he said. 'But first we're going to figure out what's going on … and then we're going to figure out how to survive it.

END

ACKNOWLEDGMENTS

Special thanks goes to Jenny Avery for all your help. These books wouldn't be what they are without your generous input.

Thanks as always to Elizabeth Mackey for the fantastic cover art, and to Gustavo Gorgone and Dom Doumy for the internal illustrations.

ABOUT THE AUTHOR

Benton Ford is a pen name for Chris Ward an author from the UK who writes under several names, including CP Ward, Jack Benton, Michael White, and Michael S. Hunter.

For more information on other releases, visit the AMMFA Publishing website at

www.amillionmilesfromanywhere.com.

Printed in Great Britain
by Amazon

39158993R00192